The Midnight Menace

by

Judy Lynn Ichkhanian

Raised All Wrong, Book 2

The Midnight Menace

Cover Art by *Jennifer Greeff*

The Wild Rose Press, Inc.
PO Box 708
Adams Basin, NY 14410-0708
Visit us at www.thewildrosepress.com

Publishing History
First Edition, 2023
Trade Paperback ISBN 978-1-5092-5150-6
Digital ISBN 978-1-5092-5151-3

Raised All Wrong, Book 2
Published in the United States of America

Dedication

To my parents: I miss you, and I hope you're watching From the 19th hole up in Heaven, all your friends and relatives gathered near, having the best cocktail party of your after-lives.

Also By Judy Lynn Ichkhanian

Arabella's Assistant (Raised All Wrong, Book 1)

Primrose and Promises (Jellybeans and Spring Things)

Perhaps she bobbed her head in consent. He wasn't certain as she moved too quickly. Even had she refused he would have darkened her door, demanding to see her father. It was what he felt, deep into his bones, though it made no sense on such a short acquaintance. Still, his mother had fallen equally as quickly for his father, by all accounts, and married in haste by others. Perhaps he had inherited her passion and temerity.

Later that night as he lay before the fire, his head once again upon the broad back of his furry friend, he considered his actions and his words. He could find no trace of regret within him, only excitement. Tomorrow, he would see what she would answer. She had to answer yes.

Reluctant to abandon his pleasant thoughts and comfortable surroundings, he rose and returned to his room. Ten minutes later, he slipped from the house dressed in rags. Underneath the rags he wore loose black trousers that tapered at the ankle and a tight black shirt. In his pocket rested a pair of black leather gloves and a black woven hat he used to cover his hair from just above his brows to the base of his neck. He checked his other pocket for his pistol, blade, and mask, before slinking down the street.

There was business to be done. He needed a grander income. His mother might take a bridegroom.

He intended to take a bride.

Praise for Judy Lynn Ichkhanian

Mid-Atlantic Authors Society
2022 First Place Romance for *The Midnight Menace*

Chapter 1

London: Summer, 1859

Anyone might be excused for thinking they fled the scene of a crime rather than retreated in defeat from another failed supper party.

Miss Honoria Cutworth rushed down the long front staircase of the Smithson townhome. Her striped turquoise and raspberry skirt ballooned around her legs and swept the pristine stone like a broom. One step ahead, Colonel Henry Cutworth, her father, tapped a quick rhythm with the heels of his polished shoes.

"All this effort. Wasted. And a new gown, too. I told you an old one would suffice." He rotated mid-stride to rap his cane in the air, marking his point. His voice, never soft to begin with, echoed between the stone walls of the townhouse and the lines of waiting carriages.

The other departing guests who lingered at the top of the stairs over their goodbyes must have heard him. Honoria did not look back to check.

"You did, Father."

"Waste of coin, too, and funds we don't have, and for goodness sakes, your dress is too…" He shook his head and waved off the liveried driver descending to open the carriage door.

Loud must be what he left unsaid, because he loved

her. Because he didn't realize she chose the fabrics no one else would choose as they cost less, not because she had the discernment of a goat.

"And what an opportunity you might have had, if only Brynley didn't already plan to leave the country." Her father snorted. "Discovering Dilmun. Ridiculous notion. Perhaps it's a good thing he failed to notice you. You might have been dragged into dangerous waters."

"Or sands. As I understand it, he posits Dilmun might be discovered in the high desert."

Having been seated next to the wealthy baron for a good portion of the evening, she had been forced to listen as he waxed rhapsodically about some mythical location. All the simpering moves in her arsenal had failed to divert his attention, though she possessed a goodly number. Batted eyelashes. Soft smiles. Napkins dislodged to the floor. She had even elbowed a spoon into his lap. His dismal response was almost enough to make her question her tactics.

Almost. If not for her practiced social maneuvers she had nothing. Youth had already crept to the portal of shelved, and wealth they had never possessed. But surely a lovely countenance and a seemingly empty head must count for something? All over London, ladies with longer faces and more vapid brains were being snatched up. What was she missing?

"I swear, Honoria, we are at the end. Only one name remains upon the list."

Her father handed her up into their carriage before hefting his larger girth within. Settling so he faced backwards, he thumped his cane against the roof of the conveyance. The carriage jolted forward. The momentum crushed her back against the plush squabs.

Once the horses settled into a rhythm, she arched her spine straight again. There was really no other way to sit given the large hoop she wore.

Honoria pet the blaring stripes and eased a few wrinkles. "Anyway, I don't believe the baron was truly available. He seemed quite taken with another."

"Yes, well, if you could have managed to turn his head, it would have saved us. Damn it to hell, what is wrong with these men?"

"Father!"

"What? Oh, pish. Never mind the propers. It is just us, after all." He suddenly surged forward to peer intently into her eyes. "You're not thinking of trying to reel in that friend of his, are you? The illegitimate fellow everyone goes on about? I saw you speaking together after supper."

The question deserved consideration if for no other reason than Brynley's friend, Peter Bartholomew, was rich as Croesus and as handsome as Apollo. He was also a rake of the first water and too... perfect. He had left her cold, but then, they all did, all the men she had tried her best to woo with practiced artifice and glamour.

"I did manage to corner him for a bit."

"And?" Her father's tone was wary.

"You needn't worry. Though he was polite enough, his attention centered upon the door. He made his escape with undue haste after a three-minute conversation. One less charitable might imagine he bolted from my company."

Her father's shoulders softened. She smiled.

"There's no interest there, I'm afraid. He wasn't on your list, was he?"

"Absolutely not. I would see you married to a man of honor, one whose moral compass is above reproach, not some rogue and scoundrel whose antecedents remain shrouded in mystery." He paused and cocked his head. "Although, the man does manage his investments well."

"*Father.*"

Henry waved his hand and slunk back against the seat again. "Never mind. Done is done, and we need not waste another moment discussing any of that lot. It's the future we must look to. Now, there's a supper tomorrow at Lord Robinson's home. I am informed Sir Lawrence Fishbane will be in attendance. His is the very last name upon the list."

The carriage jolted as if the driver pulled the horses too abruptly, but in the next instant the steeds resumed a normal gait.

Honoria held onto the wall for balance. She tried to pierce the gloomy interior to view her father's expression. "Sir Lawrence Fishbane? I don't remember seeing his name written."

"It is on the second page, top line. Only line, Lord help us. I had hoped we would not require the additional paper so I kept it safe in my top drawer. Insurance against an unmitigated catastrophe, as it were." He glared at her for a moment, and then sighed. "But here we are."

The boulder in her belly cracked and shifted. Half of it flew up to lodge in her throat. There was no need to elaborate whose fault it was they now needed the second page.

Her father leaned toward the window and dragged back the curtain. He peered out as if there was anything to see now they had turned the corner onto an inky side street. He clicked his tongue against his teeth before sitting back once more. "I had hoped Sir Lawrence wouldn't be called into play. He's not precisely our kind."

"The hopelessly poor and utterly without conscience kind?"

"*Honoria.*"

She picked at her skirts and fluffed them around her hoops. Speaking the truth didn't help matters. In fact, it tended to make her feel worse.

"We are not without conscience," he added.

Did it mean this Sir Lawrence was? She might have asked if her father's face, revealed in patterned stripes between the flickering dark shadows, didn't seem so drawn.

The silence spilled even into her thoughts as the familiar and comforting clip-clop of hooves against paving stones wove a cocoon. There wasn't much point in worrying, and besides, she was tired. Nights of constant flirtation taxed the soul. Holding oneself at perfect angles required physical rigor. Stilling her tongue when all she really wanted to do was argue and snap, and maybe even scream, required energy.

When finally the carriage rolled to a stop, she shook herself from the lovely torpor. Twenty-one steps and she could fall into bed. Fighting a jaw-cracking yawn, Honoria allowed her father to step her from the carriage. She trailed him to the stairs and gathered her unfashionably-colored skirts as he reached the top and withdrew the house keys.

Just as she was about to mount the first tread, a vise clasped around her waist. Something icy pressed against her throat as her toes whispered back across the sidewalk.

She gasped and choked on her scream.

"For Heaven's sake, don't shriek, and don't move. I would hate to bloody your dress. Mostly."

The deep and growly voice stroked her ear and washed her skin. Prickles rushed down her limbs. For just a moment everything stilled, even her breath. Then the walkway trembled as the night rushed back. Honoria closed her eyes as the entire world spun beneath her feet.

Without the male arm holding her upright, she would have melted to the pavement.

Chapter 2

"Honoria! Unhand her, you fiend!"

Her father rushed back down the stairs but came to a sudden stop upon the second-to-last step. His eyes rounded along with his mouth as the blade forced her chin higher. "Honoria!"

The villain dragged her body tight against his. His legs wrinkled her skirts and collapsed her hoops at the back so they flared out in front of her. She tried to squirm, to tear away the hand at her middle and push down the rising circle, but hard muscle held her firm.

"*Tch, tch.* Steady." His hot breath tickled her ear and goose-bumped her arms. In a louder voice, he said, "One more move, colonel, and I shall slice her to the bone."

Her father clasped the railing and swayed. "Unhand her. Whoever you are, please, please don't hurt her. What do you want?"

"I want you to go inside, Colonel Cutworth. If you don't wish your daughter to be injured, I suggest…"

He caught her as she sank toward the pavement. "Steady, I said. Breathe, Miss Cutworth. Show me your mettle."

It was an order, and Lord forgive her but she had been trained to respond to a bracing command. She used his hold to straighten, though her heart beat so fast she feared it might fly out of her chest, and her legs wobbled like aspic in the sun.

Loosening from the rail, her father's hands fluttered as if he wasn't certain what to do with them. The cane fell from his fingers and pinwheeled down the steps to land at her slippers. His expression, along with the breath she couldn't manage, leached the strength again from her legs. She crumpled, but the villain held her too close for her to risk touching the pavement.

In a softer tone, he whispered encouragement. "Stay with me, darling, please. Focus upon my voice and all will be well."

"I… I can't."

The words stuck in her throat, glued there by fear. They emerged as an unattractive croak.

"You can. You're a brave thing, aren't you? How many seasons have you navigated? How many Society doyennes? Surely a little tussle with a hapless brigand will not fell you?"

"Hap…hapless?"

Despite her quivering legs, she caught upon the characterization. What an odd adjective for a man to use about himself, especially one who held a female at knifepoint.

"Your beauty would bring the most resolute foe to his knees. I confess, I am quite undone."

She gasped. Was he… was he *flirting* with her?

Impossible. Still, his words helped clear the fog of terror, which must have been his point. She drew in another breath and steadied further. Anyway, he was right. She was no shrinking flower, although she liked to pretend the part.

"You know my name?"

"Do you think I pull my victims from the

unknown? It would be foolish of me. Now, please, remain calm and all will be well. You have my word."

His deep, dark, and growly voice, a mix of sand and molasses, doused more of her fear. At the same time his accent provoked a few questions. His wording was elegant, yes, but it wasn't so much his choice of words as the way he said them. He couldn't be a lowborn marauder. His clipped ends and rounded vowels spoke of an articulate, well-educated being. Very well educated. His tones were almost as lofty as a lord's. How... odd.

"Honoria, be brave. I will rescue you." Her father twisted his wilding hands together and stepped from one foot to the other. His gaze flitted this way and that, no doubt seeking a means to effectuate her rescue.

"Oh, she's a masterpiece of courage, aren't you, darling?"

The brigand's throaty chuckle snapped her spine. Without thinking, she shot her elbow toward his stomach. Unfortunately, he held her too close to do any harm.

"Easy, darling. You'll prevent my future children from being born. Who taught you to aim?" Laughter edged his voice until he jerked straight. "Stay right there, Colonel. Not another step if you please."

Henry, who had descended to the walkway, froze in place except for his gaze. It still darted everywhere, searching for aid.

Reaching up, she pushed against the bare wrist holding the blade. Strong bones under the velvet carapace rippled beneath her fingers.

"You're hurting me."

In an instant the weight against her skin lessened

until the knife barely touched. Then the blackguard ran his knee up the back of her leg, slow and long. The sidewalk swayed once more as a rush of fire raced up from the point of contact all the way to her hair. It settled below her belly.

Honoria gasped at the mortification. The heat had to be from shame. No one had ever dared... why, the indignation, the burning points he raised...

She clung to his wrist as he chuckled and withdrew his leg. Her gaze shot back to her father to see if he had noticed the ruinous behavior. Happily, he searched the street to the left and seemed not to have witnessed the brigand's temerity.

Her attacker leaned in and nipped her earlobe with his teeth. Something flipped and quaked at the center of her, something pooled and...

"No. You mustn't." She trembled so hard the words barely grazed the air.

But he heard her. He whispered back, his breath to her skin. "My apologies. It's just..."

She melted against him as her legs wobbled. With a loud growl on some unintelligible curse, he spread his fingers across her middle, from the bottom of her chest to the wide bell of her skirts. Through boning and layers of linen tiny flames flared where his fingers held. His lips melted down to her throat.

No one had ever held her so intimately.

Honoria tried to swallow. Failed. She inhaled deeply through her mouth. The action steadied her. He pulled his kiss away.

"I will not tell you again, colonel. Stay where you are."

He flirted. He seduced. He held a blade to her

throat and threatened. Who was he?

She could see too little of him, though light spilled from the lanterns by the front door. She had only an impression of ragged cloth, stained and begrimed. Inhaling deeply again, this time through her nose, she expected to encounter the smell of unwashed streets and the musky, acrid scent of dried male sweat.

Instead, something sweet, spicy, and dangerous tickled her nostrils. Citrus. Sandalwood. She paused, considered, and inhaled again. Yes. Ambergris. It was an expensive adhesive, musky, delicate as smoke, but…

"That fragrance."

He left off threatening her father as his attention shifted back to her. His voice softened to the murmur of a gentle stream. "You smell of summer roses, enticing as the spring." He grazed the top of her head with his lips and groaned. "Gads, but I did not expect this."

His voice, a purr of sticky sweetness, vibrated through her and tickled her skin. She swallowed. Hard.

"Not my perfume. Yours."

"Are you saying you like the way I smell?" Amusement etched his voice again.

In point of fact, it had never left. Laughter shadowed every word he spoke, except when he addressed her father. He was flirtatious, seductive, and… happy?

What kind of brigand was he?

"I do. Very much." She tried to hold onto her wits. They kept escaping "Y-your cologne. It was created for Kaiser Franz-Joseph. I would know it anywhere."

Again, she tried to push the weapon away so she could pivot and examine whoever it was who could afford such a scent. Not too many men could.

It was a bit like pushing at solid rock. Another shiver raced her spine. Terror, probably.

"Unexpected again." His blade lowered further. It rested just above her fanning neckline.

"What did you expect?"

"Not this." His voice betrayed confusion, as if he was as hapless as he pretended to be. Suddenly, he pulled her back another couple paces as her father took a careful step toward them. "He is determined, isn't he?" He muttered a few curses she had never heard, before apologizing.

Her father advanced another step on cautious feet, hands spread. "Let her go. Please. I'll give you whatever you want. Anything at all."

Her attacker retreated so the low curb slipped under her dancing shoes. The blade pressed deeper into her skin once more, forcing her chin high. She winced.

"Not another step, colonel. I don't wish to cause Miss Cutworth injury, but if you do not step inside immediately, I shall have no choice. Last warning."

Her father tossed her a desperate look before he nodded. He fled back up the stairs to the door. In between pleas, he swore he would free her. At the portal, he dropped the keys. It took several tries before he edged inside, vowing all the while to rescue her. His last gaze over his shoulder looked horror-stricken, his lined face frozen with the same panic she should have been feeling.

Was feeling. Most definitely was feeling. Wasn't she? The villain sounded resolute, desperate, and determined. She should believe his threat. Her father did. Anyone would, except...

Another tremor traced her spine. Fear. Definitely

fear. Or… something.

Honoria inhaled a deep breath through her nose to steady herself and was instantly transported to the place where a perfectly blended perfume took her. So few excellent assemblages existed. Either the bottom note was too weak, or the top one too cloying. When she found a mixture that pulled rather than pushed, it was like art. Music. A tempered bath. She needed to submerse herself in it and gulp it like a clean pool of water in the desert.

In another life, in a male body, she might have been a perfumer. As it was, she could only be an aficionado. Honoria leaned her head back against the villain's chest and rotated so her nose pressed toward his neck. Once again, she drew in a deep whiff of his scent.

Divine. Complex. Enticing. Anyone who could wear such a fragrance had to be a gentleman. A gentleman, for whatever reasons he might have for placing a blade against her throat, would never hurt her. Some things just weren't possible.

"Are you sniffing me?" The amusement returned to his voice.

Now her father had gone, his merriment struck her as dangerous. Seductive? More than that. The playfulness beneath the words glued her to him as nothing else could.

"How is it you recognize my cologne?"

He pressed his lips again to her hair as his thumb stroked the area just beneath her right breast. Her entire body quivered in response to his caress.

"I can't…"

"*Tch*. We've been over this, haven't we, darling?

Strength. Now tell me. My cologne."

"Yes. Yes, I've… a…a sample of it. It was… sent to me. By a cousin… on the c-continent." She stuttered as he created tiny ripples of aching hollowness with his small movements and his teeth again found her sensitive lobe. "It…it is quite… famous there. Impossible… to purchase. And… expensive."

She fluxed into his length before she realized she shouldn't, but when she tried to pull back away it was already too late. The brigand bent his head. His lips traced a path along her exposed neck, trailing a line of kisses. A soft mewl escaped her as lightening shot through her veins.

Oh, yes. Fear. Definitely. Terror explained the warm rush over her flesh, and how a melting thunderstorm centered in the pit of her stomach like an expanding wave of heat. It explained the ache in her breasts, a sharp pang that made her wish all his fingers could inch up to press against the throbbing unease.

His wrist rippled under her fingers, a thin covering of bones and muscle. She slipped her fingers up his forearm over the ragged-weaved jacket. Taut strength rolled beneath her touch, but his figure neither suggested the overt bulge of a working man or the scrawniness of a street person. Whoever he was, he was built upon elegant lines.

The hand at her waist, his splay of fingers, tightened and released. The pulse sounded at the vee of her legs.

She moved, slipped sideways, anything to get away from the terrible, incredible, ridiculous feelings welling up inside her. He caught her with negligent ease.

"Don't leave. I don't wish to hurt you, but if you

squirm, accidents might happen."

Odd, wasn't it, she didn't have blood trailing down to ruin her gown already? To be certain, Honoria lifted her free hand and swiped against her chest. When she held the white-gloved length up to the air, the dubious light of moon and lamps failed to reveal a single stain.

"It's clean."

He laughed outright. "Unexpected again. You do hold up marvelously under deleterious circumstances, Miss Cutworth. I find you astonishingly delightful." He turned her to face him.

Finally.

Chapter 3

Dressed in the rags of the working class poor, smelling like an emperor, her attacker sported a lithe but muscled body beneath the dust-encrusted garments. The face above the neckline of the filthy shirt ended in a strong, flat chin and rose to full, plump lips. She could glimpse the abutment of high cheekbones beneath the edge of the black half-mask he wore. In the dark, his eyes were two deep pools pinpricked with reflected lamplight.

She pressed her fingertips to his chest and felt his heart racing, but whether from excitement or something else, she couldn't guess.

"Who are you?" she whispered, searching his hidden features. "You are not who you pretend to be."

"Neither are you. I expected a beautiful, empty feather-head." His hand reached up, all long strong bones, and feathered a trailing wisp of her hair. "The beautiful part... yes, indeed you are."

Everything in her tumbled to his feet. She swallowed the honey flood and tried to focus. "Expected?"

There was the word again.

"I should take exception to your characterization."

"It was not my description. I merely repeat what I've heard. I anticipated I might well be repulsed, yet I had to know for certain. Some decisions are simply too important to leave to chance."

"Did you learn what you wished to learn?"

"More. Who would have guessed after all this time I might be undone by a bit of muslin and the scent of roses? The feel of you in my arms?" He laughed, a grating sound. "I confess, it's never happened before."

He trailed his thumb in a line across her cheek. His lips parted as he leaned toward her. Before he could complete his action and kiss her, before she could even finish drawing the deep breath into her lungs in anticipation, probably to scream... almost certainly to scream... a cry rent the hushed night, startling him back and away.

Approaching at a run from the corner of her father's property, a tall, thin man dressed in dark evening kit brandished his walking stick. With a muttered curse, the attacker released her and sped off in the opposite direction. Honoria focused upon his fleeing. At the corner, something white and sizeable joined him at his heels. A yip, a shortened type of bark, pierced the air. A dog?

She jolted forward but stopped as her feet tangled in something soft. Discarded livery littered the macadam adjacent to the curb. The gilded buttons glinted dully in the darkness.

So, the man had posed as their hired driver. Interesting.

No. Disturbing. Her fingers rose to her throat. She could still feel the pressure of the blade against her skin, but when she examined the white kid once more not a single speck of blood confirmed what had just passed.

"Are you well?" The dapper gentleman halted

beside her. His gaze chased the direction of the attacker before returning to her. "Are you hurt?"

She managed to shake her head.

"Excellent." He took several steps as if he would continue his pursuit of the disguised emperor with the blade, and stopped. For a few moments his gaze traced the path of the villain. "Gone, drat it." He sighed and rotated back to her. He studied the street around them and then her gown before shaking his head. "I suppose there's no help for it, the situation being what it is. Kindly forgive my directness, miss. Circumstances and all. I am Meriven, at your service." He inclined his head ever so slightly.

Lord Meriven? The marquess? The one the papers dubbed "The Gray Lord" because his surname was "Gray?" With his pale mist eyes and silver hair, he must be. His disquieting ashen gaze centered upon her face and raked her features as if he might see through to her core. Perhaps he merely possessed poor night vision.

"My lord."

Honoria performed a deep curtsy before examining him in turn. Fair was fair, after all, though the rules dictated she should be looking down demurely at her clasped fingers after being addressed by so august a presence. Then again, she had just been held at knifepoint and survived. The fundamentals could likely be dispensed with.

He wasn't bad looking, but he had a coldness about him. The Marquess of Meriven, if she remembered correctly, was wealthy, titled, and far too exalted ever to appear upon her father's list of potential mates. Why was he rushing about a side street on the edge of an acceptable neighborhood at this time of the night?

"And you are?"

With a start, she realized he waited for her name. She shot her hand forth. Dutifully, he grasped it between his long fingers.

"I am Miss Cutworth. I must thank you for timely intervention. I'm certain you saved me from a fate worse than death. I am most grateful."

She should be, at any rate. Why instead did she have the odd urge to kick her rescuer in the shin as he bobbed over her glove? Happily, her skirts hampered any such attempt she might be foolish enough to make.

As he released her fingers, he studied her some more, stopping at the point of her necklace where it skimmed the top of her low-cut evening gown. He tensed before relaxing once more.

"Miss Cutworth. I am only glad to have been of some assistance. I saw the rogue from a distance and watched your father's departure."

His lips turned down at the corners. The suggestion the colonel's actions had been cowardly were writ large upon his narrow features.

"There was nothing else he could have done." She defended her father whose bravery in the First Ashanti War was legendary. "He was frightened for my life, else he would have attacked the brigand."

"Yes, or course. I did not mean to suggest otherwise."

Except, it seemed to her he did. She pushed aside the icy trail of goose feet marching up her arms. This gentleman was a marquess. She couldn't grow annoyed with him over some imagined insult. Life had not given her the position to do so. Plus, he had saved her. Drat him.

He stared at her face until his gaze dropped once again to her pendant. Reluctantly, or so it seemed, he tore his stare back up to her lips. "I am happy you are still possessed of your jewels. I was afraid the miscreant who accosted you might be the infamous Menace."

"The Midnight Menace? You cannot believe so!"

He frowned. "You doubt my words?" He waved his hand as if to swat away the notion. "Who else would pull such a vile caper? What other fiend would place a blade against a throat so lovely?"

Any number of people, probably. Cutthroats and criminals abounded, according to the papers. But the scourge of London himself? The thief of ladies' purses, baubles, and virtue? The one all the press gushed about in various shades of scorn and admiration?

Honoria tumbled the information through her brain, picking out the consistencies. The fine form. The elegant speech. The cologne—the incomparable scent of him. The Midnight Menace was rumored to be seductive and dangerous. But what were the odds a housebreaker would accost a lady and her father upon the streets, particularly a rather impoverished colonel and his spinster daughter? She would be a fool to place such a wager.

She shook her head to dislodge her thoughts. "As you can see, my lord, no matter the villain's identity, you have quite readily and admirably foiled his sinister plot with your brave counterattack. The papers should write of your heroism instead of the man's misdeeds."

He straightened and preened, so much she almost laughed. "Indeed. I only did what might be required of any gentleman in such a circumstance."

"I beg to differ, my lord. Now, will you forgive me if I take my leave? My father must be prostrate with concern. I should advise him of my welfare and your timely interference."

"Yes, of course."

He bobbed his head once more though his gaze remained focused upon her pendant. Or was he staring at her décolletage? No, no he was most definitely staring at her jewelry, as if it was the most fascinating part of her.

Her gloved fingers slipped up and wrapped around the T-shaped pendant. The length of a pinky, it was fashioned of gold and studded with blood-red garnets. Because of the large bail it resembled a cross, though it wasn't. Normally, she wore it strung upon a black velvet ribbon closer to her throat, but tonight she had chosen to latch it upon her one and only heavy gold chain instead.

If her father were here, he would applaud the intensity of the marquess's attention, despite the geography of where that focus lay. Perhaps tonight had not been the total loss it seemed. Perhaps another name might be added to the list, and this one greater than any other the colonel had sought upon her behalf.

The Marquess of Meriven.

She should be excited. She should be trembling with anticipation of conversation with so high-placed a lord she might never otherwise have expected to meet.

Instead, she glanced toward the far corner and then down at her feet, her heart beating quicker once more. Who was he, the mysterious villain? Not who he pretended to be, but who was he really? And had it been a white dog at his heels? Between the distance and the darkness, it might have only been a flour sack fluttering in the wind, the imagined yip nothing but a snap of fabric through the air.

The door cracked open and her father appeared within the span. Once the introductions had been concluded and gratitude served, the marquess accepted her father's invitation to tea the next day. He touched the brim of his tall hat before clipping down the short flight of stairs.

As the door closed behind her, Honoria sagged against it. The Gray Lord had saved her from death or worse. Wonderful. It was the coup of her endless seasons. Except... the black-masked attacker might harass her again. He might take her in his arms, and this time there would be no one to rescue her.

She was terrified. She most definitely was. Why, the mere memory of him was enough to start her heart pumping once more.

Odd, though, how her skin tingled.

Chapter 4

Honoria glanced away and bit her lips together as she tried to conceal a yawn. To draw attention away from her face, she clinked her cup into her saucer, as if clumsy. Her mother, were she able, would turn over in her grave at the rough noise.

Of course, being dead disadvantaged Lucy Cutworth from movement. She could neither flop over nor dance a waltz. She certainly couldn't censure her daughter, though if she could she would likely start with the tattered state of the linen across the round tea table, the peeling paint along the floorboards of the atrium in which they sat, or the mismatched pitcher Honoria had uncovered at the market only last week. Had the marquess called before today he would have found his tea poured direct from the boiling kettle.

Perish the thought.

"… delightful in its text, don't you think, Miss Cutworth?"

Too much so, if her father was to be believed. Thinking had always been one of her largest deficits. Shaking her head, she pasted on her best smile and set out to charm The Gray Lord. Her lips said she was an idiot incapable of adding two consecutive teaspoons of sugar to her tea. What man could resist such allure?

"Oh, my lord, how fascinating." She simpered. "Do tell me more."

Meriven's gray eyes sparkled as he leaned in. "Assyriology is my passion. Nothing unusual about it, given the twenty or so clubs devoted to the study currently obsessing London Society. Although, if I might take you into my confidence?"

"Of course, my lord. I would be honored to share a secret with you."

His lips twitched and his chin lowered. Clearly, he enjoyed flirtation done by rote and without the least sign of true emotion. "Then, I confess, I am intrigued less by the study of the ancient civilization than I am by the obscure eastern religions practiced by it in the past."

He looked at her steadily, as if waiting for her shocked titter at such an unholy statement. If nothing else, it would be a pleasure to deprive him. Gads, but he was boring.

No, not boring. *Interesting.* Any marquess had to be.

"How marvelously intrepid of you, my lord. I usually save my religion for Sundays."

For a moment he held still. His eyes narrowed as if he suspected she might be making fun of him. Was she? Honoria searched her feelings but couldn't find the strand that would give her a definitive answer. At least she wasn't risking a yawn in his face anymore.

She leaned in as well, stopping just a hair too close in direct contravention of propriety that dictated she should remain ever at a remove. She held his gaze. "I'm teasing, of course. Do tell me more. I find people with passions so entertaining."

His expression cleared, which was unsurprising. Flirtation was a game she knew how to play, even if she hadn't managed to win a prize with her skills just yet.

Meriven gave every appearance of aching to lose to her. Already. Which thrilled her, she was certain. It must.

"Speaking of religion, tell me about the cross you wear. It is an intriguing piece."

"This?" She fingered the gold with garnets. Today it dangled from a white ribbon at the base of her throat. It matched the trim on her bilious green gown, an unforgivable color whose yardage had been acquired on the cheap. Had her mother been alive she might have wondered why her daughter chose her least attractive garment to have tea with a marquess whom she should be doing her level best to impress.

Sometimes, her mother's absence was less difficult than other days. Today, it seemed all important.

"Yes. Is there a story behind the pendant? It isn't from this part of the world, is it?" He reached out with his overly-long, narrow fingers. They reminded her of a spider's legs. As he gripped the gold, his hand brushed against her skin. His expression turned so feverish it appeared he might yank the jewelry and flee.

"My lord!"

Indeed, he must be quite ill to have touched her person in such a manner. At tea. In the broad light of day. In company. After the brigand's actions last night, a mind less befuddled than hers would be forced to wonder if all the men in London had suddenly gone mad.

Casting a glance toward her father across the table, she sent him a silent entreaty. He appeared deaf to it. Turning a page of the newspaper the maid had ironed twice that morning, he glanced up at the wall clock and back to the print.

Meriven did not release his grip. "Does it hail from

the east?"

"Yes. No. It was…was given to me by my uncle. How… astute of you, my lord." She tried to wiggle it free, but the marquess had grown pinchers for fingers.

"Your uncle?"

"Er, yes. Samuel, Baron Mayberry, my mother's brother. He- he traveled all over the east, claiming to have touched hewn stones as tall as a house and as wide as a stable." She laughed and fought her impulse to rip the pendant from her neck simply to escape his grasp. "We didn't believe him, of course. Er, do you mind?" She tugged as she tried to retrieve the piece without touching his fingers.

He ignored her efforts. "Baalbek. Yes. He was telling the truth. The labor to have set the stones must have been back-breaking. We suspect they had a scientific process we might rediscover. There arc rumors of the use of sound to affect levitation. Fascinating, really. The search for like processes is part of what drives us."

"Us?" She yanked. He held on, his knuckles pressed to the hollow of her throat.

"The organization of Assyriologists I lead. We believe religion and scientific invention merged in the time of our distant ancestors. Baalbek is but one example amongst a host we are rediscovering."

"How fascinating it must be to hold such a passion. Would you mind?"

"And this piece?" Instead of releasing the pendant as he must recognize she wished him to do, he reeled her closer, bringing it near to his eyes. The top of his gray head feathered the underside of her chin. "Where precisely did your uncle find such a piece?"

She cast another glance from the side of her eyes toward her obtuse father. No help from his quarter. He had turned to stone. Wrapping her fingers around the bail, she wrenched it away from the marquess by force. The piece slipped from his grasp, jettisoning her to the back of her seat. Her chair tipped upon two legs before steadying.

Meriven frowned, but ignored her indiscretion. He should, considering he was in the process of ignoring his own. He leaned back in his chair. "You were saying, Miss Cutworth?"

She breathed in through her nose before steadying her expression into her best simper once more. "I do wish I could be more helpful, my lord, since you've taken such an obvious interest in my pendant. I'm afraid I don't know where my uncle acquired it. Somewhere outside Baghdad, I believe. He told some story of trading illegal French wine for it under the guise of distributing foreign bottles, as alcohol is forbidden to the eastern people. That is all I know."

"I see." He frowned. The thunderstorm mirrored in his eyes. After several moments, he reached for his cup, drained the contents, and rose. Colonel Cutworth popped up as well, proving he was not as insensible to the other occupants of the room and their actions as he pretended.

"Leaving so soon, Meriven? I had hoped to discuss a fine pony I am considering at Tattersalls. You're something of an expert on Hanoverians, I understand?"

Meriven shrugged his shoulders, an elegant ripple under his gray jacket. He tossed a glance toward Honoria. "Yes, I suppose I could be considered as such."

"Perhaps I might pick your brain? I go to The Corner on Monday next and I've a few concerns about a filly recommended to me."

To hear her father speak, one might imagine they had the coin for such a purchase. How lovely were it true. The essential part was Meriven might not think them the grasping, poverty-adjacent grubbers they truly were, else he might not offer for her hand. She looked at her right glove. An old tea stain decorated the tiny space at the base between her thumb and forefinger. Their poverty was obvious to anyone with eyes.

She clasped her hands at her stomach and waited. As the men discussed the details of the mythical Hanoverian, and really, the colonel should try his hand at penning novels he had such an active imagination, Honoria practiced her posture.

Fifteen long minutes later, the gray-haired, gray-vested, gray-eyed, gray-demeanored John Gray, Marquess of Meriven, bobbed his head and took his leave. Honoria made her excuses and raced to her room, there to fling herself upon her bed. She plopped her head upon her pillow and closed her eyes, only to have them pop open once more.

Tonight, she was to ensnare a baronet, the very last name written upon her father's list. Except for the unexpected attentions of the marquess, Sir Lawrence represented her last chance of fulfilling her obligations to marry. Heaven help her if he was boring, had bad teeth, or an addiction to cards, but his place upon her father's list did not recommend him. It almost recommended against him.

Her throat tightened and she pushed the stone down until it lay heavy in her belly. Perhaps Sir

Lawrence would not be so bad. Perhaps he would prove more interesting than The Gray Lord, whose icy fire chilled her more than it ought. The remembered feel of Meriven's spider-fingers against her goose-bumped her skin. She shook it off. She would enthrall the baronet, and he would prove sufficient. She shivered.

He simply had to.

Chapter 5

Sir Lawrence Fishbane reclined with his head rested atop his dog's broad back. Both of them sprawled upon the crimson Oriental before the study's snapping fire. Warmth from the hearth and peace from the surrounding disarray filled their bones.

Around the room, shelves lined the walls. Books scattered in every direction instead of marching in ordered rows. Unlike the rest of the house where precision reigned, courtesy of his mother's hand, Lawry's office looked as if a whirlwind had swept through and straightened chaos just a bit before giving up. The furniture stood out of alignment, the papers on his desk intertwined like a complicated diagram of snares, and the lid stood off the crystal decanter of whiskey.

In the midst of the dustless, swept, and polished disorder, he and Hercules often found contentment. Today, though, the dog had proved agitated. Having barked at the poor squirrels and birds brainless enough to settle outside the window, he had only just submitted to pillow duties and conversation.

"Meriven. Of course, it had to be him. There's something about the man. He raises the hackles, doesn't he? Always has, the stodgy carper."

In response, Hercules whined low in his throat..

"Exactly. He rounded the bend from the alley next

to the Cutworth residence, almost as if he, too, had been lying in wait. He surprised me so much I forgot to grab the necklace. That's going to set us back, though not as much as I anticipated. Pennies, really, nothing sufficient to lessen the amount of fowl in your bowl. I'm rather glad I discovered the value before I relieved her of the thing. It's a question of principle, isn't it?"

Again, the dog grumbled, but it was a sleepy sound this time, as if he lacked interest in his person's dilemma.

"Fine. You prefer to discuss the lady rather than her questionable jewels. She is gorgeous, isn't she? Though I had heard of her beauty, I didn't expect such loveliness. Such strength. I didn't expect my arms to ache when they dropped from around her."

Snort.

"Yes, perhaps I should have met her in the ordinary way. But I couldn't risk missing something important, like the scent of roses or the way she tried to elbow me, or…" He chuckled. "Checked her glove for blood. I don't know why, but the small action near cut me in half." He chortled again.

The dog sniffed, as if disgusted. Some of Lawry's happy mood fled. Hercules was right. It had not been well done of him to have threatened her. He gazed at the portrait over the hearth of one of his ancestors, though he had never been interested in such things. The painting had been hung because the man's jacket matched the rug.

"Her father worked so diligently to throw her at my head these past weeks, I thought something awful would be wrong with her. Three arms, twenty toes, a wart the size of London on her nose. The way he cornered me for casual conversation at my club no less than six times suggested as much."

Whine. It bore a questioning intonation.

"No, I don't know why they didn't spot you lying curled upon the seat beside me. It does suggest a lack of awareness. What driver brings his dog to his employment? Then again, it was dark and they were preoccupied. Did I mention I am the last name on her list of eligible suitors? Poor lass. One might almost feel sorry for her for plumbing such depths."

Whine.

"Well, I suppose I do feel a bit sorry for myself, now you mention it. Last name on the list? I was under the impression I might garner a more promising spot given our families' history of friendship."

Distant friendship. Possibly only acquaintanceship. After all, he had known Meriven better than the colonel had known his mother, and Lawry didn't consider the marquess a friend. Not any longer, at least.

"And it isn't as if she's fishing among the grandest aristocracy, is it, so my place must be so lowly?"

But perhaps she had set her cap higher than he had considered possible or wise. Meriven's presence last night could not be discounted as mere accident. The wealthy marquess had no business loitering at the edge of the acceptable neighborhood, not when his own home rested in the best part of the city, not unless he pursued an assignation. But with Miss Cutworth?

She hadn't seemed the type, though she had gasped and purred and melted into his arms. But something had quickened in him too, something unexpected. As she had settled into him it had felt as if he had trapped a raging storm inside his blood.

Perhaps he simply needed more rest. All work and little play had left him weak and irresolute.

"Those elongated dark blue eyes. Those full, red lips. They must be naturally that color or some Society doyenne would have outed her long since. The lace at the edge of her sleeve, though. It was coarse to the touch. If she possessed significant funds she would not suffer the indignity of scratched skin. And the color choice of her dress was quite... something."

Snort.

"Yes, I know you're not blind." Lawry paused and folded what he had learned through his mind. Quite a bit. Nothing at all. The encounter had left him strangely wobbly, as if Miss Cutworth had been the one to hold the knife to his throat and not the other way around.

Grr.

Lawry raised an eyebrow. Hercules grumbled another reply. It rumbled against the underside of his head. Lawry took the retort to mean the dog thought he, Lawrence, was placing entirely too large a decision upon the quality of sleeve lace and the young lady's ability to withstand attack. Perhaps he was. She intrigued though, didn't she, especially the bit about knowing his cologne?

A rough rumble interrupted Lawry's thought, but it didn't issue from the dog this time. He raised his head just enough to view the doorway. Within the frame, Smithers, his butler, stood with his nose raised in disapproval. His wretched expression looked particularly despairing as he noted his employer stretched out upon rug and canine.

"Sir Lawrence." His nose wrinkled. He drew in a long breath and released it. "You are wanted for supper at Lord Robinson's in an hour. Might I suggest you commence with your ablutions?"

"You might, but I shan't thank you for it."

Reluctantly, Lawry rolled to his feet. Hercules protested with a low whine before closing his eyes. The dog might rest another hour. Lawry's profession, on the other hand, required an almost constant attention.

So many lords and ladies to fleece. So little time.

After completing his usual pre-dinner rituals, Lawry and Hercules descended to the carriage. The matched Cleveland Bays complimented the new conveyance. The mahogany and black steel mirrored the steeds' black manes and shiny brown coats. Each horse stood seventeen hands tall, monsters with gentle natures. One of them, Crimea, reached down to touch noses with Hercules. The two had long been fast friends.

"Never mind that now. No time for socializing, my hirsute brethren. Work awaits."

Poised to heft himself into the travelling contraption, Lawry heard his name. His mother descended from a different carriage on the arm of a man he disliked quite intensely.

"Fishbane."

"Kildare."

The fat and pompous earl slithered closer, his smile something like what Lawry imagined worms might sport at a drunken social. His random gray hairs lay in wiry lines combed over a large balding spot, and his belly shook like a wobbling tray of aspic as he pranced the sidewalk.

"Darling, are you off to the Robinson supper?" His mother gazed past him and into the carriage where

Hercules sat patiently at attention. "Must you bring the mutt?"

"He'll stay within the carriage confines and fall into a deep, untroubled sleep. He's protection, Mother. There are so many unsavory sorts dashing about, don't you know." Lawry eyed the earl, his point made when his mother began to flutter.

"Don't coddle the boy, Esmelda." Kildare patted his mother's arm where it lay over his own. "If he needs something to caress, well, better a mongrel than... another of his ilk." He cleared his throat and delicately glanced away, allowing his tiny action and oblique words to say what they all knew he meant to mean.

"I don't take your meaning, Kildare. Do elaborate." He raised his brows and smiled wide as if he were the village idiot.

"I say, Esmelda, is he also dense? Did you drop him upon his head when he was a babe? I mean, Sir Lawrence, you don't like women."

His mother gasped, frowned, and slit her glance toward the earl. Good. The earl was dangerous. Though he had pursued his mother this past week and charmed her in an onslaught of devotion, very little credit could be laid at his stinking feet. Yes, he had pulled something from her Lawry hadn't seen since his father's death, but the man was still despicable. He had ruined more women than the handsomest of rogues. He was rumored to lie and cheat. Plus, his insults lacked finesse. As if it should matter who anyone chose to love!

"I assure you I hold women in high esteem. I simply prefer a willing widow to an array of innocents whose anxious parents offer them to be misled."

His mother raised an eyebrow and turned her frown in his direction. Kildare grumbled and gruffed.

Well, the truth would out eventually. Blackguards couldn't hold their secrets forever. He would talk to his mother later, perhaps over a fizzy water, and explain just why she should guard her heart, at least with the earl. She would listen. They had always been close.

Perhaps now would be the time to steer her in another direction. The earl had reminded her she was not yet dead. Others, better men, gentlemen with an actual spine and heart, might now enter the picture. It was something to think about, anyway.

Hercules interrupted the awkward silence. He growled low in his throat, a menacing sound directed straight at Kildare. Glancing toward the beast, Lawry was surprised to see the dog's lips turned up. He stood within the carriage opening and looked set to jump to the walk.

Point taken. With a nod, Lawry took his leave. Business awaited.

If only the earl knew how they managed their bills, he might not be so quick to cavil and dance upon the Fishbane doorstep. If his mother proved resistant to good sense, perhaps he would lay out their ledger for the lord. Then again, Kildare would probably rejoice at the stream of ready revenue, despite its criminal sources.

The unspeakable cad.

Chapter 6

Guests fluttered and milled around Honoria, their ceaseless motion exhausting to watch. Her eyes began to cross for lack of anything stable upon which to focus.

Perhaps forty gathered for supper and a musical rendition afterward. Between the endless eddies of pastel hooped skirts, the men, dressed in an unvarying costume of stark black and white, perambulated like rotating exclamation points. Black jacket and trousers, white waistcoat, starched shirt, and cravat. Their costume might have provided a place of repose if not for the flurry of wide colors dragging away her attention. Their hostess, Lady Robinson, wore the widest skirt of all. It had three ruffled lengths of sky blue and white lace, extending so far from her body she must find it impossible to pass between furnishings. Hers was not the only impediment in the building, but it was the grandest.

Honoria glanced down at her own skirts. They were fashionable enough, though constructed in an unlikely shade of puce. The color was unrelentingly vile, but with her white skin, ebony hair, and dark blue eyes she could just about manage its unfortunate hue. The *modiste* had practically paid her to take the yardage. It had lain unloved for so long the outer band of rolled fabric had grown a fine film of dust. Now, with her unusual T-pendant draped upon a black velvet ribbon hugged tight to her neck, Honoria definitely stood out from the crowd of other husband-hunters.

It remained to be seen whether the contrast was a good thing.

"And are you acquainted with Sir Lawrence?" Lady Danvers appeared in front of her and drew a tall man of fine build into Honoria's presence.

The very man she wanted to meet. The very last name on her father's list.

"Sir Lawrence Fishbane. Always a pleasure." Lady Robinson swished to his other side and gripped his arm.

Her wide skirt caught him in the legs. For a moment it appeared he might lose his balance. His knee buckled, but he recovered by stepping forward. The action brought him closer to Honoria than he might otherwise have stood, so close she was forced to tilt her head back just to meet his eyes.

"He is related to Marlborough through his mother's sister, Lettice Rutheridge, who married Viscount Stalling, of course. His mother was Viscount Stilton's youngest. Their cousin, as I'm sure you're aware, is the Dowager Duchess of Shrewsbury."

Lady Danvers rattled off the man's important relatives much as if they were characteristics he himself bore, like strong teeth or a sterling intelligence. In many ways his relations were more important, at least to most people.

Honoria dutifully simpered in her most practiced fashion. In response, he lifted his brows.

She really should study *Debrett's* just as soon as she remembered to care. The peerage could quote chapter and verse of how they connected to one another. Perhaps if she paid it half the attention she did her greenhouse filled with plants and distilling equipment she could eschew all parties for the rest of her life. Attaining a husband would mean she could pursue her hobbies in peace and quit these nail-biting events.

Scents over sense, her maid, Alice, liked to quip about her mistress. She wasn't half wrong.

Honoria tilted her head back a little further and stared up at Sir Lawrence. Even a quick perusal revealed there was more to recommend him than his relationship to the Dukes of Marlborough and Shrewsbury. For one thing, he was rather good looking in a tall, mussy sort of way. Dark hair danced about his forehead, refusing to be bound by gentleman's gel. Hazel eyes sparkled above cut cheekbones. Lips full and shapely drew her gaze to his squared chin. She could find no fat around his trim figure, but still he seemed a warm, almost cuddly type.

Something passed over his eyes as she studied him, some dark shadow of awareness. Her throat constricted so she could not swallow as her skin tingled.

How odd. It was the same strange feeling she had experienced last evening. Was she coming down with some dread illness?

"Sir Lawrence, may I present Miss Honoria Cutworth? I believe you are acquainted with her father, the colonel, who is around here somewhere." Lady Danver's watery blue gaze searched aimlessly among the gentleman as she recited Honoria's own less-exalted connections and antecedents. "Like cookies on a baking sheet, aren't they? It's impossible to locate the particular gentleman required." She swiveled her head from one side to the other as she continued to look for the colonel.

"What, pray tell, is a baking sheet, and how would one recognize such an object?" Lady Robinson flicked her fan open and waved it briskly, sending her friend a pointed look from the corner of her eyes. "Well, no matter. Sir Lawrence, I believe Miss Cutworth is also an ardent admirer of, er, well, it is on the tip of my tongue..."

The fan beat faster as she scrutinized them, clearly attempting to remember their stated interests and how they might overlap. If Honoria hadn't known her father had requested an introduction be made, she would still have realized.

She darted a glance back up to meet Sir Lawrence's gaze. In response his eye twitched. Twitched? She could swear he winked.

"French cuisine, isn't that right, Miss Cutworth?" Lady Danvers smiled broadly and nudged Lady Robinson with her elbow.

Sir Lawrence's head tilted as he studied her. "Fascinating. Do tell, Miss Cutworth, what is your opinion on escargots drawn with butter, *sans coquille*?" He held his laughter barely in check. His upper lip pulling downward to avoid the smile that sparkled in his kind eyes from which the shadows had already fled.

Honoria unfolded her own fan and swished it lazily through the air. "I prefer them in the garden rather than upon a plate, Sir Lawrence, but please, do not let my opinion color your enjoyment of the dish."

His laughter broke free of his restraints. The two older women exchanged a silent look and raised eyebrows before disappearing in tandem into the crowd. Their heads rested so close together Honoria was afraid they might bump while they congratulated each other upon a fine match well made.

Which remained to be seen, of course, although Sir Lawrence seemed a preferable sort to the cloudy day marquess. Still, hers was not the decisive vote on the matter of matrimony. That joy fell squarely upon the man's shoulders, more's the pity.

"There should be a trophy, shouldn't there? But which one of them would take the prize?" she murmured as the ladies blended into the sea of eddying colors.

To her surprise, Sir Lawrence laughed again. "If there's to be a competition, I insist we enter my mother. She would say she's done all the hard work in raising me to meet expectations, though I fear if the prize depends solely upon attachment, I might not win the game for her."

"Elusive, are you?"

He laughed a third time. "Slippery as an eel."

His good humor almost annoyed. She swished her fan faster. "I suppose I should thank you for the warning. I wouldn't wish to waste my time with a confirmed bachelor, would I?"

He leaned over slightly so their faces almost touched. Three light freckles spread like stars over his upper cheekbone, urging her fingers to trace their constellation. "Is interesting conversation and a degree of accord ever wasted?"

With a start, Honoria realized she had melted toward him. Her fan stalled. She straightened her back and pressed the object to such speeds she worried it might fly through the wall. She had to force it back to a normal rhythm.

Sir Lawrence was not at all what she had expected. Her father's descriptions had neglected to mention his ready amusement or his disarming hazel eyes, or even the strength of his square chin and full lips she had already noted.

Square chin and full lips?

Shock rolled through her, cementing her feet in place. The lazy waves of her fan stalled once more. She stared at his lips, at his high cheekbones, and tried to picture him in half-mask.

Oh, no. It couldn't be.

Leaning into him just as he pulled back, she inhaled his scent as carefully and subtly as she was able. She used her fan to waft his fragrance toward her. Citrus. Sandalwood. A medium note of ambergris to draw it altogether. She straightened again, her thoughts whirling.

Surely her attacker last night was not the only man in London to wear the cologne developed for the mustached emperor? Surely there must be others in the city sporting a square jaw and cushioned pillow lips who just happened to wear the exact same fragrance?

Except, as she searched his face, her fan dropping to dangle from the cord around her wrist, he lost his laughter. His eyes narrowed and he watched her just as closely as she watched him. As if sensing her thoughts, he withdrew into himself, almost as if he waited for her declaration against him.

"You..." She swallowed.

"Perhaps I was too quick in naming our conversation 'scintillating.' Perhaps 'abbreviated' might have been a better adjective." His growly voice, dry as a sand dune but loaded all the same with a healthy measure of honey, shadowed the snap in his eyes.

So that's what made him wary. He wasn't dumb as toast, which was refreshing, if not outright fascinating. He could read a woman's thoughts upon her face. "I believe you called our hypothetical conversation 'interesting,' not 'scintillating.'"

"My mistake."

Honoria cocked her head to the side, studying him from a different angle. She let her gaze fall down his arms to his hands, those long fingers that could stretch across the breadth of her abdomen. "It was you last night. With the blade."

She assumed he would deny it and play the potted geranium. He didn't act to assumptions.

"Yes. Yes, I'm afraid it was." His gaze darted sideways before returning to hers. "I confess, I am an enormous gourmand. I believe in the healing properties of garlic, though such confession might shock you. If even snails can be made to taste so delicious, the stuff must be beneficial."

Honoria followed his glance to find Lady Robinson swishing up beside them. The older woman beamed. "How lovely to find such common interests you are still chatting over them so many minutes later! Now, Sir Lawrence, I've just changed a few place cards and taken the liberty of seating you next to Miss Cutworth. You both seem so intrigued by the various nuances of foreign cookery, I'm certain you'll want to explore the subject in greater depth. No need to thank me."

Neither of them made any move to do so.

"I am off to announce the service," she continued in a single breath. "Do feel free to wander towards the table. You'll find your names close to the end furthest from where we now stand."

Lady Robinson sashayed off before Honoria could denounce Sir Lawrence as a sneaky, underhanded, vicious villain. She eyed him carefully. Was it even safe to do so? Did he have a pistol to brandish and threaten the company? Or perhaps a bloody blade? She looked up and down his fine form, but could see no revealing bulge.

He cleared his throat and looked toward the ceiling before gazing back at her. "Forgive me, but I fear you have some reservations about sharing my company?"

"Reservations? In partaking supper with a man who held a knife to my throat? One who only narrowly missed sending me to my grave due to the gratifying intervention of Lord Meriven?"

She assumed he would deny this charge, though he hadn't the earlier, vaguer one. Instead, he smiled and stepped closer. Too close. He angled in so his face rested only inches from her own.

"Gratifying? Are you certain? I rather thought your erratic heartbeat might have indicated desire, not fear. At least, I hoped it was so. I spent the better part of the night dreaming it was so, at any rate."

All his caresses, all his pressed lips and hands, crashed back to pool at the base of her stomach. The flaming honey mixed with the rise of hot anger at his assumption, here, in a room filled with Society. That he dared to say such words to her, sentiments one might only say to one's wife... or mistress... flashed red fury through her entire body.

Her well-practiced smile fell to the floor and lay in the dust somewhere. Before she even knew what she was doing, she poked him squarely in the chest with the tip of her fan. Instead of weighing each utterance before it left her lips, she let them fly. Something very akin to exultation washed behind the rage.

"How dare you?" A jab of her fan echoed each syllable. "You loathsome, currying, deceptive toad. You lily-livered worm, crawled in to spread your filth. How dare you say such a thing to me, you, who are... Who are...?"

Something stopped her from shouting his sins to the rooftops, the real ones, the ones involving blades in dark nights and threats against her life.

His expression remained faultless, but something shifted in the darks of his pupils as he straightened. "I'm certain I have no idea what you mean. Are you quite all right, Miss Cutworth? Are you having a fit of some kind?"

"I will see you hanged, sir." She hissed the words as she narrowed her eyes, hoping to spot even a touch of fear upon his face.

Instead, he seemed as unmoved as if they discussed the weather in Dorset.

She pivoted, intending to find her father and make her accusations, weapons be damned, desire be damned, when Sir Lawrence grabbed her arm, pulling her back toward him. Spots of fire flared where he touched.

"Unhand me!"

He leaned over her shoulder just enough to whisper in her ear, "Order your expression, Miss Cutworth, before someone notices your disquiet."

She whipped her gaze around the room to see who had observed his deplorable sentiments or her reaction.

Her reaction. It was... odd. As she breathed deeply

through her nose, struggling for calm, something hot and hollow, something waiting to be filled, split open within her. A blaze heated her cheeks and flushed her chest. Her heart beat faster than her fan had, and bees buzzed along her veins.

In a fit of obvious madness, she slanted back into his hard, long length. Her reward was his audible gasp as his fingers tightened.

"Another time, another place, Miss Cutworth." He growled the words in his honey-and-sand mixed voice.

Further shivers raced up and down her spine. He spread his hand across the low of her back, flooding her brain and body with sticky, warm sweetness. He impelled her upright.

"Eyes will fall upon us any second now."

At the reminder, she gasped and rammed her spine straight. Her fingers fisted as she tried to tear away from his hold upon her elbow. Despite his words, he held on, though he stepped to such an angle his hands were blocked by the width of her dress from those grouping to eat. Without doubt, he stood no more anxious than she to make a scene.

Happily, the guests were already charging the table, intent upon filling their bellies. They were the only ones left in the room.

She forced a more even tone. "Unhand me."

"In a moment. Please." His free hand encircled her waist from the back, resting upon the skirt where it belled from her body. His touch branded her through the fabric. "How did you recognize me?"

"How could I not?"

"I was masked."

"You were half-masked. I couldn't see your eyes

clearly, but I saw your lips. Your chin. More than that, I smelled you."

"You smelled me. Yes. I hadn't considered you might mark the fragrance enough to remember. How careless of me." His voice was careful, steady, but there was an undertone of arrogance.

It goaded her.

She tried to rip her elbow away but he clung to her like a second sheathe of skin. "I am not the silly frippery I might appear, Sir Lawrence. I have an interest in the study of scent, and a laboratory in which I brew many of the household's soaps. I know fragrance like others know art. You pretended to be a laborer, but your cologne gave you away. It practically screamed money, just as your articulation decried your education and status."

Her skirts rustled and collapsed. She felt the pressure against her legs as he took a half-step closer so the front of his thigh pressed into the back of her dress.

Damned hoops. She couldn't fall into him.

Glorious hoops. She couldn't fall into him.

"You are an extremely interesting female, Miss Cutworth." He leaned over her shoulder so his breath once again fanned her ear.

Goosebumps rushed up and down her naked arms to lose themselves beneath her gloves.

"Might I beg you for a small reprieve?"

"A reprieve?" Her pulse banged against the hollow of her throat.

"Yes. A tiny one. If you would forbear telling on me, I promise I shall explain my actions. You will be… satisfied by my words. I swear it."

The way he breathed the word "satisfied," as if it

was something dirty or scandalous, tightened her muscles from hip to neck.

"You are a threat to every person here tonight." The words choked against her throat as her heart hammered against her chest.

"If you denounce me, you might well be ruined too, had you considered such? After all, I held you quite close. You leaned against me. Your body flooded with desire."

"What?" The word exploded from her lips, every part of her incensed. She looked around again. They were still alone. Thank Heaven.

"I'm afraid I'd have to say so, at any rate. Who knows? Perhaps it might even be true." His lips pressed to her earlobe before slipping down to her neck. He caressed the quivering skin there with his velvet mouth before retreating.

"What are you doing?"

"Kissing you. If you tell on me, you'll be ousted from Society, though your ruin might come with presents. I could come to you then when we're both pariahs and caress away your pain. You'll beg me for more. I promise."

Every part of her trembled. Fear. Longing. Who could tell? "You would throw me to the wolves?"

"Only if you throw me there first. I'd want company. I dislike being alone. I'm a social type of fellow."

She tried to pull away, but not very hard, not hard enough to actually accomplish the measure.

"Allow me the chance to explain, that is all I ask."

"When?" She could barely choke out the single syllable.

He paused. "Tomorrow. Might I call upon you in the afternoon for a walk in the park?"

She shouldn't allow it. She should absolutely run to her father right now, who at any moment would notice her absence and come looking for her. She should denounce Sir Lawrence for the brigand he was. Anything else was utter folly and could, by association, even lead to her own destruction.

Instead of condemning him, instead of screaming as she ought, she turned into his embrace. She stared into his hazel eyes, hoping to find, what? She wasn't certain. Something to stiffen her back and her resolve, at any rate. Instead, all she found within those sparkling iris's was a deep river of amusement, a small trickle of concern, and an onslaught of acceptance for whatever she might decide.

"Bring your dog, Sir Lawrence. I should like to meet him." She ripped away from his touch and rushed off before he could respond, and before she could gather her scattered wits and take back her ridiculous agreement.

He didn't immediately follow. She checked only once, briefly, over her shoulder.

Interesting. A man who could hold his own space without the need to hammer a point home was a rarity.

The strange fluttery butterflies took light again within her chest. A walk in the park? How would he fare under her best smile? When he pooled at her feet, she would step on him. Or maybe over him. Or into him.

Instead of seeking her chair, she sought out her father in order to plead a headache. Remaining in such close proximity to Sir Lawrence and his devilish glances required more bravery than she possessed. Between her desire to measure the width of his shoulders and the need to decry his identity, she would dribble her soup right down her chin as she spilled herself into his lap.

That was all right. She would find more courage tomorrow.

Chapter 7

When the doorbell chimed the next afternoon, Honoria jumped from the brown flowered sofa and fluffed her bright green walking skirt with its numbing orange dots. She checked her face in a low-hanging mirror and smoothed her hair. Then, bulging her cheeks and widening her eyes, she temporarily blurred her vision.

It was a technique she had learned from her friend, Marjorie Plimpton. After the exertion, once her face relaxed again, her eyes would sparkle and her skin would appear energized, though she would also be left short of breath and gasping like a beached fish. Several times, she had used the technique when late evenings had left her wan and bored with hours yet to glitter. Its efficacy could not be denied.

She let out the air in a giant *whoosh*, then inflated her cheeks once more.

"Uh-hum."

Honoria rotated and blinked her lashes. The air she had been holding escaped in a rush of wind and whine. Haunting the doorway, staring at her as if she had grown an extra head, Sir Lawrence leaned with the exaggerated negligence so much a part of him it had to be real. Despite his stance, he stared at her through narrowed eyes.

She couldn't help it. She burst out laughing.

Unfortunately, her breath choked. Instead of emulating a tinkling fountain, her cachinnation exited more like a series of grunts, gurgles, wheezes, and grates. She tried to catch back her amusement, but snorted again when his eyebrows rose and his spine straightened. She gulped, and gurgled some more.

"Er, um…" He bounced his gaze around the parlor, over decrepitating furniture and out-of-date decoration in shades of dirt, musty rose, and blue, before zigging it back to her.

More sputters escaped her lips as she tried to regain her poise. Snorts. Indelicate squawks. His face devolved into wrinkles of astonishment. She choked harder while he eyed her as if she might be dangerous.

He cleared his throat again. "Um, Miss Cutworth? Are you quite all right?"

"No," she managed to say between bouts. Tears sped down her face. She swiped at them, and hiccupped.

He continued to stare until his face cracked into a wide grin. "Far be it for me to interrupt whatever hijinks has left you in such a state. Carry on." He leaned against the doorframe once more and folded his arms across his chest. Eyes sparkling, he chuckled once or twice himself as she fought to take herself in hand.

She waved her fingers. She inhaled and sputtered. She looked at him as he began to chuckle more, at the way he tried to restrain himself, and she completely broke down. The more she tried, the harder she laughed, and the harder she laughed, the more he followed suit, until finally they were both bent double with mirth.

When the contagion finally petered out into a series

of coughs, she swiped at her face to erase the trace of hysterical tears. Was there any explanation she could give? Did he even need one?

"I say, Miss Cutworth. What a jolly greeting!"

Whatever else he might have wished to add was lost as he gulped in air and straightened. He likely thought to call her a loon but was searching for a proper way to do so.

Hoping to distract him, she gazed around the room for inspiration when she lit upon the large, shaggy, white dog sitting placidly next to Sir Lawrence's polished black shoes. The canine's head tilted sideways as he examined her, but she could swear he wore a matching grin to his person's.

"Ooh! You did bring your dog!" She crossed the room to drop at Sir Lawrence's feet as he used his palms to wipe away the moisture on his face. "And what is your name, sweetheart? Aren't you just the handsomest boy?"

She scratched the dog behind the ears and under his chin. He immediately put paid to her attention by closing his eyes and whining in a contented manner before he pushed his head against her chest. She toppled to the floor in an ungainly sprawl, only to be covered by the puddling dog. He rolled right over her, crushing her hoops as he exposed his belly.

"Hercules! You are no gentleman." Sir Lawrence pushed the dog from her with several hearty shoves before he extended his hand. When she took it, lightning sprang up her arm from the flashpoint where their palms connected.

"I say, Miss Cutworth, you do know how to gain a man's attention."

Before she could respond, as soon as she regained her feet, the dog, not to be outdone or ignored, leaned against her once more. Again, she sprawled to the floor. Her hoops flared up. She batted them down.

Too late. Sir Lawrence had seen... something. Petticoats. Pantaloons. Stockings. A new gleam entered his eyes before he buried it behind a pretend cough as his glance skirted sideways. When it returned, he addressed the wagging dog with a dramatic frown.

"Hercules! That will be enough. Remove your paw from Miss Cutworth's stoma... er... Miss Cutworth. Bad dog."

The dog rolled to the side into the position of a sphinx. He grinned.

"My apologies, Miss Cutworth. The mannerless beast makes so many a conquest with his outrageous comportment he has become difficult to restrain. It baffles the mind just why anyone would show his ugly mug affection. I suppose he draws so many kisses out of pity."

The beast woofed before pulling up his gums. Long teeth gleamed as he exaggerated a snarl. He returned his attention to Honoria and smiled, as if letting her in on the joke. "*Ahrrr.*"

She scratched him under the chin and he melted against her palm. "Anger, even when feigned, is unbecoming in a gentleman of such distinction, Hercules. I shall expect better of you if we are to continue our acquaintance."

"We shall both be upon our best behavior." Sir Lawrence stretched forth his hand. "Allow me to once more offer aid, unless you prefer I join you both upon the floor? I confess, I had not expected to have to fight the great beast Hercules for your affections, Miss Cutworth, but needs must."

When she struggled to a sitting position, she placed her hand in his. In one smooth motion he lifted her to her feet. Almost, she had been tempted to pull him into a sprawl beside her. Almost.

Honoria glanced up from her efforts at righting her green skirt with its eye-numbing orange dots to see laughter still sparkling in his eyes. "My affections are not easily won, Sir Lawrence, though it remains to be seen which of you is the larger beast."

"*Touché*." He playacted staggering back, hand over chest. "Ah, but you wound with such precision I am undone. I vow, my heart is quite cut to shreds."

After he recovered from his wobble, he studied her, making no attempt to hide his perusal. From the tip of her hair and her favorite little lime-green hat, already perched upon her head in anticipation of their outing, to the far end of her boot-clad toes, his gaze roved like fingers. Disconcerted, she rubbed her gloveless hands along her skirt to rid them of the dog's slobber before she held one out to him. Instead of simply bowing over it as was customary, he shocked her by placing an actual kiss upon its naked back.

He held his lips in place a beat too long. Once more her heart began its drumming against her chest as if it sought freedom outside her body. When he straightened, their gazes met and held. As the floor wobbled beneath her leather soles, she resisted grabbing for his arm.

"You are lovely." His growly voice purred his assessment.

With the earth spinning, maintaining a calm

demeanor posed an unexpected difficulty. Still, she managed. She jerked up her chin.

"And you are an attacker, likely a murderer, and certainly unworthy of my time or attention. If you leave now, no one shall miss you, except perhaps for your dog. Quite unreasonably, he appears to care for you. But then, who can account for the canine brain?"

Indeed, the dog had risen to a crouched position and leaned against his master's legs. He grinned across at her as if he understood her words.

Sir Lawrence's gaze chased the plain ceiling before returning to her face. For once, no laughter reflected in his eyes. "Would it interest you to know the blade was so dull it couldn't have cut through pudding without some effort? You were in no danger, I assure you."

"I felt as if I was in danger." She should have, at any rate, so she probably had. Possibly had. Well, there was no accounting for a reaction to such an unusual situation, was there?

"My apologies. You weren't."

She nodded, before shaking her head. "Then why hijack our conveyance? And what did you do with our driver, Tom?"

"Left him a couple shillings after drugging his skin of ale. He slept off the effects quite safely at the inn of a friend of mine. He was in no peril except of a woolly head the following morning."

She would have pressed him further if her father hadn't chosen that moment to march into the room. He was a colonel. He rarely sauntered.

"Ah! Sir Lawrence. My daughter has informed me you intend a jaunt through the park with your beast. Magnificent creature, isn't he?"

Her father bent down and looked the dog in the eye. They examined each other for a moment and then nodded together.

"Good dog," the colonel said, patting the white head as he straightened.

"Colonel, my mother has asked me to convey an invitation to supper this coming Wednesday evening, both to you and to Miss Cutworth. I realize it is deplorably late notice, but when she discovered my plans for today she became quite nostalgic for your friendship. I understand you two were acquainted in your childhood?"

"Indeed, we were, right up until my regiment decamped for the Indies. By the time I returned to this land, she and your father had already been wed many a year. I believe we crossed paths once or twice during the early days of my own marriage, but then, well, Mrs. Cutworth preferred a quieter life once Honoria was born. We didn't mix much in Society. Your mother, though… she always did enjoy a good party."

Honoria studied her father's face. His words were all melty and held more than a trace of fondness. How odd.

The colonel cleared his throat. "Please convey my gratitude for the invitation and tell your mother we would be delighted to accept."

"But Father, don't we have the Anderson musical that night?"

Not that she minded the change of plans. A handful of hours in the handsome baronet's company versus the screeching of Miss Penelope Anderson? The choice was hardly a choice at all.

"Bah. Terrible instruments played by inarticulate

hands beg to be avoided. We'll make our excuses tomorrow so they have a chance to fill their numbers. Now, run along, the two of you, er, the three of you, I suppose, as this lovely fellow must count for something." He patted Hercules' head once more while the dog grinned and rolled his eyes in pleasure. "Where's Alice? We can't keep such a fine specimen too long. He looks anxious for a brisk trot."

"Here, colonel!" Alice rushed in, clutching Honoria's gloves while trying to secure her own brown bonnet. "I'll see they find no trouble."

Honoria snorted. From any parent's perspective, Alice was the worst possible chaperone in the world, which made her an excellent one so far as she was concerned. Alice lagged. Alice dawdled. Alice despised exercise. They would find her the nearest bench, and quickly, because Sir Lawrence had a bit of explaining to do.

And she wanted as much privacy as possible in which to let him do it.

As a ray of heat shot from her chest to forehead, Honoria busied herself slipping into her gloves. Her father shooed them from the room and through the front door. Soon she found herself meandering the sidewalk the ten blocks to the park's entrance. Normally, she would have had to set her elbows wide to block the crowds from running her down. Today, everyone melted away from Hercules. He looked quite fierce if one didn't take notice of his comically lolling tongue or the happy spark in his large, dark eyes.

"Someone seems to be having a wonderful time." Honoria scissored her legs to keep up with the two males.

Sir Lawrence drew in a long inhalation and grinned. "I am indeed. It is a perfectly gorgeous day, is it not? The kind of day when all cares should be left behind. Do you smell that marvelous scent?"

"I meant the dog seemed to enjoy the stroll, but…"

She sniffed. Sir Lawrence's expensive cologne flitted toward her nostrils. Closing her eyes, she leaned toward his fast-pedaling form to better appreciate the perfume… and tripped. If not for the steadying hand he immediately provided, she would have fallen to the sidewalk.

"Thank you. I was, er, appreciating."

Paused, he bent toward her ear as his fingers tightened about her elbow. "Not me, darling. I meant the flowers growing upon the rail just over there." His chin jutted toward the side where riotous white flowers scented the air.

She looked up into his twinkling eyes and laughed right into his face. At the same time, her cheeks heated at the endearment.

He wrapped her arm around his and had a quick word with Hercules, who pulled on the leather leash. When the beast settled, they proceeded, strolling slower now in companionable silence. Alice already lagged a good half-block behind.

Sir Lawrence cast a glance over his shoulder before they crossed to the park entrance. "Is she always so slow?"

"Reliably so."

His arm bunched, tensed, and released. "I'm not certain whether to report such dereliction to your father or rejoice in it. I suppose it depends how many other gentlemen you intend to stroll with in the park and how dastardly their intentions."

"Could anyone be dastardlier than you, Sir Lawrence?" She fluttered her eyelashes as he flushed.

"Your virtue is safe with me, Miss Cutworth."

"Though perhaps not my life or jewels."

His lips thinned but he didn't reply. She slanted toward him in a way clearly at odds with convention. Pulling away under the guise of straightening the dog's brown leather collar, she tried to force her fast-beating heart to slow. It wasn't as easy as it should have been.

As they meandered through the park, Alice conveniently deposited upon a patch of sun-ridden bench, Honoria began to point out some of the flowers they passed. "There's lavender. It's a popular note in fragrance, as I'm sure you realize. It also dispels bugs. It doesn't grow as well in this climate as it does in the south of France, but there are certain varieties that manage the task. Oh, and look at those magnificent roses! They must be something newly cultured because they lack scent. With the breeze in this direction, one should be able to smell them all the way to my front door. It's a terrible thing, is it not, this mucking about to create longer lasting blooms? I think these horticulturists a bit like Mary Shelley's doctor. His name is stayed upon my tongue."

He looked at her, eyebrow raised. "Dr. Frankenstein."

"Yes, that's it."

"You've read the work?"

"I have. I confess, I very much enjoy fantastical novels, but I've also read much of Mrs. Wollstonecraft, Mrs. Shelley's mother. Wollstonecraft wrote, *The Vindication of the Rights of Woman*. I found it rather instructive."

She tossed him a look from the side of her eyes, studying his reaction to this last inflammatory admission. Women of her class were expected to read love poems and instructive manuals on the art of keeping a home, not politically charged treatises.

"Yes. I've read it."

"And?" She couldn't help prodding. He would put her in her place, no doubt.

Except, he didn't. "And there is merit in what she says. Men and women are equal beings, with only our education to decide us. Our rights should also be equal. Does it surprise you I agree?"

It did. Most men abhorred the very idea and found it revolutionary at best, society-destroying at worst. "I believe I'm past surprise where you are concerned, Sir Lawrence."

She turned back to the roses and dipped her nose into the center of the bloom. Still no scent. When she looked back at him, his gaze caught and held hers in a tight grasp. He searched beneath the color of her eyes, then dropped to the T pendant she wore over her high-necked white blouse. The gold was meant to play off the orange dots in her skirt, though she wasn't certain it succeeded.

When he raised his gaze back to hers, he said, "I had begun to wonder if you truly were the mealy-mouthed flutter everyone describes you as being. Apparently not."

Her lips fell open. She could not seem to close them. "Excuse me?"

"I do. I will. I am discovering I would excuse you anything. Isn't it marvelous?"

Marvelous? At the moment, his insult appeared just the opposite, but then, the day was long. Their intended route would take them next to a deep pond. Who knew what accidents might ensue?

She would show him the definition of marvelous in a way he wouldn't soon forget. Mealy-mouthed flutter, indeed.

Chapter 8

Narrowing her eyes, Honoria asked him to repeat his remark, just to be certain she hadn't dreamed it.

"Mealy-mouthed flutter." His deliberate tone and clipped consonants made it impossible to mistake his words. He drew straighter as he watched her with his steady gaze. "I was informed you haven't a thought in your head outside the catching of a husband. Most gentlemen give such reason to explain why your incredible beauty has failed to net you the prize. Yet."

Offended, as he must have intended her to be, she snapped her response. "Is this your attempt at flirtation? You're rather abysmal at the game if you think disparagement will have me falling at your feet."

He glanced toward the ground. He probably didn't require much in the way of imagination to place her there given her very recent scrambling upon the wood with Hercules. She followed his gaze but there was nothing very much to see other than gravel and grass and a very diligent Hercules sitting at attention and panting.

"I also offered you a compliment. Incredible beauty, I said. Did you catch the accolade?"

"I did, yes."

"Well then. If you are a fair-minded sort, you will be forced to admit I stand at a neutral point. Offense and praise. I balance."

"Upon a single toe at the edge of a very steep cliff. Be careful, less I push you over the edge."

He laughed. The sound sparkled in his hazel eyes. "Now, now. Temper, Miss Cutworth. Even a stalwart admirer such as myself might take exception to violence against my person."

She glared at him. "You are forgetting, Sir Lawrence, you attacked me. There are no positives to compensate for such an enormous negative."

His laughter became a smile, a devilish turn of lips. It set her insides quivering.

"Miss Cutworth. There are myriad methods of compensation a gentleman might utilize to tip the scales to his favor. It only remains to be seen which I shall choose and which might move you."

"Your words sound more warning than flirtation."

He shrugged. Still sparkling with amusement, he leaned in. "I suppose I'm just a dangerous sort of fellow. The only question is, are you brave enough to risk my company?"

She leaned in as well, so close she could count the three tiny freckles beneath his eye. "No, Sir Lawrence. The question should be: are you brave enough to risk mine?"

He reared back, roaring with laughter. Three little girls and their nurse perambulating nearby stopped to gape and stare.

"Touché, Miss Cutworth. Gads, but you are magnificent!"

He gestured toward the path and waited with arm outstretched. She hesitated before slapping her palm around it. He wrapped her fingers close to his body as he drew her forward. After Honoria punched her feet into the pavement a bit more, arrested every few feet by a fascinated Hercules who sniffed out excitement in random stones, she paused. Without releasing her arm, Sir Lawrence angled to face her.

"I take exception to your characterization, Sir Lawrence. I am not mealy-mouthed. I simply adhere to a code prescribed for young women who wish to obtain a husband and children. Is that so wrong?"

His muscles rippled under her fingers as he shrugged. "The desire? No. One day in the distant future I suppose I shall want those things myself."

"A husband or the children?"

He sputtered and barked with laughter again. "Have you been talking to Kildare?"

"Why? Have you held him at knifepoint also?"

Which set him roaring once more. He laughed so hard he was forced to drop his grip. When he settled, he shook his head. "Never mind. I will not despoil your innocence by discussing the toad." A soft smile remained to lighten his expression. "Gads, but you are funny, aren't you? I never expected it. Certainly, in detailing your virtues, your father forgot to add it to his… list." His smile stilled. He cleared his throat. "For the record, I am neither enjoined by my own sex nor endeavored of becoming a sort of rebellious hermit."

"We womenfolk rejoice." Her tone was less sarcastic than she had intended.

"I hope you, in particular, will. Rejoice." He shrugged, a careless gesture, but his eyes glowed with a sudden intensity.

Flames rushed throughout her body in mad waves. They knocked into each other and over, chaos more confusing by the moment.

He began strolling again, pulling Hercules to heel. He pulled her as well, but in a very different way. She was so drawn to him she wanted to splay against his jacket like a coating of dust rather than merely wrap her fingers around the forearm he extended.

"I want a wife," he said, his voice suddenly serious. "A family. Eventually. I suppose it makes me rather boring to admit it, but there it is. May I share a secret?"

Another gentleman who wished to bait her with a confidence? Unlike Meriven's disclosure about his search for old religions, this potential information flipped through her like a dark wave. She swallowed as her heart beat faster still. Sir Lawrence arched toward her, and once more she found herself hooked upon the edge of his tousled appeal.

She swallowed against the intrusion blocking her throat. "I suppose so. I haven't betrayed you thus far."

"True enough, for which I admire you greatly. Not many women could resist a fit of screaming and vapors. I'm not even certain I could." His fingers stroked over her arm from wrist to elbow as they continued to move forward. "Well then, my secret is this: had any acceptable female sought to capture me, I likely would have gone to the hook with only a modicum of squirming. Sadly, I suppose I am not the stuff of which dreams are made, a fault I can lay squarely upon my wallet."

"Your wallet?"

"It is quite flat with desperation. My conversation and sterling wit of a certain cannot be blamed for my unwed state." He winked, but the tightness of his expression conveyed his earnestness.

Was he trying to warn her off? But wasn't he pursuing her?

"Your penchant for insults notwithstanding, I agree your wit and conversation are not completely appalling. Yet, you mentioned last evening you had no intention of marrying."

"I didn't know you well enough then to give up the confidences of my heart."

"But you do now?"

He shrugged once more. Again, his muscles rippled, sending shock waves to her belly and beyond.

She grasped his arm tighter before forcing her fingers to loosen. "I agree you are the sort for whom a woman might repine, Sir Lawrence. Such is true enough in the normal course. However, any lady must naturally despise your propensity for attacking helpless females in the dead of night. Forgive me if I repeat myself on this subject."

"I have yet to grow weary." He paused. "You believe me a worthy object of interest? Even without the wherewithal?"

Which begged a question she could not yet answer. "I suppose it might depend. However, you do know how to charm, which I suspect such is not news to you."

"Have I charmed you?"

The heat of a thousand suns rushed to her cheeks. She studied the ground. "Except for your nocturnal activities, yes, I suppose so."

He tipped toward her. "Or could it be I was earlier correct, and my so-called nocturnal activities had your heart beating faster with yearning rather than fear?"

There wasn't much response to be made to this

question, not any she would admit to, in any event, so she punched him in the arm. No sooner had he flinched back than mortification rose to heat her cheeks again. What on earth had gotten into her? Even as a child she had never hit anyone.

"I'm sorry," she whispered, pulling away, horrified to her bones. "I... I don't know why I did that."

He nodded, but his eyes held a considering light and his lips tilted into an expression of quiet satisfaction. It goaded her more than his insult had done.

They ambled on a bit more, her heels losing their staccato rhythm, and when they came to a bench bordering a small pond, they sat. Sir Lawrence pulled another leash from his jacket pocket and hooked it through the hold of the first one, thereby giving Hercules more room to stretch his legs.

Honoria took her courage in hand and broached the forbidden subject again. Society frowned upon honesty between unwed men and women, but after all, he had raised the subject first.

"I would enjoy hearing your opinion, Sir Lawrence, of all the particular reasons you have not yet been dragged to the altar. You are not so young anymore."

He slapped his palm over his heart and fainted away from her. "Struck once again upon the barbed points you sling with terrible accuracy! And just when I was feeling rather handsome, given those melting looks you slip me from the sides of your eyes."

"What? I never—" She broke off, his laughter a balm, and sat back against the wooden bench trestles. "Oh. You're jesting."

He bowed back toward her. "Always. How else but with laughter does one deal with the ridiculousness of life?"

She smiled at his words. He drew curved lips from her very soul.

He swept the ground with his fingers and returned with a fistful of small pebbles. He lobbed one toward the water. "In all truth, as I've said, I believe my lack of fortune has done me a disservice. I've very little lucre to recommend me, and not much chance at procuring honest work sufficient to change my status. Further, my hereditary title isn't grand enough to make up for the lack of funds. Had I the sagacity to have purchased a military commission in my youth, I might fall back upon that career now. However, I despise blood and gore. Always have, more's the pity." He lobbed another stone, this time winding back so it arched higher and longer.

Honoria looked at the dog, who was relieving himself upon a flowered bush. How did a woman respond to such an admission? She should not ask him anything further upon the subject. She should let the matter rest.

"Just how poor are you?"

"Poor enough." He dropped the remaining stones. They *plink*ed to the ground as he wiped his palms upon his pant legs. He left a smear of dirt. "And I'm without an honest means of refilling the coffers."

"Surely not?"

"Alas, yes. Though many in Society have maintained prosperity through successful investment strategies, I am abysmal with such things. I always pick the losing venture. Always. Upon the few occasions I garnered some small funds through luck or happenstance, I could never manage to balance the ledger. My mother does all the bookkeeping. I am simply the scourge of all matters financial."

Her heart, which had dropped a little more with every syllable he uttered, bottomed out somewhere low in her belly.

He paused and looked to the tops of the trees before returning his gaze to hers. His tone, when he resumed speaking, contained a grudging note. "Of course, to the positive, I do possess a London home, and I've an inherited income enough to secure a modest living. Though most of our paintings are second class, and my clothing, such as it is, can generally be said to be more serviceable than stunning, my bride would not starve. She would not be forced to the streets. I cannot in good conscience pretend such horrors would await." He looked as if he wanted to, though. "Yet, why should a female consider an enjoined life with me when opera, theater, routs, and teas beckon elsewhere?"

"You spend a king's ransom on cologne." The observation slipped out before she knew she would speak the words.

He flashed a bright flight of white and even teeth. "A man must have his foibles, even one so constrained as I."

For a moment, they both stared toward the pond. She considered his words and what they meant. "My father has you penciled in upon his list of potential suitors. You are the last name, I'm afraid, but you do still make the paper. Your wealth must be adequate, if not astounding, else he would never have written of you."

"Yes. I overheard something to that effect as I drove your carriage the other night."

He had overheard them? What else had they discussed?

"Nothing of import, nothing I did not already know," he replied, obviously reading her face. He glanced at his knees before returning his gaze to meet hers. "I admit to being a tad irked by my placement. I should at least register second from the bottom, or perhaps even third."

"An impoverished baronet with no real funds to recommend him? You aim so high?"

"Sarcasm does not become you, Miss Cutworth, but yes. I am not, after all, a scoundrel who goes about seducing and ruining women. I have always taken assiduous care not to mislead the fairer sex in any manner. Some points should be given me for my consideration. Plus, I adore Hercules, but I'm not generally mad for horses and hounds as are others I might name." He paused. "There are a lot worse than me, is what I'm trying to say."

He eyed her through lowered brows, as if daring her to contradict him. She didn't. By his very honesty he recommended himself, though he didn't seem to want to.

"Except for the pesky assault business, I could see how your nature might do you credit. You do temper your insults with compliments, after all."

"You aren't one to leave a subject unexamined, are you?"

"I'm afraid not, no." Her fingers stretched the fabric of her skirt before she peeped back. "Why did you go through all that trouble the other night, Sir

Lawrence? You promised to explain in exchange for my not outing you to all and sundry. It is time to do so."

He nodded, an abrupt cut as his chin cleaved the air. He pulled the dog back from the edge of the pond where he had wandered by three gentle tugs upon his long leash. Hercules, with two wet paws, sent him an aggrieved look, but meandered over to test the smells around the back of the bench.

Sir Lawrence returned his attention to her. "Call me Lawry, will you? My family does. I realize I shouldn't ask you to use my given name, but I believe our circumstances are unusual enough we might dispense with propriety in certain respects."

"Lawry." She tasted his name upon her tongue and found she wanted more, though what the more might consist of she wasn't yet certain. "You were going to explain?"

He sighed and shuffled his bottom upon the wood. Keeping his eyes glued to the distant side of the water where trees dotted the acreage, he nodded again. "Well. Well then. I suppose, if I am on your list, even at the bottom, and I am 'the sort for whom a woman might repine,'" he added, repeating her earlier words, "then I might share another secret with you. One that could see me hang."

He swiveled his head to spear her with his gaze. His face had fallen into stone, as if what he might say could shift her world. Honoria held her breath, his last words reaching into her stomach and twisting all her insides in a vice.

"I sought you out in order to assess your person outside your normal element. I wanted to know who you might really be outside the blazing candlelight of

Society. With your father cornering me at every turn, I needed to see you in the worst sort of situation before I allowed myself to become undone by you in the best. You truly are stunning, you know. Better men than I have been felled by such beauty."

She waited. There was something more, something he sought to distract her from by his excessive compliments. She could see it in the way his gaze skittered away before returning, and the way his mouth opened slightly before closing again.

When he said nothing further, she spoke. "You wish me to believe you dressed as a coachman first, and a working class person second, all to catch me unaware? You drugged our driver, paid him, and proceeded to assault me and put my father at risk of collapse, not to mention savaging me with a blunted blade, all to find out who I was when not in the company of eligible bachelors?"

It seemed far-fetched. It was ridiculous.

He looked back out over the water, and sighed. "That was not the all of it. There is more, but forgive me, I'm not yet confident in your discretion. My secret is not mine alone to share, you see. There's quite a lot at stake for an enormous number of people."

"The hanging bit requires a certain temperance with words, I should imagine." She considered his earlier statement. "How mysterious, and the part I wish to hear left unsaid, of course. The hanging part."

"Yes." He shrugged. "I cannot make it otherwise, though I fear the mystery will only make you pry. I know I promised to explain, and within the bounds of what I might say without implicating others, I am doing so. I was there, Honoria, to ascertain your true person.

Please allow that particular transgression to be explanation enough for now."

Did that mean he intended a later?

Their conversation was so singular it was almost enough to prod her to ask. Almost. Long years training to be the perfect lady were difficult to set aside, and a lady never pried into a gentleman's personal life. Not directly, in any event, though she had already pushed him about his finances.

While she pondered how to approach the subject of the unsaid from an oblique angle, Hercules rushed from the back of the bench toward the water as if chased by a pack of Hellhounds. He peddled to a stop along the soft edge of the pond and commenced barking madly at something that swam within the water.

Honoria watched the dog's antics as she tried to ignore the sinking feeling in her chest. It wasn't lost upon her that for the first time in a very long time, maybe forever, she was content to simply be in the company of a gentleman. There was nowhere else she wanted to go, and no one else with whom she wanted to spend time. However, if he didn't have money then there was no point in pursuing the mystery of him. There was no point in losing her heart. A marriage between them could never happen. It was axiomatic of Society one of a pair must have sufficient lucre if a family was to be built. Hers was not the hand to provide it.

She would have to talk to her father. She would have to ask him why Sir Lawrence, Lawry, was on his list. The colonel never made mistakes about funds. It was too important.

She slit her gaze toward the handsome, tousled

man sitting tense next to her and reached out her gloved hand to clasp over his. When he turned his head, surprise writ large, she squeezed.

"I enjoy your company, Lawry, although I shouldn't use your first name."

To her own surprise, and almost definitely to his, she bent toward him and planted a kiss upon his cheek. His sun-warmed skin was slightly bristly and rough under her lips, and the scent of him absolutely divine. It was difficult to draw away, but she did.

"You are the least mealy-mouthed female I've ever encountered." His fervent declaration mirrored in the sheen of his eyes.

"Finally, you're showing some sense."

But was she?

Chapter 9

The opera house was too full of gawking, squawking, people. Lawry could barely squeeze between the groupings. People swarmed like varied schools of lemmings, following this leader or that in impenetrable clusters. He bounced his gaze from box to box as he was pushed and shoved, rather desperate to determine which one was hers.

Honoria. Strange how even in the caverns of his mind her name melted him to the consistency of honey.

A particularly vulgar garnet bracelet several inches wide passed by his nose as an older woman raised her hand to wave to someone else. The clasp barely held and the tiny strand of gold safety chain couldn't support the weight. The temptation to remove it from the fat glove around which it rested passed, almost before it formed. Yes, Honoria might like it, but if she wore it someone would notice. Plus, she would ask questions. She had sharp eyes and a sharper brain. His secret wouldn't rest longer than the next day's newspaper article detailing the theft.

Lawry sighed and bumped through a couple of men weaving drunkenly to their seats. He dragged his mother through the hole he made. She scooted past him in the next instant, her wide skirt catching him at the knee. By the time he righted himself she had stopped three steps up to exchange greetings with two of her friends. The three blocked the thoroughfare with an insouciance that made his teeth ache.

Where was Honoria? She had said she would attend tonight. He searched the crowd, looking for a blaze of unusual color.

A gold lorgnette fell at his feet. He retrieved it. Pressing a nail into the metal by the folded grip, he paused. Actual gold. He touched the arm of the shriveled woman draped in black who spoke with his mother and offered its return. The Dowager Lady Fishbane eyed him steadily, as if she looked through to the center of him. He ignored her unspoken question and shook his head.

He didn't have time or head space to work tonight. When his mother said her goodbyes and continued up the stairs, he trailed her. His gaze roved the red velvet seats as his heart pounded.

Honoria hadn't been as rebuffed by his lack of financials as he had intended. Instead, she had kissed his cheek. What had it meant? Did she still believe a match between them was possible?

It wasn't possible… except, maybe, it could be. Though one of a couple should possess the means to continue the family line through to the next generation, no one said the rule couldn't be bent just a little. Why, he cobbled the law every day.

Their afternoon jaunt had been unexpectedly delightful. For the past year his mother had been pushing him to make the acquaintance of Colonel Cutworth's daughter. He had pulled away with equal fervor. Her father had recently joined those in favor of a match. It had become harder to resist their combined efforts, but he had been determined for reasons only a fool might understand.

Of course, even though they had never met he had known Miss Cutworth, Honoria, was lovely. Men talked. What they said of her outside her pretty face was not kind. It had dashed any potential interest he might have held for the dark-haired beauty.

Had he really told her Society called her mealy-mouthed? It was not nice, although also not untrue. Upon several occasions he had had the misfortune of overhearing drunken nitwits give marks to the eligible females present at various fetes. If memory served, Mr. Clydesmith had compared her to a potted petunia, though he had rated top marks for her skin and a middling review of her bosom. Well, it made sense. She was small up top. Most of his class dreamed of curvaceous milkmaids. Lucky for him, he didn't care. He was a hip man, and he had stood close enough to ascertain Honoria's lower dimensions were not only the result of boning and bolsters.

If he wasn't careful his mouth might water. Bad enough he was already hardening in the wrong place. What would his mother think if she turned and found him slavering like a rabid dog?

As if on cue, Lady Fishbane grabbed his arm and tugged. "There's our box." She pointed to the next level. "Wonderful! Toward the center with an unobstructed view. We'll be able to see the performers spit. I take it business has been going well?"

As if it were a good thing, the spitting. "Quite well."

"Do I look all right?"

She touched the opera length strand of pearls with its decorative sapphire clasp. It ran past the sweetheart neckline of the deep blue gown she wore. White flowers trailed upward from hem to bodice. Pearl bobs decorated her ears.

He placed his gloved fingers over hers where they clutched his arm and squeezed. "Almost too striking, Mother. Your friends will be writhing with jealousy."

She laughed. "You do make an excellent escort, dear. What will I do when you finally settle down with a wife?"

"Spoil your future grandchildren, no doubt."

She raised an eyebrow. He ignored the question and gestured ahead. They climbed without further comment, although she stopped to chatter on five more occasions. Lawry cooled his heels and attempted to appear interested in the health of various strangers and the state of the theater.

Still, the fact he had been forced to act as her companion for the evening was a matter for which he could be grateful. Kildare had failed to send his carriage as promised. Indeed, a carefully worded message inquiring into the lack had been returned without answer. It seemed the earl had mysteriously decamped London for parts unknown, and good riddance to him, too. There were far better companions for Esmelda Fishbane.

Colonel Cutworth, for example. For weeks now Lawry had been considering pairing them up. And why not? The colonel possessed an engaging personality along with a full head of fluff and a sizeable mustache. He was kind and protective. His stomach rounded only the slightest degree. His teeth were even and mostly white. He had also been responsible for the creation of the most delightful female Lawry had ever met, a fact which had to count in the man's favor, even had he been a balding, fat toad like the earl.

While the colonel had been vetting him for his daughter, Lawry had been vetting the colonel for his mother. Funny how that worked. It only remained to instigate a few meetings where the two old friends could appraise each other. Like tonight.

Once again, he squeezed his mother's fingers. With a questioning eyebrow, she looked up at him. He smiled in return.

"Have I told you how lucky I am to have you for a mother?"

She patted his cheek, her eyes misty. Well, so were his. She had never done anything less than offer her full support for whatever endeavors he chose to pursue, even the criminal ones. She trusted his judgment. Few could make that claim about their parents.

When they reached the box and slipped into their seats, his mother withdrew her lorgnette and popped it up to her eyeballs.

"Where do you suppose the Cutworths sit?"

"I wondered the same thing. Probably off-side and back." He sank down beside her. "I don't believe they're well-off, Mother."

She shrugged, a delicate ripple of her shoulders. "I suppose not, but at my age such matters aren't the impediment they once were. As for you, if you're interested in the daughter, you'll simply have to work a bit harder."

"It isn't a question of endurance, Mother."

"Mmmm."

He caught a flash of lobster-back, what the colonials across the ocean called the English military jackets due to their bright red color. The man in question, however, looked nothing like Honoria's father. His upright posture was equally as straight, but his hair was not the same shade of white.

Lawry's gaze moved on, sighting with new hope upon every blotch of crimson. Far too many such blobs dotted the crowds in the sections too far removed from the entertainment. The military could be rewarding, but often wasn't, not if a man was honest at any rate.

He examined his mother's profile as she searched the crowds. Bright color spotted the curved moon of her cheekbones as her expression rose and fell with each hope and disappointment of spotting her old friend, the same man who had placed Lawry's name at the bottom of his list, second page.

It still stung. It filled him with a strange sense of panic, as if he might not really be on the list at all.

"There, Lawry. Behind us and to the right, I think. In the public box at the aisle." His mother waved madly in the direction her glasses pointed. She leaned backward over the rail so far he feared she would topple over into the stands beneath. "Go invite them to sit with us, won't you? They'll miss the performance from there."

Pausing only to pull his mother to the safety of her seat, he didn't hesitate further. Picking his way through the crowds with greater resolve, ignoring the titters as he brushed against young, blushing flowers, he mounted the elegant staircase. When he located the Cutworths, he bowed low over Honoria's elegant kid glove. A stain of old tea spread along the inside seam under the thumb.

No, they were not doing well at all, at least, not

financially.

"My mother asks if you would join us, Colonel Cutworth. Miss Cutworth. We've the advantage of rather good seats and an empty box. Do help us fill it, won't you?"

To his surprise and delight, Honoria jumped up without the slightest hesitation. Her smile was broad and as far from the simpering mien she sometimes donned as it was possible to be.

"We would be delighted, Sir Lawrence, wouldn't we, Father?"

She grabbed his elbow and pulled him to standing as he gruffed his agreement. Her aid had been unnecessary. The man had already grabbed his hat.

When they arrived in his rented box the lights were just dimming and the curtain fluttering. A round of quick introductions and greeting, and Lawry was able to slip beside Honoria, leaving his seat to her father. Conventionality be damned. She had already used his first name. They were as good as married. She just didn't know it yet.

For that matter, he hadn't either, not until this very moment. With the light dampened and a pregnant hush descended, the certainty of his conviction startled him, but when he looked within all he found was more assurance.

His fingers stole alongside her glove, tracing a path from wrist to pinky-tip. In the waiting theater, her indrawn breath was as audible as cannon fire.

"You're blushing." He used his softest tone and hoped his words were true.

"You're a cad for pointing it out."

"Undoubtedly. Honoria?"

"Yes."

He leaned in even closer to fan the delicate lobes of her ear with his breath. "I am much stirred by your blush."

She gasped, which ended up as a cough and shiver.

"I say, dear, are you all right?" His mother turned in her seat to examine Honoria.

"Fine. Fine." Honoria flapped her hand.

"I only ask because you are making the strangest sounds. Are you taking ill or strangling a cat?"

"She's fine, Mother." Lawry rotated his finger, indicating his mother should resume facing forward.

With a grunt of displeasure, she did so, then whispered something into the colonel's ear. His head touched hers as they exchanged words.

That was faster than even he had expected. A strange feeling of contentment stole over him. Perhaps everything would turn right after all.

"Excuse me, Sir Lawrence."

"Lawry."

"Lawry," Honoria repeated. "I…"

He covered her glove with his fingers and squeezed gently, wishing suddenly they could clasp skin to skin. It was impossible how much he wanted to feel naked flesh, even if it was only a palm.

"About earlier, when you said—"

"Never mind. It's irrelevant. Will you marry me?"

The words were out before he could stop them. Not only were they inappropriate and dangerous, should she accept, they were so insane she would have to think him mad. Indeed, her eyes widened to the size of saucers and her lips opened to a round "O." But with pleasure? He wasn't certain. It was too damned dark to be sure.

He should take back his words. He should make light of them, make them into some sort of joke. He opened his mouth. A screeching note broke the silence. A caterwaul and assorted wailing issued from the stage.

Instead of retreating, he leaned toward her and grazed the side of her cheek with his lips. "I fear I am serious. I want you naked in my bed, Honoria. I want your smiles and kisses. Marry me." His lips slid down to caress her neck. He allowed his tongue to trace a small swirl as he rose to her earlobe and nipped the tender flesh.

"Ah!"

Their parents turned around as one, just as he sank back and away from the pristine swathe of delicate skin.

"What is wrong with you, Honoria?"

The colonel's voice carried just as the singers arrived at a pause in the music. The audible swish and visible reflection of stray light upon lenses told him those in the near boxes had all turned as one to examine their seats.

"I… I am not feeling well." Honoria gasped. Not surprisingly, she did appear flustered and disconcerted. "Father, might we leave?"

Their parents exchanged a look. Lawry was not certain what it meant, but he was pleased to see they already acted as one. His largest concern with his own future had always centered around his mother's wellbeing. He hadn't wished to leave her alone and unprotected. Perhaps he wouldn't have to.

Before Honoria fled, Lawry traced his fingers over the inner flesh of her arm. "Tomorrow. We shall discuss matters over tea."

Perhaps she bobbed her head in consent. He wasn't certain as she moved too quickly. Even had she refused he would have darkened her door, demanding to see her father. It was what he felt, deep into his bones, though it made no sense on such a short acquaintance. Still, his mother had fallen equally as quickly for his father, by all accounts, and married in haste by others. Perhaps he had inherited her passion and temerity.

Later that night as he lay before the fire, his head once again upon the broad back of his furry friend, he considered his actions and his words. He could find no trace of regret within him, only excitement. Tomorrow, he would see what she would answer. She had to answer yes.

Reluctant to abandon his pleasant thoughts and comfortable surroundings, he rose and returned to his room. Ten minutes later, he slipped from the house dressed in rags. Underneath the rags he wore loose black trousers that tapered at the ankle and a tight black shirt. In his pocket rested a pair of black leather gloves and a black woven hat he used to cover his hair from just above his brows to the base of his neck. He checked his other pocket for his pistol, blade, and mask, before slinking down the street.

There was business to be done. He needed a grander income. His mother might take a bridegroom.

He intended to take a bride.

Chapter 10

"I tell you, Honoria, it is terrifying to even consider wearing jewels any longer in public. What if this menace should spot my great-aunt's bracelet and follow me home? What if I am in bed when he searches my room? I fear for my virtue."

Marjorie Plimpton's voice reflected more excitement than disquiet. Honoria understood just how she felt. Oh, not about the jewel thief the papers called The Midnight Menace darkening her own chamber. The man would find slim pickings within her box since the only pieces she owned were chandelier earrings set with garnets in silver and the T pendant and thin chain upon which it sometimes hung. These items hardly seemed worth the effort of breaking and entering, so she was certain to be safe from The Midnight Menace's evil clutches.

Nor did she believe Meriven's claims Lawry might be the brigand in question. Had he been, he had certainly had opportunity sufficient to steal her jewels. No, there was something the baronet kept hidden, but it was not his matched identity to the infamous thief who raided ladies' caches of gems and sometimes, it was rumored, their virtue. Her cheeks heated at the thought.

Too bad Lawry wasn't The Midnight Menace. If he were, he could steal her virtue without her feeling guilty, although the ruin would likely be the same. Still, he had offered to marry her. If they wed, they might touch as often as they wished.

He had asked to marry her. *Her*. The truth was too astounding.

Her gaze haunted the doorway once more. Lawry had said he would join them for tea today. So far only Marjorie had arrived, and her friend was buried up to her nose in the newsprint.

"Ooh! It says he was injured last night! Listen to this. 'Blood was spilled upon the ledge of Lady Q's bedroom window, a torrent insufficient against the pitiless torments the lady must feel at having her virtue so compromised.' How awful."

"Descriptive, anyway." Honoria shot another glance toward the doorway. Still empty.

"I wonder where Lord Q was at the time. What kind of husband allows his wife to be assaulted in such a manner?"

"Out gambling, no doubt." Honoria sent a quick look toward her father, who didn't like her to know things about men.

He was buried in his own paper, a journal more somber than *The Ladies' Periodical of Happenings and Disasters* from which Marjorie read. The newish rag was devoted entirely to scandal under the guise of offering protection to women of a certain class by apprising them of hidden dangers. In reality, it piqued the senses and sent innocent hearts imagining in unproductive ways.

Take her, for example. She rubbed her hands together, hoping to rid them of the buzzing they had acquired. She could not likewise chafe the rest of her skin as she longed to, not in public, anyway.

"It says here a gold necklace with diamonds worth over two thousand pounds was taken. Two thousand pounds! Can you imagine? Along with matched earrings, a ruby bracelet, and a large emerald ring. Oh. I do adore emeralds. Hmm." Her friend read onward and scrunched her nose. "Oh. Plain setting in gold. Circular stones. Rose cut, of course. I prefer something more decorative."

"Yes."

Another glance. How could any portal remain so empty and still be considered to be doing its job?

"The paper doesn't reveal the identity of Lady Q. There are privacy issues, I'd imagine." Marjorie folded the narrow sheets and placed the paper next to her cup. Her bright green eyes sparkled above her smattering of freckles. "Isn't it all too exciting?"

It might have been, had Honoria been able to entertain any thoughts other than those concerning Lawry's question last night. Had he been serious? Did he truly intend to speak with her father and ask for her hand? Why, they barely knew each other. And what would her father say? She had yet to find the moment in which to ask him why Sir Lawrence had been inscribed into the last possible spot upon his list when, according to Lawry's self-testimony, he was poor. Even the last line entry should have held a suitable name, someone with assets to recommend the holder as a potential suitor. One they might dupe, in a manner of speaking, though the dowry must speak for itself.

She looked toward the doorway again, and this time her fast-beating heart found reward.

"Sir Lawrence and Lady Fishbane." Giles, their butler, announced their visitors in a stentorian tone.

Colonel Cutworth threw his paper aside and jumped from his seat with an alacrity Honoria hadn't witnessed in years. She knew how he felt. If it hadn't been unseemly, she might have jumped from her chair as well.

"Come in, come in! How delightful! Sir Lawrence. Lady Fishbane." The colonel bowed low over the woman's glove and the gentlemen nodded at each other. "Alice, do fetch some hot water. The tea has gone quite cold."

Lady Fishbane colored in a pretty fashion. Possessed of Lawry's same curling hair but darker eyes, she cut a fine, trim figure in her blue dress. "Colonel Cutworth. I am surprised to see you today. Don't most gentlemen spend their afternoons at their clubs?"

"And miss the opportunity of furthering a renewed acquaintance with so delightful an old friend? I am not such a bumble guts, Lady Fishbane." He shot Lawry's mother a glance so heated it warmed Honoria's own cheeks.

Lady Fishbane, blushing further, sank into a seat adjacent to Honoria. She cleared her throat. Sliding her gaze to the side, she gestured toward Marjorie with her glance.

"Oh! Pardon. Yes, Lady Fishbane, may I introduce my dear friend, Miss Marjorie Plimpton? Marjorie, this is Lady Fishbane, Sir Lawrence's mother."

She went through the same introductions with Lawry. A sharp pang in her chest broke her concentration when he leaned low over Marjorie's pristine glove now sullied by paper ink. Too low. Too long.

Honoria glared at her friend. Marjorie looked

entirely too lovely in her sprigged green-mist gown. Rounded and radiant, she presented the essence of cool spring on a day already grown overly warm. Compared to Honoria's burgundy dress and dark hair, she shone. Together, they must present a picture of the seasons in which Honoria's own thin winter figure served a dour reminder of aged and graceless cold.

She glanced down at her skirts with distaste. What had she been thinking?

When they had all been seated, Honoria poured the fresh tea Alice brought and then studiously refused to look Lawry's way. The conversation swirled. A bit too much bright tinkling laughter ensued. She kept her gaze upon her own cup, afraid of what her expression might reveal, afraid she might stab Marjorie with her cake fork.

Under the guise of reaching for a biscuit, Marjorie leaned toward her to whisper in her ear. "He hasn't stopped staring at you. I think you may have netted him."

Honoria examined her friend's face, half-expecting to find a sly condescension there. Instead, she spied only a benevolent delight. Guilt rose to choke her throat at her uncharitable thoughts until she glanced at Lawry. He smiled and nodded as his eyes sparkled in a warm and slightly conspiratorial way, as if they shared a secret.

She couldn't breathe. Every part of her flipped, waved, buzzed, and pooled until sitting still became a form of torture.

He was here. He was gorgeous in a rumpled, heady sort of manner that made her long to run her fingers through his hair and under his shirt. She knew what he had meant when he said he wanted her in his bed. She wanted him in hers, though she wasn't certain what might happen there besides a kiss or two.

Still, her body jumped and sizzled as she remembered the feel of his lips upon her neck. Her skin itched from toe to head. If she could feel more uncomfortable in her own flesh she might certainly die. Why had she considered desire to be something applauded? It was horrible.

Didn't it just figure when she finally felt the cursed emotion for someone, for something more than his hand and purse, at any rate, he was too poor to actually be considered as husband material? She peeped at Lawry from beneath her lashes, luxuriating in the curls brushing his high forehead and the way his mouth curved into a pleased smile at something her father said.

There had to be a reason Lawry was on the list. There simply had to be.

"Are you still feeling sickly today, Miss Cutworth?" Lawry's voice cut across the chatter, silencing the others as they all turned her way.

"She does appear pale, doesn't she, Henry?" Lady Fishbane elbowed Honoria's father.

First name basis? Already?

She met Lawry's gaze and saw the contented knowledge there. He already knew. He seemed satisfied with the matter. She studied her father while he studied her.

"Pale?" He squeezed his eyes and peered at her with an anxious expression before casting a quick glance toward the baronet. "Do you think so, Sir Lawrence?"

"Positively peaked. Perhaps her social calendar is

too fraught. I understand it can happen." Lawry rose as he spoke. He circled the table and drew her from her chair. "Come, Miss Cutworth. Why don't you rest upon the couch, your back pressed against a nice pillow? I'll fetch you your cup and a lap rug." His eyes glittered, a small half-smile tilting his lips in a provoking manner. "Perhaps you've caught a sniffle?"

His fingers slipped up under her sleeve. Her flesh burned where he stroked. Devouring flame raced through her blood until every part of her writhed in scorched, twisting agony.

"Stop it," she hissed so only he could hear.

He bent to her ear. "Lean upon me, darling. I've got you." His words seemed to contain a double meaning, and maybe a triple one if she permitted herself to imagine it.

Unresisting, because she couldn't, not with everyone watching, she allowed him to maneuver her to the brown, flowered furniture. As her cheeks warmed, she feared he would next insist she was fevered. He would be right. Instead, he drew the ochre velvet blanket from the back of the seat and draped it solicitously across her lap. As he did so, his left palm lay revealed. A nasty, long, red scratch cut the underside of his hand down to the base of his wrist.

She gasped. Her fingers covered her lips to keep the sound within as the discomforting desire retreated.

Too late. The sound alerted him. His gaze followed hers. Slowly, his hand fisted.

"You're injured."

"It is nothing. Too wild a play session with Hercules. He doesn't mean to hurt. He simply forgets the length of his teeth sometimes."

Lawry scurried away and fetched her cup before retaking his seat at the table. Everything in his manner said he lied, most especially the way he forbore looking in her direction. Honoria sipped the cold brew. Images of his skin kept flashing before her eyes. She pushed it away, again and again, while she waited for him to pull her father aside and broach his last night's declaration.

Besides, the paper said The Midnight Menace had left a pool of blood behind. Could a tiny line, no matter how deep, leave such an amount?

Fifteen minutes later, Lawry had still failed to take her father aside. Since setting the blanket upon her lap, he had avoided even glancing in her direction. Her pulse beat faster as her heart sank lower and lower, all the way to the pit of her stomach no matter how she attempted to bolster it back up.

"Until tomorrow then." Her father's booming voice interrupted her thoughts.

Honoria startled. The table had risen. The Fishbanes were saying their goodbyes. She threw off the blanket and jumped to her feet. Pasting on her very best simper, grateful it had become second nature, she echoed her father's delight. When her gaze met Lawry's, her smile faltered.

"Miss Cutworth." He bowed low over her hand and took his leave without saying anything further.

She looked after his retreating back. The Midnight Menace? Could it be true, unlikely though it must be? A dog's tooth made more sense. But if Lawry's explanation for his injury was correct, his distance must mean he had reconsidered his imprudent proposal.

Both ideas were untenable.

Marjorie chatted aimlessly as she gathered her

bonnet. Honoria crossed the room quickly, belying any rumors of illness, and grabbed her friend's arm.

"Come help me to bed, will you? I vow, I do feel a bit dizzy. Too much tea, I'm certain."

Ignoring her father's concerned expression and Marjorie's befuddled one, she railroaded her friend out to the hallway and up the stairs. Once the bedroom door shut behind them, she rounded on the pretty redhead, all pretence put aside.

"Marjorie, how was that thief injured? The one who stole from Lady Q? Did any of the other papers say?"

Marjorie flipped back her head. Her red curls bounced merrily. "Nothing other than the words I read to you earlier, no." She tilted her chin to the side and gazed at Honoria with concern before sighing. "It's important to you?"

She nodded.

"Well, you know how much I dislike gossip..."

Honoria almost snorted. Her throat was too full of misery to do so.

"—but Anna, my maid, heard from Lady Quinlan's maid, Debra, er, Lady Q, I mean, well, no. Quinlan. You know I wouldn't normally divulge her identity, but—"

"Marjorie! What was the man's injury?"

"Yes, well, only a trickle of blood was found, not the deluge described. As Debra told Anna who told me, a loose nail along the ledge caught the thief's skin as he slithered from the room. I imagine The Midnight Menace bears nothing but a scratch. The Devil protects his own."

As the room began to spin, Honoria grasped at the

bed's poster. A scratch. Lawry bore a scratch. It looked quite inflamed.

Cards tilted upright as they fell into place. Could it be possible, or was she simply imagining a scenario that would allow for why Sir Lawrence no longer seemed interested in continuing his pursuit? Perhaps she truly was coming down with some illness, because so fevered an image had to be the product of a diseased mind. Lawry? Her gentle, rumpled, laughing Lawry, The Midnight Menace?

But Lord Meriven had suggested as much. She had thought him wildly speculative in his assertions and put them from her. He didn't know Lawry had had a reason for his dissemblance, for pressing a blade to her throat. And there had been ample opportunity for the baronet to have stolen her pendant if such had been his goal. He hadn't seemed to pay it any mind at all. No, all his attention had been upon touching her.

A shiver rode her spine, but once again she suspected it had its origins in desire rather than fear. Otherwise, why would she be picturing his palms sliding the length of her arms as he bent to press his lips to the sensitive skin of her neck?

Yet, what if?

Her heart beat faster as her contradictory thoughts swirled. She had so many questions, and not a single answer. All she had to clutch onto were his careless words in a darkened theater against a single scratch. And his words... he had told her he wasn't the marrying kind at the Robinson dinner, but reversed his decision the next night.

Imprudent words. Still, he could not take back he had asked for her hand, not even if he was a dread thief. Plus, it would serve him right if she accepted.

Chapter 11

Lawry, dressed in black once again, angled his body so he stood in the deepest part of the shadows. Pressed against the building, out of the way of the main thoroughfare, he didn't fear remark unless the remarker also embarked upon some nefarious deed. Even then he could almost depend upon the courtesy of a blindly turned eye among his fellow nocturnal marauders. He would do them the same politeness.

Tonight he wasn't out retrieving baubles from those too spoiled to appreciate them. The treasure he waited to purloin had far greater value. Besides, stealing Honoria's heart was only fair. She had already stolen his.

His knees popped as he crouched against the wall and settled, waiting for a more opportune moment to rise. He delayed as his soft-soled boots grew damp. When the butler turned down the lamps, his pulse increased. He cooled his heels a little longer until he could be certain Giles had sought his bed.

When the butler passed by the window carrying a candle, his umbra dancing across the gap in the drawn curtains, Lawry unhinged his stiff muscles and crept toward the front door. He held two long metal picks in his damaged left hand. His flesh throbbed where they pressed.

Idiotic nail. Idiotic him. Last night, his information

had been wrong. He had almost paid for the error with more than a bit of skin and blood. Lady Quinlan, whose absence he had presumed, had barely allowed him to flee her room unscathed. She had chased him even up to the window sash, leaning so far over the opening he had feared she might tumble to the street below. As he scrambled from sill to stacked boxes to street, she had shouted suggestions after him he would have blushed to have heard whispered.

At least she had thrown her jewels at him. What fit of madness had prompted her to do so he didn't know, but the funds would come in handy. The gems were already being cut, the gold melted. Her pieces had been too noticeable to leave whole.

He mounted the stairs and reached for the Cutworth doorknob before pausing, with the cooled metal beneath his bare fingers. Not for the first time, he wondered if he hadn't lost his senses. It was one thing to break into an unoccupied house and purloin a flash of gold. It was another to force entry into an innocent's room for the purpose of conversation. Accosting Honoria on the street, in plain view of any who might lay witness, hadn't risked her reputation. If he was discovered within her chamber, she would be ruined.

He grunted. Conversation? Lady Quinlan's erotic suggestions still threw themselves about his brain until all he could visualize was Honoria spread before him, tied to the posts, as he used every ounce of restraint he possessed to taste her from neck to...

He shook his head and blew out a gust of air as he forced his body to heel. Not now. He couldn't think of it now. He had to go in there and explain why he had raced from her parlor as if the hounds of Hell chased his heels. They did. They had. And she knew it.

Despite the simpers she donned, the ones he hated, the ones she applied like a cudgel, she possessed a razor-sharp mind. Its quickness frightened most men because her mask slipped too often. Behind it she held up a sort of revealing mirror in which a gentleman was undressed to his basic layer, and what man wished to see himself as the fool he truly was?

Few. Happily, he was one of their small number. Introspection didn't bother him at all. He didn't mind appearing as bumble-headed as he sometimes was, not if it gained him the most magnificent female ever created as reward.

Lawry raised the picks to the lock and paused again. He gave the deserted street one more cursory glance out of habit. He was glad he did. A gentleman dressed in evening kit emerged at a rapid pace from the shadows at the corner. The man studied the street in the opposite direction before turning his head toward where Lawry hesitated.

A millisecond before his gaze would reach the Cutworth landing, Lawry leapt over the railing and crouched down amidst the bushes under the windows. The man clipped closer, his heels beating a staccato rhythm against the pavement.

Lawry waited for him to pass by the Cutworth residence. Surprise stilled him when instead those soles passed within a few feet of where he rested and swished up the stairs. Had the newcomer glanced to the left he would have seen Lawry ducked there. Instead, he focused upon the door. As he crossed from the stairs to the portal moonlight unmasked his features.

John Gray, the Marquess of Meriven.

Lawry pressed himself tighter against the shrubbery and eyed the self-complacent lord carefully. His heart beat a fast rhythm against his chest as he contemplated what the man's presence after midnight might almost certainly mean.

Honoria was playing fast and loose with her affections.

His stomach pitted. He wanted to vomit. A low buzzing sounded in his ears.

He drew in a long breath through his nose and fought the impetus to slump back to his own home in wretched defeat. Then he stopped breathing altogether at the astounding sight before him. Lord Meriven, heir to all he surveyed, the most grandiose of gundiguts, greater than the greatest among them, pulled picks much like Lawry's own from his front pocket. They were so shiny they glinted in the starlight. Meriven's use of the implements was not as expeditious as Lawry's more practiced hand, but a few scrapes and a loud *click* moments later indicated this was not the first lock he had brasted.

The door opened, and Meriven disappeared within.

Remarkable. Gentleman were generally unfamiliar with the apparatus of forced entry. Was Meriven a fellow thief? But why? There was nothing of great value in the entire house. Even Honoria's jewels were of the third water, if not the fourth, and barely worth a trip to the pawn unless one found himself desperate for a crust of bread.

Lawry stood and studied the closing door despite the inadvisability of retreating from his hiding place into plain view. His insides twisted into pretzel shapes.

Of course, there was the lady herself, a jewel of

unparalleled value. She was worth any risk. But why break and enter when the marquess might have had her to wed at a word? Though her station was too far removed from his to make a match between them easy, it was not impossible. He could ask, she could accept, and he could insist the match was perfectly reasonable. After all, who would gainsay The Gray Lord?

What if… what if he had insisted, but upon a different sort of relationship?

Sudden rage trembled Lawry's hands so he had to grip them into fists. Meriven had interrupted him three nights earlier. Lawry had taken his ostensible rescue of Honoria for chance, but The Gray Lord had slid from the Cutworths' property. Perhaps he had awaited her arrival in order to indulge in a sweet assignation. Perhaps breaking into her home was a kind of lover's game.

He should go home. He should forget Miss Cutworth and her ready wit. He should ignore how Hercules haunted the door, waiting for her to reappear into his life once more, or how he had barked and whined an entire opera at the chance to accompany his human friend on tonight's mission to her residence. The canine was never subtle about his desires.

He straightened further. Nor was he. Whatever pain it caused, he had to know if he still had a chance or if she had played him for the fool he was.

Lawry stomped up the stairs, took another few steadying breaths, and thrust his picks into the lock. A few twists later and he followed Meriven's path through to the entryway. No sooner did he press the door closed but he saw movement rounding at the top of the stairs. Using the outer edges of the treads to avoid creaks, he wasted no time in following. When he arrived at the second floor, The Gray Lord stood only a few yards ahead. He must be unfamiliar with the home. He slunk his way with care, pausing every few feet.

The first door he opened made only a whisper of sound. Belying his attempts at silence, the marquess rubbed something against something else, producing an odd clicking noise. A small, dim light flared, barely strong enough to carry into the room, but obvious in the otherwise dark hallway.

A battery light. Such a thing had been known for the last half century, ever since Humphry Davy, an English scientist, had invented the electric cell. When connected by wires to a piece of carbon, the carbon would glow for a short period of time, long enough, anyway, for a miscreant to do his worst. Lawry had used one himself on one of his earliest ventures but found the light more annoying than worthwhile.

What on earth was Meriven doing with such a thing in his pocket? Where had he even acquired it, and to what end?

The marquess shut the door and moved across the hallway. On silent feet, Lawry followed him, door by door, staying to the deeper shadows until Meriven opened the last portal on the left. This time after he waved the light around, he dampened the flame and slipped inside the room. Lawry peeked around the open frame but the space was too dark to see much more than shadowed movement. Five times the light flared, illuminating only a small portion of the space, each time with less success. The final time, the clicking sound was followed by quick footsteps back towards where he stood.

Ducking around the edge, Lawry slipped into deeper gloom to watch Meriven tap his way back down the hall, the stairs, and out of the house completely. For a moment, as relief spread through him, dizzying him, he remained where he stood.

It appeared Miss Cutworth had not been the object of Meriven's early morning entry. Lace swathes across the bed had been visible in those flashes of low light. A figure lay within. Given the decoration, it stood to reason the room belonged to Honoria and not the colonel. Meriven had only skirted the furniture, not been drawn towards it.

But he had stopped by a dressing table. What had he taken?

Lawry's body made the decision for him. He followed the marquess's trail, out the door and down the street, just in time to see The Gray Lord jump into a waiting carriage at the end of the block.

That was all right. Lawry knew where he lived.

Chapter 12

Early the next morning, Lawry hastened his ablutions, sped through his dressing, evaded his dog and mother as best he could, and made his way to Honoria's door. The process still took longer than he wished so it was closer to luncheon than breakfast by the time he arrived.

"Miss Cutworth is not receiving today, Sir Lawrence. Should you care to leave your card, I shall be certain she receives it." Giles blocked the door as Lawry attempted to pass within. He bobbed and weaved to match Lawry's movements as if he had taken classes at Gentleman Jim's boxing ring.

"She'll wish to see me." Lawry tried to duck under the butler's arm.

"I fear she will not." The servant's tone was firm as he bent his knees in return to block.

Lawry looked the man up and down before plunking his tall hat back upon his head. Not having anticipated a rebuff, he had already removed it. "Is she ill?"

"Not at all, sir."

"Is the colonel at home then?"

He tapped his walking stick against the stone to remove some of the extra energy coursing through his veins. Normally, he hated carrying the implement as it tied up his hands, but after last night's exertions the better part of valor had dictated preparedness. A sharp and lethal sword lodged within the wooden frame. Thus far he had not been called upon to draw it, but the day was young.

"I'm afraid he is not, sir."

Could he kabob Giles and jump over his prostrate body? Both Honoria and the colonel would likely object. They seemed rather fond of the man. Plus, the blood, and the fact he was against violence as a general rule. Lawry squinted at the butler, just to be certain his mind hadn't changed upon the subject, and sighed.

Temperance, then.

"Could you tell me where I might find him? I have a matter of some urgency to discuss." When Giles failed to look impressed, Lawry leaned in as if about to confide some secret. Which he was. "About Miss Cutworth, if you take my meaning."

A fellow could hardly fail to understand his purpose or what it might signify. The only conversation a gentleman might have with a lady's father about his daughter had to be a declaration of intent to marry. The butler, however, remained unmoved, except he backed up and began to shut the door.

Lawry gripped the edge, risking his fingers. "Please, Giles. You've given me cause for concern now. Don't leave me hanging."

Giles hesitated. He eyed Lawry carefully before studying the street in both directions. He pitched his voice low. "The colonel is currently in conference with the Metropolitan Police at their station. Miss Cutworth's jewels were taken from her room last evening."

Before Lawry could process the information, Giles

bent closer and softened his tone even further. "Might I rely upon your discretion, Sir Lawrence?"

"Of course."

Giles straightened, looked uncertain, and gave every appearance of already regretting his words.

Before he could dither further, Lawry said, "I am a friend of the family, Giles. My mother has known the colonel since they were children. The Cutworths, Miss Cutworth in particular, is held very strongly in my heart. Whatever you say, I shall not compromise her with my knowledge."

The butler studied the sky. "While she was within."

"Pardon?"

In his stentorian tones, Giles conveyed the problem. "Miss Cutworth was within her chamber when her jewels were taken." He met Lawry's gaze. "She was alone. Sleeping."

Which was scandal enough to rock him if he hadn't already known of Meriven's foray. He knew firsthand The Gray Lord hadn't touched her, then or later. Having followed the marquess back to his home, Lawry had returned and watched this house from across the street into the dawn. Just in case.

No one else had entered except Meriven. He knew it with a certainty. Nevertheless, his pulse leapt unpleasantly against his skin.

"She is uninjured, but rightfully disquieted at the violation. The theft has left her... upset."

Those three words, uttered in a soft, even tone, banged into him. They reverberated around his brain for a bit before settling in his stomach. Disquieted. Violation. Upset.

Strange, the weight they held. He stared at the

butler as he wondered how to respond. His stomach clenched. Rolled. When he understood why, he gripped the walking stick so tight he feared he might snap it in half.

Surely, the other females from whom he lifted a trinket or two were not likewise disquieted, violated, and upset?

Yet, the thought held him in place as if it glued his shoes to the landing. He folded through his memories, shifting them as he searched for whether those same three utterances might be applied to his unknowing and largely unwilling benefactors.

There were some differences. Lady Q was the first and only female he had ever encountered upon his midnight jaunts. His Society connections usually landed him with good information and empty rooms. Plus, some ladies never even realized their boxes had been rifled. Of course, some knew, especially of late, now notoriety dogged his footsteps. Upper class women had taken to inventorying their possessions.

In the hope he would visit, or in fear he might? It was difficult to be certain.

Still, he had never stolen from anyone who could not well afford to replace what went missing. And Lady Q hadn't seemed to mind his presence. She had actually chased after him. No, he couldn't believe she had felt violated by his presence. He was almost certain of it.

Some sense of quiet returned, although an uncomfortable niggle of doubt remained.

Like the mythic Robin, he had always chosen his exploits with care. The items conscripted to his cause described wealth, not sentiment. He kept just enough of the proceeds to allow himself a life at the lowest ebb of his class, but no more. His new carriage and his cologne were the only two expenses upon which he had ever splurged for his own sake, though he had, upon occasion, gifted his mother with items he shouldn't.

What he didn't keep he spread among those who broke down the jewelry for him and sold the parts, along with a list of ten charitable causes he ardently supported. Because of his nocturnal activities, four different orphanages were able to hire tender wardens. They each served three full meals a day and provided schooling and trade opportunities. Various animals lucky enough to be captured in Marleybone were transported to a life of ready food and sunny fields in Shropshire. The remainder of the funds helped educate girls and boys who otherwise would have been forced to a life of crime.

A little more of his own disquiet fled, but some remained. He couldn't exonerate himself completely, could he, not and still believe he was an honest man at heart?

"May I be of further service, Sir Lawrence?"

Blinking, Lawry focused upon the butler who stared at him with hard eyes.

He shook his doubts away, though it was more difficult than it should have been. More immediate matters required his attention. He loosened his grip upon his stick.

"I'm sorry, Giles, but I must see Miss Cutworth at once. Move out of my way or I shall be forced to remove you. The matter is beyond me, as I believe you must understand."

The butler either noted his resolve or had grown tired of dancing in the doorway. Though he tossed various entreaties and threats after Lawry in a monotone voice, he moved aside.

Up the stairs, down the hall, last door on the left. Lawry pushed it open and froze, arrested by the sight of Honoria in naught but her chemise, raven locks flowing down her back as she stared out the window.

She turned as he entered. Tears wet her large dark blue eyes. Surprising him, she gave a little cry and ran across the room to throw herself into his arms, sobbing. What could he do but wrap her tight to him? He kissed the top of her head and inhaled the rose fragrance she wore.

"I heard. Your jewels." His words sounded muddled against her hair.

She tilted her head back and wiped away the moisture trailing down her cheeks. "Just the necklace. He left my earrings, which is unfathomable because they are worth more. But he was here, Lawry. He was in my room while I slept. The Midnight Menace. It must have been." Her voice ended in a whine much like Hercules's when he was denied too long a part of his supper. She gripped his arms. "I thought, that is, with your cut, and the blood in Lady Q's chambers, I considered—"

"You considered I was the infamous rogue?"

So, he had been right. When she had looked at him at tea yesterday something had shifted within her eyes. She had noted his injury and put it together with the circulating story. He had hoped to dissuade her from the inevitable path to realization by departing her company, even though it had meant forgoing his intended conversation with her father. Last night he had hoped to confess all to her, but then Meriven had arrived and upstaged him.

But now? With the words disquiet, upset, and violation banging about his brain and constricting his chest, how could he ever explain? She would hate him. She would see him as equal to the vile criminal who had made of her a victim.

Everything in him contracted at the thought she might not be wrong to do so.

He cleared his throat of its strange obstruction. "Honoria, I-I did not break in and steal your necklace. I give you my word." Such as it was. He wasn't lying. He was merely answering in the particular.

She dropped her gaze to the point of his cravat and slid her hands to the front of his jacket. Delicately, she tapped a rhythm there, stirring more than his pity and guilt. "Then someone else must have been... I have only been able to bear the trespass by believing it was just you."

"*Just* me?"

"Not like that. Or perhaps, yes." She shook her head. "I don't know. I am too horrified by the loss to make any sense right now."

She sighed and moved from his arms to cross the room. Two chairs bracketed a small table. She sank down into one. "You should leave. If my father catches you here, he will insist we wed."

He moved to the other chair. "I'd prefer a different path to reach the altar, but it doesn't disturb me to be nudged there at the point of a pistol. I meant what I said, Honoria. I would like us to marry." More than like. He had a need. It made his fingers itch. The fact she was so scantily clad he had seen the full outline of her lush bottom as she swished to the chair didn't help relieve the demand.

She gazed out the window once more. The only view visible through the narrow slice of glass between the heavy drapery were the windows of the building on the opposite side of the street.

"I don't understand why he took the pendant. It is only hollowed gold. Garnets might be cheaply had. There's a Czech merchant in the next quarter who sells them by the handful." She shrugged, but tears pricked the corners of her eyes once more.

"Did you purchase your necklace there? From a Czech merchant in London?"

"No. My uncle brought it from the desert. He said it was fashioned to resemble a necklace held by an ancient ruling family. The "T" shape is a symbol of their gods. Given its pagan origins, I should be happy to be rid of it, and yet I always thought it might be the only interesting thing about me."

His spine jammed straight. "Honoria!"

She twisted her gaze toward him, eyes widening at his exclamation.

"You are being an utter goose."

She blinked. "Excuse me?"

"I'm sorry, but you cannot expect me to sit here and allow you to abuse yourself in such a manner."

"I can't?"

"No gentleman worth his salt would..." His fingers drummed against the table. "Yes, your privacy was invaded and a sentimental trinket was taken. I do not deny you have cause for upset. I understand. You may sob and wail to your heart's content and I will do my best to jolly you into better humor. I would not wish to stifle your feelings. However..." He paused, too many emotions warring within him to easily find the reason for his own agitation.

"However?" Her voice was so small it was almost indecipherable.

"To believe a pagan fob is the most interesting part of you is ridiculous. You are an astounding woman. Your wit, when not covered by a wet blanket, is extraordinary. Just now, however, you are retreating into that mealy-mouthed shell you have so assiduously created to protect you from the censor of lesser individuals. It is offensive of you to lump me with them. I am insulted. I won't tolerate it."

She blinked several times. "No?"

He shook his head. "No, of course not. I want you to be who you really are, even if it's all anger and annoyance and demanding tantrums, all of it." He waved his hand and tried to tamp down on his ire. He breathed deeply through his nose, inhaling roses.

It calmed him enough to even out his voice.

"Honoria, you are strong and capable. You are quick and fascinating in your own right. This feather-brained humility is unattractive. It makes me feel you don't trust me enough to show me the full portion of you, but you can. I assure you, you can."

"I can?" She sniffed. She appeared more contemplative than angry.

The constriction in his chest lessened. He leaned his forearms upon the small table. "Yes. And if I ever try to mold you into some sniveling, simpering Society female you have my permission to hit me about the head with your bumbershoot until I apologize."

She smiled. It lit a tiny portion of his heart. Then she sniffed, and his world darkened.

"Don't, please. There's no need for tears. I promise you, Honoria, I will retrieve your piece. You have my word I shan't rest until it is recovered."

"Thank you." She blinked some more, long lashes betraying her doubt as they fluttered against ivory skin, but her lips curved.

Gads, but he would do anything for her smiles. He cleared his throat again and spread his fingers wide upon the table as if anchoring himself to the ground. "I beg you to believe as my wife you will be guarded and protected at all times. This incident will never be repeated." Or he would kill the cad, his feelings about violence be damned.

"Do you think me unguarded now?"

"I think, until such a magical time when we might all agree to your lawful place as my bride, I shall be forced to rely upon your father and Giles to keep you safe from sunup to sunup. I shall insist their attentions be so assiduous you will long to run to my arms simply for a spot of freedom from their affection." He sat back. "When you consider the matter, it is an excellent plan on my part to assure your defection to my home."

"You are a wily one, aren't you, Sir Lawrence?"

Her smile transformed into something mischievous. It matched the sparkle in her eyes. He didn't think the sheen was the type brought on by tears because every part of him hardened to stone in response.

A man knew. He just knew when he was being flirted with.

"I am as wily as I need to be, which is quite a bit where you are concerned."

She leaned over the table and crooked her finger in

a come-hither gesture. It raced through his veins like wildfire and matched the reckless spark in her dark blue eyes. He complied until their noses almost touched.

She batted her eyelashes again, revealing and concealing by turns the devilish gleam within. "Perhaps you imagine I shall tumble to your puffery? Shall I beg you to take me to bed and have your way with me, all upon promises written in vapor-covered glass?"

He swallowed, but an obstruction blocked his throat. His pants grew uncomfortably tight.

"Beg me," he said. He closed his eyes while he tried to catch his breath. "By heavens, I hope so." He opened his lids. "But not before I've made it official. I'm not some gal-sneaker, you know."

Her lips, pouty and crimson, parted. She leaned in further still, so only a mere hair-width of air separated hers from his. "But what about me? What if I seduce you before it's official? What if I tell you how I am longing for you to show me all manner of wonderful things I've never dreamt of in my wildest imagination?"

Which was more than any man might stand.

His thoughts fled as he gripped the back of her head and drew her into a grinding kiss. He told himself to be gentle. Screamed it. He couldn't. The ground beneath his chair tilted as her lips, tensile and pliant, moved against his. He thought he might fall. Precious satin skin melded to his own as he pulled her over the impediment of the table to tumble into his lap. The small furniture crashed to the floor as her arms wrapped around his neck. Giggling under his questing mouth, she sobered as he pressed her breasts flush against his chest.

He sank. He rose. Honey sweet, dark as wine. Her

mouth, her body… he couldn't taste her enough. Her lips parted under his and he used his tongue to tickle, to tempt. She groaned and he swallowed the sound, his hunger made greater by the strange exultation filling him from toe to tip.

He had embraced his share of women before, but it had never felt like this, as if he were drowning and reviving all in one measure. She trembled as she tried to draw him closer, and when they parted, she looked at him as if he were… what? A god?

Maybe better than that. It certainly felt better than that.

"Will you marry me, Honoria?" His fingers tightened in the silk of her tumbled hair, and then loosened while he waited. She looked set to speak, but didn't.

"Honoria?"

She bit her lip, those plump, succulent pillows, and he groaned. Never mind, he would ask her again tomorrow, and the day after, and the day after, until she said yes. He pulled her closer to him again, but before he could kiss her the sound of a banging door down the hallway distracted him.

"My father." Her eyes rounded as she scampered off his lap. "We can't…"

For a moment he clung to her hand. He brought it to his lips. "As I've said, one path or another suits, but for the sake of your modesty I shall try to convince you both the natural way." It took him a moment or two to stand, although the thought of meeting the colonel under such circumstances did at least have the desired effect of softening him.

She bit her lip and her brow crinkled.

"You are to dine at my home tomorrow night. We shall talk then."

He left before she could reply because he was afraid she might cry off both supper and the future. Though she obviously wanted him in a physical fashion, she seemed uncertain of his suitability as a husband for reasons he couldn't quite comprehend. Yes, their initial meeting had been unfortunate, and yes, he wasn't a wealthy man. Still, he had been on her father's list, even if his had been the last name on a separate page. Perhaps he had been too successful when he had tried to push her away at the park, before he had realized she must be his.

Well, he would just have to prove to Honoria his name should have appeared further up her father's dratted list. Perhaps not in the first space or the second. He didn't possess so much of an ego. But the third entry from the top was not such a stretch, not considering how much he and Honoria suited.

The fact he didn't place better rankled, so much more than was reasonable. At least he had only to compete with Meriven, now the others penciled in before his own name had been eliminated. Despite the marquess's wealth, the stiff-necked lord was little competition.

It only remained to convince Honoria it was so.

Chapter 13

The Meriven townhouse sprawled almost a city block long. It boasted a walled back yard cut by a wide gate through which a carriage might be driven and stored. Wealth and privilege dripped from the squared gray stone facade, but it still bore the air of a prison. Perhaps it was the austere breadth that lent the impression. Maybe it was only Lawry knew the general manner of the man who inhabited the place.

Were boyhood hatreds ever really resolved? His certainly hadn't softened over time and distance.

Once, so long ago it barely bore thinking, they had been friends. At fourteen, matters had changed when John Gray stole the headmaster's favorite book and hid it within Lawry's trunk. Perhaps he had expected Lawry to have discovered it before the school's disciplinarian searched his chambers. Perhaps he hadn't cared if his friend was caned, and worse. The result, however, had been that Lawry was sent up from school, enjoined never to return, and John had gone on to fulfill the duties of his father's title.

When they chanced to meet in Society now, an infrequent event, they nodded politely. To his credit, Lawry had never once actually lifted the blade to Meriven's throat, which had to count in his favor, didn't it?

"Steady," he whispered to himself for courage.

The imminent breaking and entering did not worry him. He had slid through tighter security than what he noted present in the sprawling manse. Retrieving the item should be simplicity itself, though he still could not fathom why Meriven had taken it. The dangerous action of burglarizing the chamber of a young Society female, even one so low-ranked as Miss Cutworth, should not be taken without the hope of ample reward. But what could that possibly be?

No, aside from the mystery of why Meriven wanted the pendant, what worried Lawry most was what he might do to The Gray Lord once he had gained entry and the necklace. Honoria had been nigh on distraught before he had managed to turn her attention. The man should be made to pay for his sins.

Lawry's fingers reached down to fluff Hercules's shaggy head but came up empty. The dog hadn't joined him for the night's festivities. This retrieval was too important to divide his attention. His word and future rested upon his success. He had promised Honoria, after all.

Taking a deep breath, he crossed the street. The usual course of events followed: picks, locks, open, shut, creep, climb, search. All of it went like clockwork, his movements so precise he might set the newly finished Big Ben in the Parliament House to ringing his lauds for timeliness. The problem he encountered came with the next step, when his seeking fingers failed to find the pendant.

He leaned against the polished inlaid marquetry hallway wall and considered. A search of the marquess's private rooms, the place where he would be expected to store the pendant, had revealed little except a card sewn with a complete set of heavy silver buttons, three gold rings set with dark stones, an ivory comb inlaid with pearls and tiny emeralds, four ten-pound notes, and a pair of diamond shoe clips hailing from a distant age. He took them all without the least twinge of guilt, their loss laid entirely at the door of Meriven's own thievery.

After shutting the portal carefully behind him, Lawry maneuvered down the corridor. He stopped at each door to explore within. Though the rooms were lavishly appointed and spoke of current as well as ancestral wealth, they were barren of personal effects. Unless Meriven was hiding pieces under the floorboards, the pendant was not within the guest chambers.

Ignoring the servants' quarters, for only an incompetent would hide their haul in such a place, he chased the stairs to the lower floor. Before the bottom tread slipped under the soles of his thin leather shoes, he stopped. Voices, muffled but unrestrained, floated from the right. Taking care to remain silent, he crept through the parlor and to the office beyond. The door stood closed. Glancing around to make certain no one watched, he lowered himself to the rug and pressed his ear to the space between floor and portal.

"… inferior weight, and why would we think it will open anything but a lady's legs? John, you took a great risk for little reward."

Lawry didn't recognize the voice.

"Not much of a risk. The chit was asleep, probably dreaming of ways to angle a betrothal out of me. While I do approve of well-executed manners, there is something about her that rubs me wrong. I cannot explain it. Her smiles are quite lovely, and by all accounts she was raised correctly, albeit without benefit of a female influence. Perhaps such is the problem."

Meriven. Lawry knew his voice. If Miss Cutworth was the female under discussion, it was probably her intelligence and humor bothering The Gray Lord. Those aspects in any person must surely put the stodgy carper on his guard.

"Still."

A tapping sound ensued like a pipe drummed against the desk. The scent of tobacco wafted under the door. A glass lifted with a scrape. It banged back to the table. Glass clinked against glass, followed by a sloshing noise.

Lawry's mouth watered. Having just gone through Meriven's upper stairs with thoroughness, he found himself a bit parched.

Something tinged and slithered upon a surface. The pendant?

"The piece appears to be the correct shape. It hails from the right part of the world. The back is angled and cut, as if in a pattern. Yet, is it too light and too small? And do the stones matter?" A pause ensued. Meriven sighed. "How should we recognize the key when we have no idea what lock will be in place? All we have are ancient tales. My instincts tell me this pendant is, however, a trail we might follow. I have to believe it was copied from the original key."

"Wishful thinking at best."

"Perhaps. Yet those initials engraved upon the underside of the bail are our best lead, Sebastian. We must send the piece to Baghdad and direct our members there to investigate further. The jeweler might know something more. In any event, it is the first clue we have uncovered in an age."

Silence. Cloth slithered and shifted. A glass *plunk*ed to a desk.

A sigh. "Yes, I suppose it is a clue. I don't wish you to think I question your instincts, John. They have proved right more often than not. As soon as I received your note last night, I packed my bags to return to London because of those instincts. I just don't wish to raise our hopes too high." More scrapes and drags, as if one of them took up the pendant. "I will see what we can uncover. The cause of Assyriology is a difficult one, is it not?"

"Assyriology? Yes, I suppose, though I never forget our genesis calls for greater investigation than its cover. Imagine, Sebastian, the knowledge of the ancient world laid at our feet!"

"Hear, hear."

The louder grating of a chair being pushed back alerted Lawry. He jumped to his feet, ignoring the twinge sounding in his lower back, and drew himself behind the thick velvet draperies. No sooner had he concealed himself than the door pushed open and Sebastian St. Clair, Earl Morray, shuffled his way past.

"Be sure to make a plaster mold before the item leaves your possession, most especially the bail," Meriven said from the doorway. "We cannot afford to lose it now should the seas prove uneasy and it sinks to the bottom."

"Never fear, John. You worry overmuch."

Morray trudged off in one direction, and from the sound of it, Meriven returned to his library. Lawry heard him poke at the fire, sigh, and lift a glass.

Taking care to do so without making noise, Lawry withdrew from his hiding spot to follow the earl, in whose possession he was now almost certain the pendant lay. Instead of exiting through the front, he circled the building through the back, arriving just in time to see the earl's carriage spring down the deserted street. He jumped into his own conveyance and ordered the driver to follow.

They arrived at Morray's home almost at the same time. Having already donned his half-mask, he pulled down his hat and grabbed his pistol, jumping from the carriage before it had come to a full stop. He raced toward the fat man wobbling up the stairs.

"Your money and your jewels. Be quick about it." He poked his pistol into the back of the earl's jacket.

"Pardon? What?"

"Hey! What are you doing?" The earl's driver jumped from his seat.

Well. How unfortunate. An earnest employee.

With no more time to waste, Lawry conked the earl upon the head with the butt of his pistol. Morray wobbled and grabbed for the iron railing. Bent over it, he clutched his pate and moaned. Lawry ignored his sniveling and reached into his pocket.

Nothing.

The driver was almost upon them. He reached into the other pocket and pulled out a chain. Pivoting upon one foot, he raised the other leg and kicked out. The driver stumbled down the steps to land in a heap at the bottom.

After stamping after him, Lawry knelt and checked the man's pulse. It beat strongly. Already, his eyes flittered. By way of apology, Lawry withdrew the card of silver buttons and laid it within the injured driver's hand. He reconsidered and took the buttons back and left him with two ten-pound notes instead. No sense stringing the man up for the noose if his pockets were inspected. Cash was ubiquitous, silver buttons not as much.

"The inconvenience is entirely my fault, but I hope this tiny offering will offset your aches. Stay down and do not follow or worse will occur."

He retreated to his carriage, not waiting to see if the servant would comply. In the next moment they were off, even before he had firmly latched the door. When he opened his palm, a sense of victory filled him.

Honoria was going to be very happy. Perhaps she might even be grateful.

A man could hope.

Chapter 14

The full damask-rose skirt swirled around Honoria's ankles as she checked her profile in the mirror. Two years old and therefore out of fashion, it was the very dress she had worn for her first supper after her debut. Though it was a bit tighter than it had been then, especially at the skinny part of the belled sleeves, she still felt beautiful within the voluminous length of fabric.

Donning it was like wrapping herself in all her past hopes and dreams, before she had realized a pretty face and a functional brain weren't the draw she had been led to believe they would be.

She touched her throat by habit. Instead of gripping the pendant her fingers came back empty. A pang of fear slid icy through her veins but she resolutely pushed it aside. Hope she could handle. Fear, not as well. She tried to focus upon the positive emotion but disquiet followed in upset's wake.

Mealy-mouthed. Was that why she had been targeted for theft? Because whoever had stolen her only necklace had considered she wouldn't make a fuss, and even if she screamed no one would listen to her ramblings? She couldn't deny she transformed into a featherhead when in public. The line between what was allowed and what wasn't was so thin she had always tried to err on the side of acceptability. With their limited finances and her very small dowry, it had seemed the better course.

Maybe, though, she should have acted more like her natural acerbic self. Yet if she had, would she have ever met Lawry? Might she not have been picked up by some lesser male well up the list?

If she had created the list, Lawry would have found top billing. His tousled strength, the length and firmness of his well-shaped muscles, set the bees buzzing along her limbs. Almost, she could smell his scent, the wonderful, expensive fragrance, yes, but also the clean essence of his skin below it. And his kiss… sinking into the pillows of his lips, tasting the mint upon his tongue, she had found excitement. Possibility. Joy. The butterflies winging and dancing within her chest felt an awful lot like Christmas morning. They pinked her cheeks and made her eyes glow. She could see the truth there in the mirror.

Soft rapping sounded. She pivoted to see her father standing in the doorway. Dressed in proper evening kit rather than his uniform, he wore an expression she had never seen before.

"What's wrong?" She flew across the room toward him.

He held out his hands and took hers as he shook his head, his eyes glassy.

"Father?"

His lips lifted into a sad smile. "Sshh. Nothing is wrong. For a moment you reminded me of your mother. I was taken aback. You resemble me so greatly I do not often spy her features within yours." He studied her, tilting her chin into the candlelight. "Something in the eyes tonight, I think, though I cannot fathom what has changed, or why. Is it the theft?"

"Perhaps. Perhaps it is only life." She slid her gaze to the side and tried not to think of the kiss she couldn't forget. "Father, I keep meaning to ask, why did you include Sir Lawrence's name upon your list? Were you unaware he has little income to recommend him?"

Instead of answering, the colonel dropped her hands before he lifted a finger to tap the place her T-pendant usually lay against the hollow of her throat. His chin firmed and he smiled. "We can discuss the matter in the carriage. Come. We don't wish to be more than fashionably late, do we?"

To press him would prove futile. He was a military man, after all. Honoria gathered her things and met him again downstairs. Once they were seated within the conveyance, she could wait no longer.

"Father? Sir Lawrence and the list?"

"Ah, yes. That." He cleared his throat. "Honoria, I know you have been thus far unsuccessful in your attempts to catch a decent husband. Not your fault, of course. The marriage game is cutthroat, and even more difficult to find a groom whom you might admire."

"True."

He gazed out the window into the dark night. "It is why I developed the idea of a list, some way to organize the disordered lot and focus your attention. I had hoped you would find some nice young man before we reached the lower levels, because, yes, the problems mount as we descend, if I am to be completely honest. As you surmised, Sir Lawrence lacks funds. There's also, well…" He paused.

"There's what?"

He cleared his throat and looked back at her.

"Nothing marked in stone." Before she could question the vague response, he continued. "To the positive, the Fishbanes are good stock. On the assumption dogs don't make cats, I presumed the lad developed a moral backbone. So far as I can tell, he is what I expected. In some ways better, in some worse."

Moral backbone? But then, her father was unaware it had been Lawry with a knife to her throat. A man who could lower himself to such action could not be called moral, even if, in a very short span of time, he had managed to bury himself like a burr beneath her skin, a constant itch in need of scratching. Though he seemed the trustworthy sort despite what she knew, perhaps he shouldn't be considered so. Some secrets still remained.

Like that tear across his skin, though he swore he did not steal her pendant. She believed him. Didn't she?

She shook her head to free it of its wayward train of thought. "So, you placed Sir Lawrence on the list as the last possible chance I might find a mate at all, though you hoped I would not descend to his level?" Grueling thought.

"I wouldn't put it in such a manner."

"I'm not certain there are many other ways to put it, Father."

He sighed. "Honoria, every man has his foibles and failures. Frankly, any of the last ten names bore difficulties I would prefer my only daughter do without. I admit funds dictated the greater portion of my decisions as to the pecking order of gentlemen, but such is only natural."

"Is it? If Sir Lawrence possessed a greater livelihood, would you have entered him upon a higher line?" Though she disliked dogging her father in such a manner, she needed to know what he thought of Lawry.

"Of course, else he would not have made the list at all."

"But what if… what if his, er, backbone, as you've said, is not as moral as you believe?"

The colonel regarded her with a steady gaze. "Do you suspect the man of ill-doings?"

Yes. "No, of course not. I merely wished to establish whether lack of funds was Sir Lawrence's only disqualification."

Her father settled back, though he continued to study her. "If not for the problem of income, Sir Lawrence would have made the very top of my list. The way he cares for his mother, his gentler nature, his ready wit: these qualities recommend him as a suitable husband. The truth is, I like the man. I have no doubt he would protect you to his death, which eases my heart. However. It is no secret life is easier when financial needs are readily met."

She picked at her skirt. "Or met at all."

Her father nodded. "True, but here we are. Fishbane is the last name on the list, but would I be wrong in thinking he is the first to engage your heart?"

"No." She swallowed. "No, you would not be wrong."

He rubbed at his pant leg. "The truth is, many marriages are successful even when funds are curtailed, though the way is often more fraught." He held her gaze. "If you wish to set your cap for Sir Lawrence, Honoria, you need not fear being rendered penniless upon the street. I do have some coin, after all, despite my egregious losses of late. There is also another ray of hope: Peter Bartholomew has agreed to accept my investment in the new consortium he is founding. The man always makes a profit. Some kind of damned rogue luck. So, you see, even if Fishbane hasn't two pence in his pockets, you might get on. You won't have any advantages, and you will almost certainly have to economize, but a match is possible. If you choose."

"Shouldn't we worry about whether he will choose me?"

Her father burst out laughing, all his features melting into good cheer once more. "Oh, I doubt that's much of a concern. He seems rather smitten from what I can see."

Before she could admit he had asked her to marry him, the carriage rolled to a stop. Honoria stretched her gloves tight, as a lady never pulled at her gloves in public, and gave her hand to her father as she descended to the pavement.

Before they could mount the stairs, Honoria stopped. "Father?"

He looked at her with brows lifted in question.

"I just wanted to say, though I don't know much about Lady Fishbane, I did find her to be warm... the times we've met. Just in case you were wondering."

Her father turned several shades of red and matched the lowering summer sun. He cleared his throat and patted her hand. "I'll take your words under advisement."

She very much hoped he would. It bothered her, the thought of marrying and leaving him alone to knock about the drafty house. Perhaps if he opened his heart, she wouldn't have to worry any longer.

****

Minutes later they perched in the Fishbane drawing room. Hercules, having greeted the guests so expansively Honoria's best white kid evening gloves were coated with fur and dog slobber, lay at her feet. He hummed contentedly through his nose. Lady Fishbane, her father, and Sir Lawrence engaged in a counterpoint of convivial conversation. Lady Fishbane's laughter rang like bells at accorded intervals.

Honoria, by counterpoint, sat dumb as a toadstool. She could not find a way to speak over the boulder lodged in her throat. It had appeared when Lawry had greeted them in the hall, practically pushing Smithers out of the way to do so.

From the first moment they had met upon the sidewalk, he had pricked something within her, some sense of wanting and rightness, adventure and fun. Now, he boiled her blood, so not touching him had fast become a form of torture. It required all her concentration not to jump into his lap and kiss those cushioned lips to distraction. He was everything. Handsome. Charming. Warm. His smile lit the room like an extra lamp.

She wove her hands together so they would not desert her control, and tried to focus upon the gilt-threaded dark-blue draperies over his shoulder.

She squinted at the fabric. How odd.

Behind the baronet, tall windows filled the expansive wall. They were draped in elegant cloth that pooled to the floor. The color and style of the curtains complemented the designs of the embroidered chairs and couch, all of which matched without quite matching. Blood reds, deep blues, hints of green, and shiny dark wood melded the room together. A large potted palm stood tall in the corner, planted in a jardinière molded in the shape of a blowing wind god. The pot was more art than domestic accessory.

Her gaze circled the space. Paintings adorned the oxblood-red walls, all contained by ornate gilded frames. Their subjects ranged from portraits to landscapes, but all had been created by fine hands. She didn't know much about art but she always instinctively knew what was good.

And what was expensive. It was a bit of a gift and a bit of a curse, the ability to know quality when she saw it, yet not be able to purchase it.

She interrupted the conversation about squirrels and their training. In America, according to Lawry's mother, such pets had long been considered superior to dogs. "This room is delightful, Lady Fishbane."

"Why, thank you, Miss Cutworth. I do take pleasure in creating a certain aesthetic in my environment. My son indulges me terribly, don't you darling?" The elder woman reached over and patted Lawry's hand where it lay splayed against the arm of his chair.

His gaze pinpointed upon her as his eyes narrowed. His laughing lips froze. She saw the question there, but she ignored it.

"And the paintings. They're marvelous. Do tell me, that one, there. Would I be familiar with the artist?"

She nodded toward a masterpiece in which two expressive women were joyfully decapitating a male. The movement of the characters was so persuasive they looked as if they might next roll the man's head toward the carpet. Lady Fishbane rotated in her seat to look behind her. "Oh, the *Judith Beheading Holofernes*? Yes. Lawry, do you recall the artist? Something Italian."

"Artemisia Gentileschi. Early 1600s." His voice was dryer than the desert. He shot her a look she couldn't interpret, but laughter and resignation seemed to vie together within it. He tapped the upholstered arm before stilling his fingers. "You've a good eye, Miss Cutworth. In my opinion, her work is superior to any I've seen elsewhere, but not yet in vogue due to her sex. It is rumored Artemisia used the face of her own rapist as that of Holofernes." He paused. "I do adore avenging angels, meek on the outside, all fire within."

If he hadn't meant the tone of his last words to be suggestive, he had been lucky to stumble upon just the right note.

"And that one?" Honoria quickly pointed at a landscape before the heat spotting her chest could rush to color her cheeks.

Bathed in light dappling from a fluffy-cloud sky, the work was as soothing as the other was invigorating.

"Er, John Constable. The scene is of Salisbury Cathedral. One of the brighter ones. He did many quite dark."

"Ah. Yes, I've heard of him." She examined the small landscape more carefully. "Quite popular, I understand." And costly. She couldn't say so in public, of course, but she could think it.

Lawry smiled across at her before removing his attention toward her father. He jumped into a conversation on the management of squirrels.

Odd. Very odd. Hadn't he implied he sat inches from destitution? How did a poor man acquire at least two masterpieces, maybe more? All the paintings appeared to be of quality. And how had he afforded the furnishings, not a single piece of which bore an unsightly scratch, stain, or threaded edge? By contrast her father's furniture looked middling and decrepit.

"Oh, thank you, Smithers. It appears we are to go in to supper." Lady Fishbane rose.

The men popped up beside her. Honoria had to first steady her legs.

How could a gentleman with little to recommend him financially come to own such objects? But why would he lie to her about the state of his funds when the falsehood placed him in a negative light? Did he think her a fortune-hunter, someone to be dissuaded by misdirection? Perhaps the objects were entailed, or…

Or what? How could such an open, amusing soul be so mysterious at every turn?

The dining room contained its own brand of displayed wealth. Rendered in Pompeian red, trimmed in dark wood dentil molding and gold Greek-key-patterned curtains, it transitioned seamlessly from the drawing room. The white-draped table bore seven forks and a flight of four glasses bracketing the heavy sterling flatware and gold-rimmed porcelain. A lovely centerpiece comprised of folded ivory silk and pink-tipped roses scented the air. Above the flowers, a crystal chandelier refracted its own lit candles. It sparkled across the table and down to the floor.

She eyed the seven forks and three spoons set around each plate. Ten courses? With only four of them to supper, such opulence seemed excessive.

She slipped into the chair next to Lawry which the footman held at the ready. There were two such servants, both comely in their navy and gold-trimmed uniforms. With their identical brown hair, even height and build, and square cut jaws, they presented an elegant matched set. Any duke would consider himself fortunate to have procured a similar service.

Which meant, what? Paintings, perhaps, could have been acquired through his late father's estate. Furnishings could have been installed in a distant age and cleaned upon a regular basis with a gentle hand. Perhaps. How did Lawry afford a matched set of servants?

She studied the baronet carefully as the first footman spread her napkin over her lap. Lawry saw her examination and slid his gaze away.

She considered the table once more. The only contravention of etiquette she could see lay in the fact the four of them sat at the center of the long table rather than spreading out along its perimeter. Two to each side, they lacked a firm head. Most men of any class would object to being ousted from a clear position of authority. Little upsets caused the greatest upheaval.

But not Sir Lawrence. He laughed at something his mother said, his eyes sparkling in the candlelight. If he was uncomfortable at losing his place of power, he hid it well. But wasn't it the very quality she found so attractive in him, the way he had of making the rules seem silly and life feel easy?

Lawry's strong wrist bones peeped from his jacket as he settled them upon the pristine tablecloth. His ease, in combination with the room, along with the memory of his lips and hands upon her, rolled in her belly as she stared at his long fingers. Of a sudden she dreaded the numbered courses to be spread in front of her. How was she to even taste them without running to the retiring room to deposit her supper?

An appetizer of blanched fish in pastry slid before her. She pushed it about the porcelain as best she could. A hearty crayfish soup followed. She sipped it once, then drank a large draught of the flat water in the etched crystal goblet. The wine she left untouched. Her wits were addled enough.

The next course contained a lovely salmon in Dutch sauce. It was her very favorite meal. She began to pick at it with the hopes of finishing the small morsel when she glanced to the side at Lawry. Waves of heat spread from her toes to the top of her head as he studied her. A flash of sharp desire mixed with her disquiet so she swayed toward him before she could draw herself back.

"Is something amiss, Miss Cutworth? Is the fish not to your liking? I believe the next course to be a calming *chaudfroid* of chicken with minced veal, topped with a light béchamel. Is that correct, Mother?" Hidden from their parents across the wide expanse of table, Lawry's elbow rubbed against hers. Where his jacket touched her bare skin, little fires lit and burned. The flames rushed heat throughout her body and climbed to her cheeks.

"Yes, dear. You chose the menu yourself, if you'll recall." Lady Fishbane exchanged a glance with the colonel before centering upon Honoria. "Is Lawry correct? Are you feeling ill again, my dear?"

Honoria nodded, shook her head, and nodded again. Lawry's knee angled to rest against hers. He wrapped his lower leg so it fixed between her calves, though the skirt kept most of his offense from settling.

It didn't matter. She couldn't breathe. "I'm afraid, my stomach... it isn't quite settled this evening."

Before she had finished the sentence, Lawry had thrown down his napkin and jumped from his seat. He pulled back her chair before extending his hand.

"Come. I have just the thing. A little fizzy water with medicinal syrup. I find it soothes a rolling belly. Mother. Colonel Cutworth." He bobbed his head as he placed Honoria's hand upon his arm. He seemed anxious to drag her to privacy. The thought made her blood pool in uncomfortable places.

At the mention of fizzy water, or perhaps at their sudden movement, Hercules, who had passed the time beneath the table no doubt dreaming of scraps, danced around their legs. Lawry barked an order at him as he almost tripped over the canine, before cursing under his breath. The dog raced toward the doorway and turned, panting.

But it was too late. Lady Fishbane had already risen, a helpful footman adjusting her chair. "Oh, Henry, you'll adore the new contraption."

"We can find the kitchen on our own, Mother." Lawry tossed the words over his shoulder as he sought to evade the dog.

Hercules rushed between them, spinning Honoria away from Lawry.

Quick as a hare, her father popped out of his seat to offer the dowager his arm. In the process his chair tipped back. One of the matched servants caught it just in time, but neither of the two parents noticed. They were too busy sharing a smile and a hooked stare.

Honoria repressed the instinct to roll her eyes. Still, at this rate there was almost certainly going to be a match between their families, but it probably wouldn't involve her. For someone who insisted he wanted to wed her, Lawry was awfully slow to ask her father for her hand.

The baronet sighed, a long, low exclamation of resignation as he regarded their parents. "Oh, good. Company." Lips pursed, he stuck out his elbow, offering his arm to Honoria again.

Once she wrapped her hand around his muscled forearm, she peeped up to find him staring. His eyes blazed, some odd combination of heat, humor, and ire mixed in such a way it captured her breath and balance.

He leaned to whisper in her ear, "Foiled again, but I'm the patient kind."

Or, it might involve her. Perhaps a double wedding?

What was she thinking? She gazed up into his hazel eyes and knew she wasn't using her brain at all.

Honoria's body tingled the entire way to the kitchen. It was her first experience of visiting such a room outside her own home. How did Lawry even know where his lay?

Once through the doorway, he led her to a huge, hulking polished silver contraption almost as tall as she was. Shaped like a miniature church replete with a tall steeple, the central spire rose in a high, delicate thrust toward the copper ceiling. However, instead of a cross figuring upon the tallest point, a half-draped female posed there. Her downcast eyes and up thrust arms drew attention to, and mirrored, the angle of the two spigots jutting from the front panel. A row of small glasses stood on a shelf beside four crystal decanters: one dark, one palest green, one golden, and one pink.

"The water is carbonated through some mechanism I've yet to examine. I have, er, been otherwise occupied of late." It seemed Lawry blushed, but in the dim light she couldn't be certain. "I have four types of syrups to offer. The darkest one is flavored with vanilla bean and citrus. It is quite delicious, as well as being known to solve the problem of a rolling belly. The pink one is strawberry. I have mint as well, the pale green there, and ginger, which is the sort of yellowish one. Excepting the strawberry, I understand they all work wonders upon the, um, nerves. Perhaps you might like to sample them all?"

She did, if only because she had never seen such a machine or tasted the results before. She and their parents moved to a small adjacent table and sat in a circle as Lawry worked the machine. Watching the bubbly brew fizz from the spigot was almost as exciting as tasting the flavors he added. With each round he filled a small dish for Hercules to sample, though with less syrup. The dog grinned from ear to ear with each course.

Perhaps because their venue was so unlikely, or maybe simply because their formal dinner had transformed into such a heretical gathering, conversation turned to giggling and laugher as they told stories of the worst meals they had ever tasted at Society supper parties.

"I win, of course." Her father smiled broadly. "Until you've tasted boiled crickets, you cannot know the depths of human cuisine."

"One of the many reasons I'm happy to have avoided the military, colonel." Lawry laid his hand along the back of Honoria's chair. His finger lightly grazed the most sensitive part of her nape, sending shivers down to her toes.

After the strawberry course, Lady Fishbane used her glove to dab away a smear of pink on the colonel's white mustache. He returned the favor by accidentally toppling one of her glasses when he startled. The dark residue of the first decanter spotted her dark green skirts. He jumped from his seat and dashed to the sink where a bowl of fresh water stood. Apologizing all the while, he wet his handkerchief and raced back to dab at the discolorations, only he couldn't find them. He raised his spectacle to his eye and frowned in dismay.

They all burst into laughter. Lady Fishbane raised her stained glove and stroked the side of his face, before turning the color of a bright sunset. She folded her fingers in her lap. Honoria exchanged a look with Lawry. He smiled his gentle smile. In response, she nodded.

It was good. It was better than good. Her father hadn't ever expressed an interest in remarrying, claiming his memories held him better than any new wife could. If she were the betting type, she would wager his opinion had changed with this renewed acquaintance.

"Which one?" Lawry demanded, after they had sampled them all. "Which one is your favorite, Miss Cutworth?"

Honoria, already laughing at Hercules's pleased and sugar-drunk expression, examined the grouping of discarded glasses Lawry had placed upon the counter. Residual colors stained the bottoms. She looked at him, the glasses, and him again, suddenly at a loss. Her smile died. Deciding which flavor best pleased her shouldn't be difficult, but a wave of nerves fluttered up her spine. Her ability to form her own opinions and spout them dried upon her tongue. Instinct forced her to paste her best simper across her lips as she sought refuge in a role she had practiced all her life.

"Why, they're all lovely, Sir Lawrence. Which is your favorite, pray tell? I'm certain we'll find ourselves in accord."

His happy expression melted. He leaned back against the counter and folded his arms across his chest. "I very much doubt it, Miss Cutworth. I refuse to hold the same opinion as someone who pretends to be a featherhead."

"Lawry!" Lady Fishbane gasped. Her eyes rounded to saucers.

"I say, son, apologize immediately." Her father scraped back his chair and rose.

Lawry ignored them. He raised an eyebrow, his gaze never leaving hers. In his eyes, she saw a challenge.

She cleared her throat as her father advanced upon him. "Father, please. Don't."

The colonel pivoted. His face flushed red. Both his fists clenched at his sides. "I'm not certain if you noticed, Honoria, but the man just insulted you."

He rotated back toward Lawry, whose gaze still rested steadily upon her. Not by a single inch had he changed his negligent stance, not even with her irate father advancing upon him in a menacing fashion.

The man was brave. She had to give him that. Or foolish. Or suicidal.

"Father, please. Sit down."

Honoria jumped to her feet. She turned the other

way around the table and caught her father's arm before he could reach Lawry. He didn't shrug her off, but he also didn't raise one of those fists and punch the baronet.

She met Lawry's gaze. "Father. Lady Fishbane. In this instance Sir Lawrence is correct to call me out about my nerves." She cleared her throat again and crossed to the counter. She slipped her finger gently over the tops of her group of discarded glasses until it came to rest upon the darkest stain. Lifting it, she handed it to him. "Would you be so kind, Sir Lawrence, as to pour me another vanilla and lime? It is most definitely my favorite."

The smile that split his face beamed so bright the entire kitchen lit up like the courtyard under a high noon sun. "I would be delighted, Miss Cutworth. You've made an excellent choice. As it so happens, it is also my favorite. I do adore coincidences." He twisted his back to their parents and winked at her.

Heat coursed down her limbs again, and it was all she could do not to slip into him. She cast a quick glance toward her father. His furious expression had resolved into one of approval. He nodded at Sir Lawrence before he sank back into his seat.

When they returned to the dining table for the next seven courses, Honoria was able to swallow once more. Lawry's fingers often drifted, under one guise or another, to touch her arm, her back, and even once, her leg.

The food might stick in her throat each time the tiny fires flared, but she wouldn't have dampened them for all the delicacies in the world.

Chapter 15

Lawry sat behind his desk and pondered. He drummed the fingers of his left hand upon an open ledger and the scattering of papers covering it. The sheets were replete with expenses he had yet to enter into the household ledger. He ignored them.

In his right hand he held Honoria's pendant. He examined it from every angle. Earlier, he had used a magnifier to scrutinize the markings. Try as he might, he could find nothing unusual about the piece to explain Meriven's theft of it.

"I shall ferret your secrets, you lowly bugger. Perhaps the garnets? What do you think, Hercules?"

The dog lifted his head, snuffled, and flopped over to lie upon his side. Lawry rubbed his fingertip over the dried-blood-colored stones. They felt cool and hard against his skin. Nothing out of the ordinary. Nothing very valuable. As Honoria had said, like stones could be purchased by the handful from the Czech merchant some districts over.

From what he had overheard, it was clear Meriven thought the piece some kind of key. But to what? And did it matter?

Yes, if he returned the pendant to Honoria and Meriven tried to steal it again. He brushed away the thought. Only a fool would dip his hand in the same vat twice. Still. The entire venture felt off. Everything had a logic behind it, even those actions which at first blush appeared illogical, but he couldn't find a thread to chase.

Unless... could it be Meriven knew Lawry moonlighted as The Midnight Menace? What if he had intended him to overhear the conversation with Morray? What if the marquess knew his old friend wouldn't be able to resist stealing the piece back, and had laid a trap for him? He couldn't discount it, but...

A single rap upon the doorframe startled him. He jumped in his chair, the pendant clinking upon the sole barren spot on the desk's surface.

"Mother! I didn't hear you approach. Practicing your burglary skills?"

"Should you fall ill, someone will have to take your place. Whatever would Society do without The Midnight Menace's exploits gracing the front page of the latest rags?" She glanced around the room. "I heard you speaking and thought you might have company."

"Just Hercules. Damned chimney. What were you doing in the guest bedroom?"

The acoustics were such any sound made in his office traveled through the flue to the room above. Since they rarely had guests, it wasn't a pressing issue. Still, he should really hire someone to correct the problem. He glanced at the papers and sighed. Gads, but he hated domestic tasks.

"I happened to be passing by." His mother swished through the door and nearly stepped upon the dog who lay sprawled before the entrance. "Move, mutt."

"*Rrrr.*" Hercules lifted his chin, but his growl sounded half-hearted.

Lady Fishbane sank down to pet him behind the

ear. He rolled onto his back to offer his stomach to her fingers.

"Bad doggie," she cooed before rising. "Well?"

Lawry tucked the pendant back into his pocket. "Meriven stole Miss Cutworth's pendant. I stole it back and have yet to return it to her as I'm not certain how to explain my possession of it."

His mother's face creased. No matter how she tried to hide her concern, it showed in her pinched brown eyes and mouth. "I see. Unusual, isn't it, for a marquess to steal from a young lady?"

"Meaning it is not for a baronet?"

She sank into one of the chairs before the desk, her pretty pale blue and yellow skirts puffing around her like a cloud of meringue. "One might imagine it would be out of the common for you as well." She glared at him before her expression softened. "Lawry. How long do you believe you might continue in your ill-advised pursuits, especially now you seek Miss Cutworth's hand?"

"Excuse me?" He straightened. "I never said…"

"Though children often think their parents dumb as toast, it is a fact we don't lose all our wits when we give birth. I saw how you folded yourself around her last evening. I believe the colonel marked your attentions as well. I advise you to use discretion else he pin you to the wall upon the point of his pistol." She patted a strand of graying chestnut hair into place even though not a whisper of it dared fall out of order.

"I hope you're not implying I have taken any advantage of Honoria." His mother raised an eyebrow and he quickly corrected himself. "Miss Cutworth, I mean."

"I am implying you have gotten into the habit of taking."

Lawry narrowed his eyes. "Say what you mean to say, Mother. It is not like you to be vague."

She raised her right eyebrow. With the simple gesture she censored him for his tone. How was it she could reduce him to a boy in short pants with such ease? Were all men such pudding?

"Pardon, Mother."

She turned her gaze toward the mess of papers and sighed before gathering the lot closest to her. She began to organize them so they rested top side in the correct direction. A peculiar kind of love filled Lawry. She could annoy him to his depths and at the same time move him to awe at her devotion.

"You do hold honorable intentions toward Miss Cutworth, I hope?"

"Honorable?"

A few quips meant to needle lodged upon his tongue. He bit them back. The way she peeped at him from under her lashes demanded an honest response. He sighed.

"Yes. I intend to marry her, if she'll ever agree to have me."

Her shoulders eased. He hadn't even realized she had been tense. "You've been acquainted what, a week?"

"Just about, yes."

There was no hope for it but to lay forth his heart. He took a deep breath.

"I cannot explain what happened. One moment I was whole and sane, and the next I felt as if the earth had opened and swallowed me whole. I could barely draw breath. All I wanted was to hold her near enough to feel her pulse beat beneath my skin. Even before she spoke, even before I gazed into her astounding eyes, it was as if lightning reached down from the heavens to spear me to the earth and set me aflame. It burned away everything I was and left me a puddle of need. Need and… ecstasy." He shook his head. "I cannot credit it, and yet…"

"*Le coup de foudre*. That's what the French call it." His mother smiled, her expression soft. "I remember it well. It was similar for me with your father."

He asked the question that had been gnawing at him. "And the feeling, was it real?" Because how could it be when it had happened in an instant? Yes, it might drive him to wed, but he needed to know what would happen in ten years, or twenty.

"Very much so. And to your father's dying day my love for him never changed, except perhaps to deepen." She straightened and tapped the pages on the edge of the desk. "The thing is, I'm learning there are many kinds of love. They come along at different points of our lives. Some arrive on a bang and upend one's world. Some slide in gracefully, with old friendship and ancient attraction."

"Colonel Cutworth?"

She blushed and waved her hand. "Never mind. Listen to what I'm trying to tell you. The lightning strike kind, it's impossible to resist. If it is *le coup de foudre*, dear, there's really no point in trying to evade it. You have to work with it, even if it disarranges your entire life."

Which warmed him from inside like a toasty beef pie on a winter's day. At the same time it chilled him to the bone. How was he to pursue Honoria when he couldn't tell her the truth about himself? How could he fit her into his life of crime even if he managed to be truthful?

When she had finished with her small pile of papers, his mother laid it to the side. He pushed the rest of the mess toward her.

He cleared his throat. "Speaking of folding around someone, and though I am loathe to press a point, I couldn't help but notice how close you have become to Colonel Cutworth. First name basis?"

She flipped papers as a darker pink stain highlighted her cheeks. "I suppose we've fallen back to our childhoods. It isn't at all the same as you calling Miss Cutworth by her Christian name."

"No?" He tilted his head to examine his mother from a different angle. He straightened. "Perhaps it isn't. I can't help but notice, Mother, how you fell to Earl Kildare's charms just days ago."

She stopped shuffling the papers and met his gaze. Her eyebrow lifted again. "Are you implying I'm a wanton?"

It was his turn to grow over warm. The heat rushed from his chest to the roots of his hairline. "No. No, of course not."

She nodded. "Good. I'd hate to have to send you to bed without supper as I was forced to do several times during your childhood." She tapped the papers on the desk to even the lot. "The thing is, Lawry…"

When she hesitated he leaned forward upon his forearms. "Yes?"

"The thing is, I didn't believe I would ever want another man in my life after your father died, but it's been so many years. When the earl came to call, I knew at once his determination bore all the signs of skullduggery, yet it lifted something in me, some hope, maybe, I could be more than your mother."

Despite the irrationality of it, the thought she might want more stung.

"I had no real interest in him. How could I?" she continued in a soft voice. "He insulted my son. I was planning on the best way to cut him in public when he disappeared. And then you sought out the Cutworths and I… Once upon a time, I harbored a rather large devotion for Henry, you know."

She blushed again, a pretty pink. The color sent sparkles to her eyes. Of a sudden she looked younger than before, or perhaps he was only seeing her in a different light.

"The colonel was sent away to war and you married my father."

"And loved him with every fiber of my being, though a love match wasn't what our parents contemplated." She shook her head and sighed. "It's water under the bridge now." Her gaze sharpened. "I want to discuss your activities."

Lawry slouched back again. "I don't."

"You cannot continue, not with Miss Cutworth in your future. I doubt she and her father will take kindly to learning who you are. What you are."

Which was true. Her words mirrored his thoughts. If he couldn't tell Honoria who he was, he couldn't marry her. He was not such a cad he would lure her into a lifetime with him under false pretenses. And yet, she would leave him if she found out, wouldn't she? Those three words announced in Giles's stentorian tones still haunted him. Disquiet. Violation. Upset. Strange how they had taken on the poundage of an anvil poised to fall upon his head.

His mother laid the second batch of papers upon the first in a neat and tidy pile he could never have managed. "When you came to me after your first lark and explained how you would subsidize our income, I said nothing. I knew you needed an outlet for your energies, and Heaven knows we needed an income. I also knew you would never harm anyone in the process, though I worried you would end up being hurt."

"Yet you never once criticized the morality of my activities."

"No." She laid her palm flat upon the stack of documents. "I never did. Moreover, I encouraged you, I'm afraid. Last night, at dinner, I looked into Henry's eyes and I realized. I imagined telling him your secret. I imagined his reaction. He will tell me I did wrong by not helping you find a different outlet for your energies. A different manner of securing an income. And he will be right."

Lawry rose from his seat and walked around the desk. Perching upon the edge next to where her skirts bloomed out around the seat, he laid his hand over hers. "The fault was never yours. If you had objected, I would have sought my success anyway. And I truly believe I've done much good with what I've garnered."

She nodded. "I believe it as well."

He shrugged and removed his hand. "Then there is no problem. Yes, the narrow lines of morality might squeeze me a bit, but on the whole, I believe I've done better than not."

Hercules lifted his head and sniffed through his

nose.

His mother shook her head. "You've been lucky, Lawry. I say a prayer every day you continue to be so, but I have a terrible feeling in my heart. Here." She covered her chest with splayed fingers. "There are other avenues to pursue. Perhaps the military? Colonel Cutworth has connections. If we were to sell some of the paintings you inherited, and I were to let go the folly of those matched footmen, you'd have enough to buy a commission."

And lose Honoria? Be parted from her by the width of seas and not just a few London streets? The idea was a knife to the chest. It cut through bone and sinew.

Yet his mother was right. His days as The Midnight Menace had to be nearing the end. Either he would be caught and hanged, or he would be caught and killed by the colonel for his disrespect of his daughter. In all events, he would lose Honoria.

And that he could not do.

Chapter 16

Surrounded by her herbs, flowers, and distilling equipment, Honoria stripped the dark, sticky interior from a vanilla pod. She drank in the aroma.

Last night's fizzy flavored water had given her inspiration. The soaps and scents she created usually centered around flowers, but what about baking ingredients? Certain fragrances already used vanilla as a base, but rarely did they focus upon it. And what about sugar? Was there a way to distill its essence for use? Surely she was not the only one to delight in the smells of cakes or her favorite fruit tartes? And what about milk? Cardamom? Cinnamon? An entire fragrance world had opened before her.

After pushing her sleeve back up when it fell down her arm, she carefully scraped the black seeds clinging to the blade into the beaker before adding a dash of alcohol. Once it rested and melded, she would add another draught before bottling it.

She grabbed a jug of olive oil, an expense almost unjustified in their current situation, and poured out half a glass. Three more vanilla pods met the edge of her knife, the seeds tossed into the oil before she set the mixture within the metal ring over the small flame. The heat would fuse the scent to the oil. If the olive undertone was still too strong, she could add another scent to distract the nose. Cinnamon or cardamom, but what about sage? Or lemon? Or peach?

"Miss Cutworth?"

Startled, Honoria pivoted. In the doorway, framed against the brighter light of the exterior yard, a tall, thin man stood. When he removed his high hat and stepped forward, she recognized Lord Meriven. A sudden wallowing of her heart reminded her she had forgotten him quite completely.

"Lord Meriven. What a lovely surprise." So much so, she forgot to simper. She quickly pasted on one of her best fake smiles before dropping it again.

No. She wasn't going to do that anymore. Lawry didn't like it when she hid her true self behind the mask Society approved. More importantly, she didn't like it much either.

"Forgive the intrusion. Your butler indicated I might find you here." He chuckled. "I'm afraid I insisted upon seeing you."

Her fingers tensed upon the table. "How odd. Giles rarely recognizes station as a reason to abandon his senses."

Meriven shrugged. "I do have a way with words. I did threaten some rather awkward results should he refuse me. Few men of reason would have resisted."

"How kind of you to come to his defense."

He gazed around the small room, a separate space outside the kitchen erected with stone walls. Her father had ordered it built when she had been just a girl, a way to avoid the eventuality of her burning down the house when she forgot a distillation set over a flame.

"Interesting sort of place. What is it you do here?"

He sauntered toward her and leaned over the oil. Sniffing, he donned a slightly puzzled expression.

"Baking?" He stepped back. "How unusual, especially for a female of your class." The tightening of his mouth, the small flaring of his precise nostrils, indicated he did not find her activity unusual in a positive manner.

"I'm not baking, no. I am creating a fragranced oil. For… personal use. I have a great interest in scents. For instance, yours smells of small white flowers and musk."

He glanced at her, a frown upon his lips. Of course. She should not comment upon his person, most particularly his odor. To do so must place her in a lower genus.

"Pardon the observation, my lord. It is the space." She gestured to the walls. "It leads me to forget my manners. I become immersed in the art of perfume. I meant no disrespect."

He grunted his response and resumed his perusal of her equipment, circling the counter as he bent from time to time to stare at a flacon or beaker or burner. Every so often he would reach forth a gloved finger to wiggle something. When he came to a wax-sealed crock, his eyebrows rose. He lifted the jug in question.

"Er, well, yes, I suppose that particular jar might be classified as baking. It's a vanilla bean syrup for use with a water dispensary. I've recently tried fizzy, flavored water and found it quite delightful. Have you ever experienced the pleasure? What you hold is my first attempt at recreating the additive. Unfortunately, the consistency is a bit off, as is the sweetness. Would you like to try some? I can fetch a glass of water – normal water, but I think…"

He replaced the jar as if it might bite him and

withdrew a handkerchief from his pocket. He wiped his gloves and repocketed the square. "I don't approve of sweets. Rots the teeth and guts." His gaze roved over her as if checking for such deterioration.

Gritting her perfectly fine dental appointments, she fisted her fingers before loosening them again. "And what brings you here today on this surprise visit, my lord? Is there something with which I might assist you?"

His excoriating stare centered upon her neck. "I notice, Miss Cutworth, you do not wear your customary pendant. Might I inquire as to why?"

She touched her throat. She lifted her head. "It was stolen from my bedchamber. I no longer possess the piece, I'm afraid."

"Stolen from your bedchamber? While you were within?" He sounded scandalized, but there was an exaggerated aspect to his expression. His eyes rounded too wide, his tone undulated too syrupy-sweet. It was as if he already knew and mocked her.

She drew up her spine. If she admitted she had been within when the crime had been committed, she would be ruined. That she had done nothing wrong would prove irrelevant. It was why the theft must remain a guarded secret, at least the particulars of it.

Yet she had had no qualms in telling Lawry the details of the event, had she? Whereas she would rather die quite violently than relate the experience to this gray lord, she hadn't hesitated a single second before informing the baronet.

How odd, now she considered it. Her fingers fell to the table and thrummed against the edge. It must mean she trusted Sir Lawrence with her very life, for a reputation once lost was irreplaceable. Society acted as a herd, one hand helping another to the trough. Once ousted, no means of acquiring wealth exited for a rejected female. There wasn't a legitimate position she would be able to fill, from governess to wife to laundress. Her demotion would reflect equally upon her family.

"Miss Cutworth?"

She met his gaze. "I was with my father in his study at the time, going over some watercolors my mother had done. We often reminisce and remember her thus. I suppose some hours passed before I returned. I noted the absence of my pendant immediately, but thought nothing of it until I could not locate it in any of the usual places the next morning." There. Let him accuse her of lying. He couldn't, not unless he chose to insult her directly.

"How... convenient." He approached and she stepped back, her spine angled against the workbench. "Have you alerted the Yard to the theft? One of your servants is no doubt responsible. Set the authorities to the inquiry. You'll soon see it sorted. That is, if it hasn't already been returned?"

He stood too close for comfort, too close for etiquette. Carefully, she slithered to the side, but he stepped with her.

"Yes, well, I shall have to do so, my lord. Report it. Of course. Capital idea."

"So you are still without the pendant?"

"Yes. Obviously. I mean, yes."

She drew in a deep breath. The cloying sweetness of the white flowers he wore coated her throat.

"I wonder if you wouldn't mind taking a small step

back? It is rather close in here, isn't it?"

In response, he stepped nearer. With his long fingers he lifted her chin. "I believe I would mind. Very much. Tell me, Miss Cutworth, Honoria, where exactly did your uncle say he purchased the piece you've lost to thieves? I might find you a copy. I feel it is my duty as a gentleman to try to do so, especially after you have been so compromised."

Honoria's limbs trembled, whether from his actions, his insinuations, or his use of her first name she didn't know. From all three, most likely. His audacity was unacceptable, but what lay behind it all was something more terrible: for whatever his reasons, he no longer believed he owed her the duty of treating her like a lady. If he didn't think of her as such, it meant...

Her knees buckled and he caught her, bringing her against his chest.

"My lord!"

"I could be. Yours. In a manner of speaking, of course."

Before she could object further, a rough growl sounded from behind his back. Around his arm, a shadow resolved.

"Lawry!" she cried, relief filling her.

Too late, she realized she had used his pet name when she should have used his title. She cast a quick glance up at Meriven. His tightened lips told her he had noted the mistake.

"Unhand her, Meriven." Lawry's voice, always deep and growly, reverberated off the glass windows and beakers so it echoed.

"Ah, Sir Lawrence. Always in the wrong place at the wrong time." He loosened his grip and stepped back. "To what do we owe the dubious pleasure?"

"If pleasure is owed, you are its debtor." Lawry stalked forward. When he reached her side, his hand jerked as if he would touch her, but he did not. "Are you quite well, Miss Cutworth? You appear unsteady upon your feet."

"The fumes." She arched her eyes sideways toward the marquess, just in case the baronet had grown dumb as toast and missed the reason for her upset.

The marquess frowned down at her once more, not certain, perhaps, if her words had been the insult they seemed or if she truly did refer to the smoke erupting from her latest distillation. "If my presence undid Miss Cutworth, well, it is not unexpected. I am used to causing vapors when I pay my address. Ladies are often overcome by the honor." Meriven preened as he drew himself up taller.

"Tell me you are not such a coxcomb as you sound." Lawry laughed, but the sound seemed forced. Deliberate.

Meriven's lip raised. He looked as if he might growl.

Lawry swiveled toward Honoria. "Miss Cutworth. I've come to fetch you for our outing today. Have you forgotten we are to attend the séance of Madame Rose at the Duchess of Shrewsbury's home?"

His eyes, soft and warm, told her what his words could not. He was saving her.

She let him.

"Of course! I am so sorry, Sir Lawrence. Time ran away from me. I shall change right away. Will you kindly await me in the front parlor? I shall return in a thrice. My lord." She bobbed her head toward Meriven, a sort of curtsy, the best one she might make under the circumstances. "It was lovely to see you again. I'm certain you might find your own way out."

"I had matters to discuss... Miss Cutworth."

At least he didn't use her given name in front of Lawry. It was unimaginable what might occur if he had.

"Perhaps we might have a word over tea tomorrow? Or a walk, or an event? Well, I'm certain something can be arranged. My hours are not filled after all." She began to laugh, a Society laugh, and caught it. She bobbed again. "In any event, I must be off. Er, thank you." Though what she thanked him for, she couldn't imagine. For raising her hackles? For pointing out once more, if she was at all still uncertain, how much she preferred Lawry's company?

She raced through the doorway, into the house and up the back stairs, pausing only to grab Alice along the way. With every step she left her disquiet further behind her. Lawry would make it all right again, whatever it was had been wrong. The thought made her pause at her doorway.

How had she developed such faith in a man who had held her at knifepoint less than a week earlier?

"Miss?" Alice slipped by and moved to the wardrobe. "The bright blue?" She pointed to a dress made of all the wrong fabric, its skirts too narrow and its neckline too low.

"No, it won't do at all." She pressed past her maid and prayed to find something suitable.

The Duchess of Shrewsbury? What on earth would she wear to attend a séance at so lofty a home? She pawed through the usual assortment until she came upon a brown cotton calico skirt with matching jacket, embroidered with an India print in mustard yellow. It was horrible. It was the only thing she might consider.

And why on earth was Lawry attending such an event? His invitation was decidedly odd and last minute, but not so odd or late she did not welcome the reprieve from what might have happened.

She rushed her toilette, aware he waited downstairs. Her heartbeat counted out the moments until she could see him again.

Chapter 17

With Meriven paced in front of him, Lawry swiped upon The Gray Lord's heels, practically pushing him from the residence.

"A word, Meriven."

With his fingers upon the knob, the marquess pivoted. He raised his arched brow. The gesture contained a question and a sneer. As Lawry stopped a pace from him, Giles rushed into the hallway. His jacket hung askew as if he had rapidly donned it.

"It's all right, Giles. I'll see to his lordship's exit." Lawry held The Gray Lord's gaze. He could swear he saw laughter in his old friend's twitching lips, but he must be mistaken because Meriven did not possess a sense of humor.

Giles cleared his throat. "Ah, yes, Sir Lawrence. How kind of you. And your own exit, Sir Lawrence?"

"I shall await Miss Cutworth in the parlor. I merely required a word with the marquess before he tumbles down the front steps, never to return."

The air stilled as the three waited, Lawry's words a clear provocation. A pregnant sense of violence underscored the responding silence. After looking between the two men, Giles bobbed his head and made a rapid escape.

Smart man.

"So nice to see you again, Lawry. How many years

has it been?" The marquess withdrew a walking stick from the stand. He leaned upon it, both hands covering the snarling silver beast topping the cane. His lips tipped upward, a challenge in his narrowed gray eyes.

"Not long enough, John."

"Oh? You're using my given name now? I don't recall granting you permission."

"You used mine." Lawry steadied his gaze. He refused to unlock it from Meriven's.

The marquess shrugged. "I am at a station where I might be informal with a mere baronet, don't you think? You stand only one step removed from the common fluff, and I stand only two steps removed from a king. It's a very different thing." He waved his hand. "No matter. Say your piece. I grow weary of resting in this derelict environment."

The marquess broke their stare first to glance about the hallway. Lawry's gaze followed, seeing it all as the marquess must. A tear in the umber-colored papered wall revealed a line of brown paste just to the side of the stick stand. Someone had not been careful when removing their cane and had rent the decoration. The hall mantle rested slightly off-level, propped up from beneath by a narrow-hewn board. The marble top bore a crack down the middle. The dark veneer of the chest below peeled in places, revealing lighter, cheaper wood beneath. It matched the scuffed wooden floorboards covered by a wisp of threadbare carpet.

The signs of poverty glared. Strange he hadn't noticed them before. On all his prior visits he had been most anxious to see Honoria, so anxious, in fact, he had neglected his environment.

He skewered the marquess once again. "I earlier

chose to spare Miss Cutworth's feelings, John. I did not call you out for your unsolicited advances, but—"

"Call me out? You?" Meriven reared back, but his upside-down bumbershoot-smile goaded. "As for 'advances,' I merely saved Miss Cutworth from dirtying her skirts when she grew faint. Surely you should be congratulating me for my gentlemanly actions, not lambasting me?"

As an excuse, it was impeccable. Lawry was searching for a scathing reply when the tap of heels sounded upon the stairs. The colonel descended.

"You could call me on my explanation, Lawry, but you must do so in front of the chit's father." Meriven's voice pitched low enough so only his ears could hear his words. "Whatever the result, you will not benefit."

Which was true. He had no standing to challenge Meriven to a duel, as The Gray Lord had correctly pointed out, not without besmirching Honoria's reputation in the process. Tongues would wag about the exact nature of their relationship. And when the colonel's inevitable challenge ensued after he heard of Meriven's embrace, and when Meriven refused to marry Honoria, as he would, and Heaven help them all if he acceded, life would only grow more disastrous. The colonel might be killed if he lost, or jailed if he won. In either event, Honoria would stand disgraced.

"So good of you to see reason." Meriven chuckled.

And he had thought the marquess without humor?

The colonel greeted both men, surprise written across his face to see them hovering like well-dressed crows in his hallway. He looked back and forth between them. "Have you both come to call upon my daughter? I didn't realize she had become so popular."

"The marquess was just leaving, colonel. I am retiring to your parlor to await Hon… Miss Cutworth." Lawry rectified his error, but not before Honoria's father frowned. "Er, we are to attend a séance this afternoon at the home of my mother's cousin. The Duchess of Shrewsbury."

"Impressive." Meriven sounded anything but awed.

Lawry felt heat upon his cheeks. It was The Gray Lord's fault he had name-dropped like the worst sort of climber. Even as a boy, John had had that effect upon him.

The colonel's brow furrowed as he looked between them again. "Very well. Allow me to see you out, Meriven. I'm just on my way to promenade with Lady Fishbane, as it happens. It is a splendid day for a stroll about the park, don't you think?" He slid his gaze towards Lawry though he could not read the silent message written there.

Giles appeared from nowhere as if summoned by magic, his jacket freshly squared. He slipped through them to open the door, his shoulders slung low and narrow. When the colonel and the marquess disappeared through the frame, he shut the heavy wood and heaved a pregnant sigh.

Lawry nodded. "I feel much the same."

"Marched right past me. Insisted I direct him to Miss Honoria or he would have me taken up for theft. Can you imagine? Me?" Giles shook his head. "I couldn't let the family suffer such indignities, of course, and after all, what harm could he do? He's a marquess, after all."

"You directed him to Miss Honoria's laboratory."

"Pushed past me, I said. There's a bit of that going

around these days."

Lawry patted the butler on the sleeve. "Yes, but from this point to forever you only have to keep one of us away from Miss Cutworth. I'll leave you to guess which one."

Before Giles could respond, Lawry marched his way toward the front parlor. The house was not overlarge. He found it in not so many footsteps. Sinking into a plush chair before the empty hearth, he noted for the first time the decrepitating furnishings. Nothing matched. Nothing invited. Despite the shabbiness, as he drew in a long, calming breath, his pulse steadied. The room already felt like home.

Family. In an odd way having nothing to do with the burgeoning romance between his mother and her father, Honoria already felt as if she had been attached to him forever. It took no large stretch of his imagination to picture them celebrating Christmas together, the four of them, with perhaps a few assorted children running around. Their fingers would be sticky with pudding. Hercules would rejoice in licking them clean. Honoria and his mother would fuss about it. Her father would wave them off. And Hercules, perhaps he would find a canine love of his own, settle down, have some offspring. Each child could have a puppy to safeguard.

Odd, how Honoria had become the centerpiece around which all his secret familial longings now centered. They had been a secret from him, at least, until the night of the opera. She held within her a wealth of opportunity, with her open humor, her joy at the simplest things. Under her lady-like exterior she held a tiger in her heart. It would be a privilege to protect the wild beast, to nurture it out of its mask and set it upon Society.

All he had to do was convince her to see him as something more than the penniless scamp he presented. Perhaps it was time to let his own tiger shine in the clear light of day.

Terror chased the thought through his veins. He jumped from the chair and strode to the window. How easy it had been to demand honesty from her.

How difficult it would be to set free his own.

Chapter 18

Dressed in her brown calico skirt with its matching bodice, green feathered hat, and white gloves, Honoria raced to the salon. She tucked a falling strand of hair back into a pin as her eyes searched the room. Happily, the marquess was nowhere to be seen. Lawry stood by the window, his face in shadow, his hands clenched behind his back.

"I gave Meriven the boot. Politely. I hope you don't mind my little ruse and the lack of proper invitation to do so." Lawry looked her over from head to toe. A gentleman to the core, he did not comment upon the hideous colors.

How awful it must be to hold such exquisite taste and yet have to pretend the presentation in front of him didn't require a cringe and darkness. Honoria firmed her shoulders. If he could dissemble, so could she.

"Mind? Not at all. I must thank you for your efforts, and your restraint. He was, he is… Well, never mind."

Words of appeasement and explanation slipped her searching tongue. Perhaps it was best to ignore what had transpired in her distillery. She stepped into the room.

"Are we truly to attend a séance? The sort involving moving tables and ghosts and whatnot?"

He shrugged. "Yes. I'm sorry I forgot to mention it

166

earlier. I suppose I also failed to extend an invitation, didn't I?" He looked at the ground. "To be perfectly honest, I had intended to avoid the affair, but when I saw Mer..."

He shifted his gaze to the place where wall met ceiling. A dark moisture stain spread in an uneven pattern there.

"But?"

He shrugged and returned his gaze to her. "Though I try not to bandy it about, the duchess is my mother's cousin. They don't get on. Elizabeth was gravely disappointed in my mother's choice of husband. Esmelda, my mother, was born the youngest daughter of Viscount Stilton. As such, she was expected to aim not so high as a duke, like her cousin, but certainly not so low as a baronet, like my father."

Honoria approached nearer to where he stood by the window, her pulse jumping as she studied the way his jacket hugged his muscular shoulders. He was rock beneath, she knew it now, though he bore an air of softness. Perhaps it was the result of his melting eyes.

"As the daughter of a mere colonel, I understand the levels of ascension and descension, along with how many degrees of title are appropriate."

"Yet your mother was not without standing." He flinched. "Pardon."

She waved her hand. "One of the very many aspects I enjoy about your company, Sir Lawrence, is our ability to state truth plainly. Yes, my mother was the younger sister of Baron Childes. We do not consort with the Childes as the family became quite upset with my mother for her disastrous marriage. Disastrous by their standards as my father is untitled, not by hers."

"My mother suffered a like reaction when she married beneath her station." He smiled, his odd remove fleeing as he lit from within. "Far be it from me to upset propriety. Tell me, would a baronet be censured for consorting with a colonel's daughter?" Once again, his eyes laughed. Even when he was serious, his humor could not remain hidden for long.

"I suppose it depends upon the type of consorting the baronet might wish to undertake."

He blinked. He cleared his throat. "Are you flirting with me, Miss Cutworth?"

"More like seducing, Sir Lawrence."

She couldn't be certain because the strong sun at his back shadowed his face, but he appeared to blush. She knew she did. The heat in her cheeks was almost unbearable.

His gaze flitted to the doorway. When it returned to her, he again appeared earnest. "I confess, at the moment the usual course of roguery is not on my mind." He paused. "Honoria."

"Lawry."

He frowned. "Honoria, do you wish me to have a word with Meriven? Or your father? The colonel might forbid him entry without creating a scandal, or see he is made to..." He bit his lips between his teeth. His gaze traced the ceiling once more before returning to her. "He touched you, Honoria. If you would see him pay for his indiscretion, I shall oblige."

"Pay? As in forcing him to the altar?"

She nearly laughed. Only his torn expression stopped her. She shook her head and approached him on careful feet until she stood almost toe-to-toe.

"No, Lawry. Though I thank you for your

sentiments and offer of aid, the scandal of your intervention would prove appalling. Moreover, Meriven is not someone I would wish to marry, no matter how reduced my circumstances might become." A shiver traced up her arms at the notion.

He must have noticed. His entire body tensed. Had she just considered his eyes were never without laughter? They had grown cold, hard, and sharp, almost merciless. His anger rolled along her skin. She reached out to touch him on the sleeve but withdrew before making contact.

"It is fine. No real harm was done."

"No?"

She shook her head. "A private moment of discomfiture will not fell me. Not I, who have taken on Society doyennes and lived to tell the tale." She referred to his exhortations to bravery the first night they had met, when he had sought to reassure her while his blade pressed to her throat.

He sighed. The danger retreated from him as quickly as it had arrived to end in a rough burst of laughter. "There you go, forcing me to agree with my own words. How dastardly of you, Miss Cutworth."

"I am a menace."

Her agreement leached the brief bout of humor from him again. Before she could ponder why, he scuffed his toe against the ragged carpet.

"Actually, I have delayed speaking with your father upon my own behalf. One thing or another has prevented me, most particularly your lack of acceptance. Should I seek him out now, Honoria? He walks in the park with my mother. Or would you prefer more time to become acquainted? I don't require the extra hours. I am certain of my mind, but I would not push you."

"Push me? Why ever—"

Proving they could never have a full conversation, Alice rushed into the room. For once Honoria was very glad of her maid's presence. It was so easy to forget the secrets Lawry still carried, though his reassurances he still meant to speak with her father put her concern at a distance.

Except, shouldn't she hold it closer?

Instead of becoming annoyed with the interruption, Lawry laughed again and shook his head. He leaned closer, all his ice melted. "If Hercules was here, he would drag her off at my command. How foolish of me not to have brought him."

She wrapped her hand around his proffered arm. "I can save myself from unpleasant scenes, you know. I do not need interloping servants."

"Indeed you do not. I hope, however, I have not created the need for such salvation?"

She met his gaze. "You have not." A tremor passed along the edge of her voice. She swallowed it back. "It is just I am not quite ready to address the matter. First, before I consider your, um, proposition…"

"Proposal. Of marriage. To me."

"I must be assured the secrets you hold are not so terrible. You do make me forget the need, but I cannot ignore what is hidden forever. Charm can only take you so far."

He reached up and touched the feather upon her brim, the one sliding inconveniently over her right eye. "Touché. Foisted on my own petard. Et cetera." He sounded pleased and worried, all in the same moment.

"Please don't confess to anything too terrible, Lawry. I don't believe my heart can stand it."

In response, he squeezed her fingers. "I knew from the moment I met you your bravery would put me to shame. Now come, we have miles to travel."

She tucked away her disquiet and allowed him to lead her to his carriage with its matched steeds. It was a great deal of fun to be able to speak her mind, even the hard things she didn't quite wish to say. Mealymouthed Miss Cutworth, indeed!

The trip to the Shrewsbury home was not so far. While Alice sought the servant's rooms, they were shown into the library. Stacks of books reached to very tall ceilings where scenes of gamboling putti, fluffy clouds, and blue sky had been painted. Birds held banners spouting Latin phrases, but Honoria had never been very good at the language and hadn't a clue what they meant.

"'Honor, Valor, and Perseverance.' The left one reads, 'Chosen by God.' His Grace's family has never been remarked for their modesty." Lawry shot her another of his dazzling smiles, the kind that sent her blood pooling below her belly.

"Ah, Lawry! How wonderful of you to join us." The Duchess of Shrewsbury sat facing the door, her back to a large desk.

Six others waited around a round table set with nine chairs. The gray-haired lady held out her hand and stilled with limpid wrist while Lawry crossed the room and bowed over it. Dressed in a white frilly dress far too young for her age, the duchess surveyed her new guests by looking down her long nose.

"Your Grace, may I present my friend, Miss

Cutworth? Miss Cutworth, Her Grace, the Duchess of Shrewsbury."

The duchess examined Honoria carefully from hair to toe. Her single raised eyebrow conveyed the impression she wasn't impressed. "Miss Cutworth. We were not expecting you, but any friend of Lawry's is, of course, welcome."

If so, the lady's voice was singularly unable to match the warmth of her sentiments.

She introduced the both of them to the others, some three ladies and two gentlemen. "And this is Madame Rose, of course," the duchess added, placing her hand upon the woman's arm who stood to her right. "Madame comes to us from the colonies, where I am told there are ghosts aplenty. It's a wild land, isn't it, Madame Rose?"

"It is indeed, Your Grace. All the murders make for spirited spirits in the United States of America."

The woman's rough, nasal voice sounded as if it had been dragged over coal several times and hung up over flame. It grew cavernous as she corrected her hostess, a *faux pas* to match the deep red gown she wore. It looked an awful lot like Lowry's dining room walls. Constructed of velvet and silk, it was far too heavy for the afternoon, especially in the heat of summer. Everything about the woman seemed off, most of all her American accent. It twanged unpleasantly to Honoria's ears.

"Duchess, if you intend to add guests, I must insist my fee be increased likewise. Two guineas a head."

Which was another thing a lady would never say. To discuss money in an elevated circle was simply crass.

"Yes, yes, Madame Rose. You will be compensated." The duchess waved a pale tapered hand through the air. She sent Lawry a look and scrunched her nose.

Lawry gestured toward one of the footmen and signaled an extra chair should be added. "I hear tell Mrs. Hayden only charges a guinea a head, Your Grace, and hers is, as I understand it, the ultimate voice upon these shores in matters pertaining to the dead."

The duchess slapped him playfully on the hand in a demonstration far too flirtatious for her age or station. "Oh, you silly boy. What a trial you must be for my dear Esmelda." She simpered and laughed gaily, a tinkling, bell-like sound.

Honoria glanced toward Madame Rose again. The woman's expression was unreadable, but it seemed to contain a sort of masked delight at the duchess's ridiculousness.

It was the way people looked at her, too, when she tried to appear a flutter. Lawry was right. The artifice was unbecoming.

"Oh, dear. More unexpected guests." The duchess flipped open her fan and fluttered it as she looked past them to the entrance.

Lawry glanced over his shoulder before leaning in close to Honoria's ear. He nipped the lobe before he whispered. "I could forgive many things, darling, but not such hair. Do reassure me you haven't a purple wig hanging about your closet."

She used the action of rotation to hide her shiver at his inappropriate, well-hidden caress. Approaching at the speed of a snail, an elderly woman pecked her way with a cane the final steps to meet their hostess. She sported an outdated beehive wig in a bright purple hue. On her arm, a dashing, military-postured gentleman caught Honoria's eye and smiled. The turn of the man's lips said he ate dragons for breakfast and more for dinner.

Honoria nodded in what she hoped was a polite manner and tossed a glance toward Lawry. By contrast, the baronet's smile had nothing of darkness in it. Everything in her lightened.

"And I believe, Lady Aimsbridge, you are acquainted with my nephew, Sir Lawrence? This is his friend, Miss Cutworth. And this, Lawry, is Mr. Havisham. I'm afraid I know little about him." The duchess waved her hand as if Mr. Havisham, he of the dragon-eating smile, was of little account.

Mr. Havisham studied Lawry. Something dark, maybe dangerous, flitted past his eyes, but the cause of his peculiar emotion eluded her. He turned away, and with his pivot Honoria's unease lifted.

Attend a séance and suffer nerves. It only made sense. Still, Honoria gripped Lawry's arm tighter. He lifted an eyebrow as his eyes sparkled.

"Don't go eyeing other men, darling. I vow, I'll melt into a wobbling heap of jealousy, and I don't trust Her Grace's servants to know how to clean jelly off the carpets."

She laughed, for no other reason than he made her so happy.

After introductions had been made, the group moved to the table. The duchess declared Lawry must sit at her left, while she placed Honoria to the farthest side of the circular table by claiming there was more room there. Madame Rose rolled her eyes before hiding the expression behind a cough into her palm.

As Honoria nodded politely to the two men who bracketed her, the footmen extinguished the lights and closed fast the draperies. The only illumination to the room trickled in from the hallway until a small flame was lit upon a tiny candle. The light was placed before the medium so her face flickered with patterns of dark and bright.

Across the way, Lawry nodded and smiled. His warm gaze gave her strength. It wasn't she believed in spirits. It was she might be wrong.

"We will now join hands," Madame Rose intoned in her rough voice. "As our company is majority female, we shall almost certainly be visited this afternoon. The female nature is considered superior in matters of communication with the departed. We are more sensitive and receptive to the messages of those who have passed beyond. I have great hopes my spirit guide, Juniper, will help draw our favored deceased near to us. Now, I beg you all to rest absolutely silent. Fidgeting makes for a disastrous and oft-times dangerous session."

Madame Rose turned her baleful glance upon Lord Carnoven. He stopped twitching, arrested with one cheek raised off the sprung upholstered seat. Quietly, he sank down flat again.

"Might I pose a question?" Lawry smiled. Even the dim couldn't hide his sparkle.

"Lawry, don't disturb her now," the duchess ordered. "We rent her by the hour, don't you know?"

"Just a simple question, aunt. Madame Rose, will it be possible to ask the departed to locate a necklace Miss Cutworth recently lost?"

All heads turned her way. Honoria tried to remain expressionless.

"Really, Miss Cutworth? Where did you lose it?" the duchess inquired.

"In my bedchamber." The words came out harsher than she intended, but she had never much cared for attention. Then she recognized what she had said. "Er, um, it was stolen while my father and I sat below. Together. My maid was with us. In the early evening. When it was barely dark. Servants everywhere. The villain must have climbed through the window or entered through the back."

She met Lawry's gaze. He winked in response to her fabrications before pretending to have something in his eye.

"Why, how horrid," Lord Carnoven said.

He took the opportunity to fidget some more. Perhaps his laundress hadn't sufficiently rinsed his garments.

"I had some jewels stolen once," Lady Adelaide Swinson declared. "It was a horrible ordeal. I fired my maid, of course."

"Sensible," Lady Clinton agreed, nodding her head. "It is always staff."

"Well, who else could it have been? Funny, though, where the girl left my ear bobs. You'll never guess."

"Ooh, do tell," Lord Clinton said, leaning forward in an expectant manner.

Lady Aimsbridge echoed the sentiment in her deep voice. Besides her, Mr. Havisham's lips tipped upward.

"In the library, on the very desk I use to write my correspondence! She must have meant to hide them away to retrieve later, but my quick actions in having her immediately escorted from the premises put the matter to rest. I hope she's in prison still, or transported."

Honoria gazed into the darkened faces around her. Of them, only Lawry and Madame Rose seemed to think accusing a maid on such grounds was not well done. Both frowned. Of a sudden, she felt a certain sympathetic camaraderie with the medium, although she still doubted she could communicate with the dead.

Madame Rose cleared her throat. "We start, or I must leave."

The group quickly settled.

"Do not break the chain of hands at any time. Do not speak. Do not fear whatever shall come to pass. I have harnessed the power over the dead and they will do my bidding. Often they choose to speak through me. It is not generally pleasant, but I do my sworn and sacred duty as a vessel. I repeat, no matter what happens, you must not break the chain."

Goosebumps dappled Honoria's arms despite her belief séances were nothing but organized chicanery. Her hands gripped those of the strangers she sat between.

And then, Madame Rose began to hum.

Chapter 19

A wordless tune, eerie and frightening, swallowed the room. When it seemed as if a crescendo would never be reached, Madame Rose relented. Her tune snapped off mid-bar. She mumbled some meaningless, sing-song words. Her voice rose again, this time to a loud exclamation, as if she might be exhorting the dead to arrive. Honoria glanced about. Hers was not the only study of the room.

The medium switched to English. "We urge you, oh loved ones, oh spirit guide, to reach across the veil and visit us in this cruel and intrepid world. Join us, and speak. Tell us you are near!"

The table thumped, as if someone had rapped a knuckle upon it.

Everyone jumped, Honoria included. She quickly looked at Lawry and amended her thought. Everyone jumped but Lawry. Instead, he studied the medium, a small smile stretching his wonderful pillow lips.

"Is that you, Juniper?"

Another knock, twice.

"Juniper, we thank you for attending. Is there anyone with you on your side of the ethers who wishes to speak to one of the living?"

Two more raps.

"Is it for Lord Carnoven?"

One rap, then silence.

Madame Rose continued through the group, stalling only to ask for a reminder of Honoria's name, before finally obtaining a double-rap for the Duchess of Shrewsbury.

"Ooh," the duchess trilled.

Lawry flinched. She must be gripping his hand too tight.

The candle flickered with some sort of breeze and then went out. Gasps resounded.

"Do not fear," Madame Rose ordered. "Now, who comes before us?"

Another breeze, and suddenly the medium doubled over and screamed. Her head shook back and forth with a certain violence, then flipped back and forward again. When she spoke, it was in a high-pitched voice, tipped with an English accent rather than an American one.

"Elizabeth, do sit up straight. Have I taught you so little you would slouch in my company?"

The duchess sprang up even straighter, though her posture had been impeccable. "It's Cordelia! My nanny!"

"I wish to bring you news, Your Grace. Here, in the blue sky of the afterlife, we remember and watch over you. Your mother, Lady Margaret, asks you remember to be generous with those less fortunate. Your uncle, Lord Smiles, reports his hunting has been superb. Most importantly, your grandfather, Lord Roger Wilkerstein, asks you to remember your German cousin, Hildegarde. She is in need of your aid, Your Grace, a sum of fifty pounds, eighteen shillings is required if the estate is not to go to taxes. Your generosity will be rewarded in this life and the one beyond."

The duchess turned to Lawry. "Do you know this Hildegarde? I don't remember hearing of her."

"I'm certain if we check the family tree, we shall discover her perched quite carelessly upon a removed branch, though she may hail through your father's side. Wasn't Wilkerstein your father's father?"

"No. His name was Wallerstein. I'm almost certain of it."

"I must go," the ghost of Cordelia said quickly in her English-tipped voice. "There are others who wish to speak. Remember me fondly, Your Grace, and sit up straight."

Another *whoosh* of wind. More questions. More tapping.

Though at first interested in the proceeding, Honoria soon found herself stifling a yawn. It seemed the spirits arrived to talk to each member of the table. All of the dead exerted their living brethren to be generous with those less fortunate. Every single one of them mentioned a distant cousin or aunt who required assistance. The sky was, apparently, quite blue on the other side. The trees were emerald green. All was right and fine, excepting the numerous gossips and voyeurs populating the realm. Even Lawry received a message, though it was only from his old horse, Duncan. He asked Lawry to forgive him for the tumble he had taken on Regent Street.

Lawry winked at her across the table. She suddenly recalled a story reported in the papers last year. Sir Lawrence Fishbane, a name she had not known would be important at the time, had been tossed into the bodies of the perambulating Misses Peppersworth when his horse had missed a step and broken his foreleg.

It had been good of Madame Rose to include the horse in Heaven's number, but odd she hadn't found at least one dead relative to exhort Lawry into generosity.

Sighing heavily, as if she had born the weight of worlds upon her shoulders, Madame Rose opened her eyes. "They are gone. We might safely unclasp—"

Suddenly, her head tipped back and a low moan rose from her gaping mouth. "The key is here, the T-shaped pendant. Guard it against those who seek it for their ends." Madame Rose's head returned to its normal position. She continued speaking in regular tones as if the odd conversation regarding the key never happened. "—hands. Your Grace, your servants might open the blinds."

Chills raced up and down Honoria's spine. She searched across the table. Lawry frowned, his expression tight. Around her, conversation increased to a voluble level as the room returned to normal.

Lawry rose and took her arm. He made their excuses and rushed them to the door before they could partake of the repast spread along the buffet in the next room. Honoria followed his lead willingly, disquiet still goosing her skin. An unsettled, quietly nauseated feeling swept over her body. As their carriage pulled away, with Alice perched on the outside seat with the driver, Honoria looked at the grand estate, a city palace, and hoped she would never have to cross the threshold again.

"An interesting afternoon." Lawry studied her as if afraid she might break into pieces. "How do you suppose Duncan occupies his time in the afterlife? Lots of hay and no riders, or do you think he's hooked himself up to a carriage by now? And how kind of him to remind me of my public embarrassment."

"Yes, I thought so. I suspect Madame Rose has perused *Debrett's* more than once, as well as the local papers. How fare the Misses Peppersworth, by the way? Has Miss Peppersworth's arm healed well?"

He shrugged. "I wouldn't know. I took care of the physician bills and sent flowers every week for a good three months, but the ladies refused to see me when I attempted a call. They hold me responsible, as if I purposefully flew from Duncan's back simply to injure the less attractive of the two."

She laughed. She hadn't intended to, but... well, both Peppersworth sisters were sullied by unfortunate noses that hung a bit too precipitously over razor-thin lips. Covering her mouth with her fingers, she glanced away. "You do know how to chase the blues, Lawry. Tell me, do you think the final, er, conversation, was about my pendant?"

He tapped his knee with his forefinger. "Perhaps."

There was something about his mannerism. It caught and held her attention. Lawry was never vague unless he concealed something. She didn't know how she knew it about him, but she did.

"What are you hiding?"

Unbelievably, he blushed.

"You are hiding something!" She surged forward on her seat and peered into his face. "Lawry, you said you did not steal my necklace."

"And such was true. Is true." He shut his eyes and took a long breath through his nose. He reached into an inner pocket of his jacket and pulled out the chain.

She gasped, and covered her mouth with her fingers so as not to scream.

The golden T-shaped bob dangled there, swaying with the carriage. He reached across and unfurled her fingers to deposit the jewelry within her palm.

"I did not steal it. I merely retrieved it from a man who got it from the thief. I meant to give it back to you earlier but I could find no good way to tell you about it. Leave it to the dead to spill my secrets. I had thought only to prove the medium a fraud when I mentioned your necklace."

The metal was warm from having lain so close to his body. Instead of burning her skin, it seemed to burn right into her chest.

"I don't know whether to be angry or relieved. I'm not sure whether to kiss you or slap you."

"Both? Here. Let me help you decide."

He reached out without warning and pulled her onto his lap. His arms wrapped around her like a vise, strong and certain, but he made no move to draw her lips to his. Instead, he studied her, searching deep within her eyes.

She should pull away. She should slap his face. She reached out her hand – and caressed his cheek. Her finger traced the fullness of his upper lip and scooted down to lie within the mild dimple of his chin. He made no move at all, and simply allowed her to explore.

"You lied to me."

"Never. Not about the pendant, anyway."

"You will tell me everything, right now?" Her fingers moved to stroke his jawline. Remembering the feel of his breath against the sensitive whorl of her ear, she leaned into him so he might feel the same thing when she said the words she needed to say. "We cannot continue without truth between us. I'm afraid I must insist upon it."

To her own surprise, she touched her teeth to his lobe and pulled gently. He groaned in quite a satisfying manner.

"Honoria!"

She moved her lips to the pulse beating erratically in his neck just above his collar. The skin beneath her tongue was taught, firm, and softer than she had imagined it would be. Fire sprang against her flesh.

Distantly, she heard a groan and realized it was her own.

He grabbed her face between his hands and drew her mouth to his. As she melted into him, her breasts pressed to the hardness of his chest, the world tilted. The raging flames flashed brighter, dampening by comparison the world outside their tiny confines. The horses' clatter, the sway of the carriage, joined the rhythm thrumming beneath the surface of her skin.

The next instant, she was lying on her back. Lawry hovered over her, his hands slipping across her waist, around her hips, and up to her breasts. He ran his thumb across the tenderest part and she jumped, her shriek lost beneath his lips as he pressed them again to hers. Had she thought he brought fire before? It was nothing to the rage of heat swamping her entire body.

He ripped his mouth from hers. "You will marry me." It wasn't a question.

She pressed the back of her hand against her lips, trying to catch her breath. When she didn't answer, couldn't answer, he sank back upon his heels.

"All right." His voice was a ragged whisper. Returning to the seat opposite, he straightened his jacket and cravat, then ran his fingers through his hair.

"Fine. You want the truth. Prepare yourself, Miss Cutworth, for you will not like what you hear."

She swallowed, but could not speak.

He took a deep breath, and latched his gaze to hers. "I am a thief. I steal for a living. Others have named me The Midnight Menace. You may have heard of me."

A gasp escaped her. She shook her head.

"Like it or not, it is the truth. I didn't steal your necklace, not from you, but I did take it back from the man who took it. If I hadn't honed my skills with my more spurious exploits, the retrieval might have been impossible. I would ask you to remember this fact."

Honoria froze. She tried to blink and couldn't. Fire might have traced her veins just seconds before, but suddenly she was carved from ice. She couldn't even breathe.

What? She wanted to shake her head and ask him to repeat himself, for surely she had heard wrong, but a terrible sense of rightness held her still. The scratch. The blade at her throat. Had he intended to rob her?

"May I explain?" His voice was whisper-soft, almost silent. Tousled and devilishly handsome, he glowed with a funny, amusing, kind, and gentle light. It shone from deep within him and made those around him radiate in response.

How then could he be a thief? The Midnight Menace? Yet she had known, hadn't she? Suspected, at any rate.

She scrambled to an upright position, banging her hoops down as they threatened to reveal everything to the man sitting across from her. The man she trusted. The man who had kissed her and sent her into swoons.

The man who had held a dulled blade to her throat.

How had she forgotten that? Forgiven that?

"Honoria?"

Resolutely, she swallowed and inhaled through her nose. The carriage swayed again, sending her against the squabs, or maybe she simply couldn't sit straight anymore.

"I would have said yes." Impossible not to hear the high-pitched whine in her voice. The thread of disillusionment.

"You still can. You must. I… I need you, Honoria. Please don't make me live without you."

She shook her head, half a movement, slight, but it was all she could manage as disappointment welled from her belly to squeeze at her throat. Unbidden, tears pricked her eyes. Until this moment, when shock made her body realize Lawry—Sir Lawrence, now he could no longer be hers—could never be a viable option for a husband, she hadn't realized the depth of her feelings for him. There had been desire, friendship, trust… but no, the trust had all been on her side, and greatly misplaced.

He sighed. It sounded much like she felt. "I had to earn a living, Honoria. I had a mother to support. I still do. After I was sent home from school, my father died. His heart stalled at the news of my failure. We were left with too little funds. I had caused our destruction, my father's death, but I had no ability to rectify any of it. A few months after the funeral, we depleted the coffers. I was going to be forced to sell the house, and if that happened…"

She knew what would have followed. The world would have turned out of sync with them, and they would have been left penniless and fodder for the reaper at the ragged edges of it.

"I tried investing. I attempted to gamble. For a while I thought I might earn my way at the card table, but it turns out I am as bad at the game as I am at other sorts of ventures. Just when I had grown desperate enough to try to find an heiress, I was invited to a week-long party in the country. I noticed there one of my aunt's friends, the wife of an earl. She positively dripped in precious stones. I can't tell you when the thought struck me, or how it translated to action."

"Did earrings magically appear in your pocket?"

Her tone was meant to whip him like a lash. Instead, he smiled, just a tiny twist of his lips. Even that warmed her. A bit.

"No. I noticed during the week she had an enormous selection of jewels, a set for every change of clothing, and as you are aware, women generally change outfits at these things at least four times a day, sometimes more. Rubies. Sapphires. Pearls. She was so careless with her adornments, I remember feeling angered. I looked at the maid and three footmen, all standing ready to serve. They appeared both harried and grateful for the chance to be there, and I suddenly thought, why? Why should some people have so much when others have so little?"

"You're a follower of those awful working-class radicals?" For a while the mob's political theories had been the boogeyman upon every noble tongue, their ideas whispered in the dark as if open discussion might allow the monster through the door. "You intend to upend Society all by yourself?"

She could hear the sneer in her voice, the demanding tone as if she had any right to challenge his beliefs. A strange sense of triumph rose within her at her unexpected attitude, even though it stood in opposition to her utter devastation. At least he could not accuse her of being mealy-mouthed now.

"Not quite."

He moved the curtain at the window and glanced out before letting it close. He sighed once more as he drummed his fingers against his knee. She waited.

"It is true I began reading Hardy and Owen. It is not true I undertook any decision to join the co-operative socialists or the Ricardians. I saw, and still see, too many potential flaws in their theories. Humans are not yet ready to live with love for their fellow man etched deeply into their hearts. I believe their philosophy might be the fastest route to collapse, in point of fact. However, I began to see the world differently."

He looked away and back again. "Despite the failings of these political ideologies, I began to see our class differently. Yes, I do realize my own hypocrisy, for if my father had lived, if he had amassed rather than lost assets, I might have never questioned my place in Society. As it was, I did."

"And so, you decided to steal from Society. What a venerable occupation you chose."

He nodded. "Sarcasm aside, you are not wrong."

"*Please.*" All her scorn centered in the single word.

"I waited for the next ball when I knew the countess would be occupied and out for the evening. I crept in through the kitchen with my top hat pulled low over my brow. I wore a blondish wig I had cobbled together from trimmed horse tails and pasted on a false mustache. I'd used padding around my waist so my jacket pulled tight. Later, the servants, who let me pass without a single word as I looked the part of a gentleman, described me as old and fat." He smirked, saw her frown, and cleared his throat.

Patting down an imaginary crease in his pants, he continued to speak. His gaze no longer met hers. Instead, he studied his knees. "I had heard her tell a friend how little she cared for her diamonds. They were estate pieces and she longed for something more colorful. I decided to take her at her word."

"And then what? What did you do with the jewels?"

"I sold them about a month later after careful investigation landed me with a few names of fences. Over the next few years, I made many mistakes, some quite costly, but finally I settled upon my current co-conspirators. One breaks down the pieces and reformulates them into new ones, and the other sells them. I receive half of the profits and they share the other half. My end is considered the most dangerous, you see."

He smiled again. It was becoming difficult to keep rebuffing him.

"And you pay for your matched horses and footmen with the results of your ill-gotten gains?"

He shrugged. "Yes. I splurged on the equines. Those footmen you sneer at, however, are grateful for my aid. I don't disavow your natural disdain of my nocturnal employment, but I am not such a dandy I could not live without matched servants. I pay them more than they warrant, and without my intervention they would now lie buried beneath ground, in need of Madame Rose's services. Before I discovered the twins through my nocturnal wandering, they had been lost to an opium addiction." He slid his gaze sideways before returning it. "I shall accept your censor, Honoria, but not where they are concerned."

His voice was steady, firm and certain. She reached for another way to bring him low, to strike back as his admission of thievery had struck her.

"I suppose your brigandry explains the paintings on your walls. They were not so middling as you described."

He lifted his eyebrow before understanding crossed his face. "Ah. I confess, I did purchase the small Constable and Gentileschi. Of course, you focused upon those two. However, the other works of art comprise my inheritance from my mother's father, Viscount Stilton, along with most of the furnishings you saw. When Stilton died, my mother insisted on replacing my father's rather dilapidated décor."

"Did he mind?"

"I doubt it. Theirs was a love match, but it did not render her blind to his atrocious taste." He smiled again, a fond turn of lips this time. "I learned from them, Honoria. I was raised all wrong, in a home filled with affection deemed unseemly by most of our class. I would treat you with every respect my father showed my mother, and every largesse."

"Affection, and beautiful furnishings."

He nodded.

Despite her disquiet with his revelations, she couldn't help but respond. "I was raised a bit incorrectly myself. My mother's death left me with one parent who raised me in a very masculine fashion. I can bark orders like the hardest military general. I keep a clock and a home on precise hours. My distillery is a model of organization. It has all become my nature."

"I do admire your clean, crisp corners."

He laughed again, and peered at her as if delighted with her self-analysis, so she decided to continue.

"Perhaps it's why I sublimate too much and present such a... mealy-mouthed guise. I am not altogether certain of how to act the part of a well-behaved, emotionally overwrought female. If such was ever my nature, my upbringing has overshadowed it."

He leaned forward, earnest again. "Then we are perfect together. For most of my life, I have had only my mother's influence. I believe it has made me more sensitive than I might otherwise have been under a father's tutelage, though I stop short at naming myself effeminate. The two of us raised at odds with the norm, how can you deny we are the perfect fit, Honoria?"

The carriage rolled to a stop in front of her home. She drew back the curtain and peered out onto the street, expecting to see a line of policemen waiting to take Lawry off to prison. The only person she saw, however, was someone's harried maid, hunched over and rushing past as fast as her feet would take her.

He drummed his finger against his leg some more, serious again. "I keep about a quarter of what I take, so a quarter of the half, if you care to do the math, which I never do. I simply divide my portion of the current haul in four bundles, keep one and give the rest to select, trusted charities whose work I admire. Agencies which care for abandoned children, mostly, although there's a farm I subsidize. It collects dogs who would otherwise find Heaven too soon."

Pride edged his words. A wave of anger swept over

her again.

"And you believe your charity excuses your immorality?"

A rush of red, as quick as her ire, covered his features. "I do. It balances, anyway."

"Then you are playing false with yourself, Lawry. Having been the victim of a theft, even of a practically worthless trinket, I cannot begin to tell you how deeply I am affected. I hurt down to my bones. I shall not easily trust again. Moreover, there's this-this indefinable feeling of shame. It swarms here." She made small circles in the area of her stomach. "It makes no logical sense for me to be ashamed of having been victimized, yet it stays. That is what you bring to people, Lawry. A sense of deception and violation. No charitable donation will remove the stain you leave behind."

He flinched away from her words. Not even a trace of a smile marked his eyes. "Honoria, I beg you—"

She shook her head. "No. I cannot deny we match in every way, but this one difference between us..." She took a deep breath. The words stuck in her throat but she forced them into the air. There was no other way. "I cannot see you again, Lawry. Do not call upon me. This is goodbye."

Just as the driver opened the door, she descended. She didn't look back, even though the pain radiating from her heart begged her to turn and run into his arms. Once at the door, she heard the carriage pull away.

She didn't look, even as everything inside of her crumbled.

Chapter 20

Lawry paced the front hallway of Honoria's home as he waited for Giles to return. It was too late to call upon her. In any other circumstance, he never would, but he had been so miserable after she descended the carriage without a backward glance, so absolutely cut in half, he had no choice.

Besides, he had to return her necklace, didn't he? In those intimate moments in the carriage, the jewelry had been dropped to the seat and forgotten. Afterward, well, what fool passed a thought for gold and garnets when his heart was cracking?

Hercules whined a high-pitched question. Lawry placed his hand upon the shaggy fur. "She'll see us, boy. She'll want to see you, at any rate. Never fear."

But the dog only stared straight up the stairs leading to her bedroom. He wagged his tail in slow, tentative arcs as he waited for Honoria's descent. If even Hercules had become mesmerized by her, what chance did a lonely baronet have of keeping his heart?

A rapid click of heels clomped too heavily. Giles's legs appeared, and then the rest of him. "I'm sorry, Sir Lawrence, but Miss Cutworth is unavailable, as I suggested she would be, given the hour. She's asked me to tell you her father has gone to visit your mother and she hopes nothing between the two of you will be made to affect their burgeoning relationship. I trust you understand her meaning."

"I do. Yes. Of course. Hercules, however, does not possess my patience and comprehension."

He met the dog's anxious gaze and nodded. As if the canine understood all sorts of things humans regularly didn't, he dashed past the butler, taking the steps in wide leaps.

"Wait! He can't go up there!"

"Naturally not. Allow me to catch him and relay the information. Pardon me." Lawry squeezed around the sputtering butler and mounted the stairs two at a time, just in case Giles proved more determined than he imagined.

He was. This time he chased after Lawry, shouting for him to stop. On the fifth step from the top, the butler snagged his ankle. Lawry shook him off and redoubled his efforts. The hapless servant bumped and rolled down the staircase. He sat at the bottom and glared up at him.

Lawry paused. "Are you hurt, Giles?"

The man huffed, his hair all askew along with his jacket. "Just my pride, Sir Lawrence."

"I'm sorry, Giles, I truly am. I'll make it up to you. I promise. Just rest there a moment. I won't be long."

Having already discovered Honoria's bedroom, it was easy to bolt for her door once he reached the second level. It was already opening as he sprang in front of it since Hercules had possessed the forethought to scratch at the wood. The dog didn't need an engraved invitation to enter. He bounded inward.

When Lawry followed, he came upon his intended bride sprawled upon the rug. The dog lapped at every part of her he could reach with his long tongue. Her laughing giggles and protestations floated in the air as she tried to push the beast away.

"Enough, boy. Heel. I worry you will take all Miss Cutworth's soft caresses and smiles."

Hercules shot him a look from beneath his overgrown eyebrows. He gave Honoria one last lick across the chin and crossed the room to the line of windows. There, he curled into a ball and laid his head upon his legs, his gaze steady upon them.

"Good dog. I may just keep you yet."

Snuffle. Growl. Yawn. Wag.

"I see Hercules possesses a larger vocabulary than your own, Sir Lawrence. Better manners, too."

He drank her in, all long limbs and sprawled beauty. "If you are attempting to make me jealous, know you have met with great success. I suppose it is no surprise you have garnered more than one ardent admirer, Miss Cutworth."

"How nice to finally enjoy multiple suitors. I choose the dog." She sat upright, her nightgown pooling above her knees. With a swipe, she hid her lush calves from his view before wiping the dog-licks from her face with her sleeve.

Too bad. He had much enjoyed the expanse of delicate flesh. It could lead him to, well, he shouldn't think such things, though he did.

"Miss Cutworth! I... he..." Giles gripped the doorframe, almost doubled over as he tried to speak between panting breaths.

"Never mind, Giles. I'm fine. Sir Lawrence will not harm me as I've Hercules to protect my virtue."

"But..."

The butler required a great deal more convincing

before he agreed to take himself off. Perhaps it helped when Lawry cursed a blue streak. The man visibly paled, huffed, and executed a precise three-point turn, threatening all the while to seek out the colonel immediately.

Lawry laughed and extended his hand to Honoria. "We're a package deal, I'm afraid, Hercules and me. Rather like when the butcher tries to dispose of some slightly-off tripe by running a special sale in which the price of liver is increased and the tripe added to the deal."

She glared at him but placed her fingers within his. He lifted her easily from the ground. Her white eyelet nightgown fluttered around her body, touching her nowhere. Long black hair floated to her waist, the tresses so soft and shiny his fingers itched to run through them.

She was lovely. She was beautiful. Her face could melt him to a puddling heap. The tears staining her cheeks exacerbated her comeliness, but they cut him to the quick.

"You must be the tripe in such comparison." Her frown was impressive. It even mirrored in her eyes.

"Of a certainty, I am. I detest tripe. To compare myself to the dish requires a humility I do not normally possess. I feel it, however. Here." He touched his chest. "Honoria, if I have to belittle myself every day for the rest of my life, I shall do so. Just please, please marry me. These few hours have been the worst of my existence."

She nodded, as if she understood.

"When you plan dinner parties, you can keep my preferences against offal in mind."

"Aren't you the optimist." Her limbs trembled.

He longed to take her in his arms and support her, but her upset stalled him. "Please forgive me, Honoria." He ran the back of his fingers over her soft, dewy tear-stained skin. It was the most he would allow himself until... well, until. "I would never hurt you."

She swatted his hand away. "You already have. I was beginning to fall for you, Lawry. It even began not to matter you don't possess a livable income." Her laugh grated the air. "I began to imagine a nice country cottage, something we might rent for twenty pounds a month. You could raise dogs, breed them or something, and I could sell perfumes and soaps. Instead, I must realize my dreams are made of a person I'll never meet. You have no idea the injury you do to others, do you? Their pain hurts me too."

He winced as her words struck his chest like poison-dipped arrows. "What would you have me do?"

Hercules whined softly, his meaning unclear, unless he was simply as sad as his master. Perhaps he saw the parting as permanent and was as undone as Lawry.

She shrugged. "What is there to do? The damage is done. There's no conceivability of returning the items you've taken, is there?"

That tiny, hopeful note pushed the arrows straight through to his spine. He had to focus to prevent his knees from buckling. He shook his head. "No."

"Then what more is there left to say?"

He took her pendant from his pocket and crossed to the tiny dressing table near her bed. With a *clink*, he deposited it upon the wooden surface. For a moment he contemplated through the mirror the pale lace bedspread. It looked like a wide sky, on top of which it might be possible to live a simple life in the country somewhere, in a little cottage, raising dogs and selling soaps.

He snorted. Next, he would be telling himself tiny fairies could plant a garden with which he might earn an income selling cucumbers.

Hercules barked one short staccato note. Apparently, he could now read minds.

Talk about crazy. He had gone round the bend, and he couldn't even figure out when it had happened or how. From wanting to avoid the mealy-mouthed female his mother kept pushing at him to needing to make her his... the journey had passed so quickly he felt wobbly from the flight.

Le coup de foudre. His mother claimed there was no fighting the lightning strike, though lives might be irrevocably changed by acceding.

Lawry turned back to Honoria. "Twenty pounds a month is a bit steep for rent, don't you think?"

She watched him carefully. "I don't know. I've never considered such things before our walk in the park the other day."

"And since then, you've thought of little else?"

It would be impossible to miss the hopeful note in his voice. When she blushed, something moved through him. He took a step toward where she stood, clutching her hands.

"Then allow me to consider them for you. I propose we find some rambling place falling down about its own ears and purchase it instead."

"Purchase it?" Her eyes widened. "I don't und—"

"Before I fell into my current occupation and

notoriety, before I saw a chance to remain in London, I did a little searching. I considered my mother and I would almost certainly be forced to sell our townhome and relocate. I learned the further one progresses beyond the city, the less expensive it becomes to survive. However, the outer regions are short on accommodations. One of us will have to learn to cook and the other clean, I'm afraid. There's little help for it."

Her brightening eyes released some of the muscles he hadn't been aware he had tightened. So, all was not lost. He crossed the room and took her hands within his. The pleasure of skin upon skin made him woozy.

"Marry me, Honoria. I shall give up my thievery, you have my promise. We will find a not-too-terrible home and live a simple and contented life. We can even bring our parents with us."

Woof!

"And Hercules." He smiled, unable to contain his delight. "We shall eat white bread and eggs and all the cucumbers I can grow without magical intervention."

"Pardon?"

"Never mind. The point is, yes. I agree. No more stealing. I shall live the life of a quiet gentleman farmer and allow you to make all decisions regarding morality for the both of us. Anything, Honoria, not to lose you. Please. Will you marry me?"

She narrowed her eyes, but the happiness shining within them did not dim. "You would forsake everything? For me?"

"I would forsake a great deal more if it meant you might entwine with me forever."

In response, she blushed, the color strong even in

the candlelight. "You really think we might manage?"

"I know it. We can move near Salisbury Cathedral and walk the footsteps of Constable. The beauty will uplift us. It will nourish us when cucumbers fail." He paused. How to convey his earnestness? "I cannot change the past, Honoria, but I swear to you on my very soul, I will not make the same mistakes in the future."

He willed her to see the truth within his eyes. When a slow smile lit her face, fireworks zinged and exploded throughout him.

"Then it is my honor to accept your kind proposal, Sir Lawrence." She laughed, giggled, and jumped up upon her toes. "Is this real?"

"Most real."

"I thank you for the honor you do me, Sir Lawrence, though I feel I should warn you, such is the very last mealy-mouthed response you will ever get from me."

He drew her in and kissed her. It felt like falling into golden, warmed honey. She leaned into him and the hot, sticky heat spread wherever her body touched his. His hands trod her contours, the rounded curves and the bony abutments. Without her hoops and layers, she was tinier than he had imagined, though her hips fit nicely into his grasp.

He groaned into her mouth as she wrapped her fingers in his hair and pulled him closer. Breaking away, he said, "We must stop. In another few moments, I may not be able to."

"Do you possess such a weak constitution, Sir Lawrence?" She murmured the words against his skin, nipping at his jawbone. She trailed fire kisses down his neck, each one sending a knife of agonizing pleasure straight to his favorite body part.

"Honoria…"

"We will be married. It will be fine. I want to see what I am getting." Placing her hands against his chest, she pushed him. He backed up a step. She pushed again, and again, until the backs of his legs touched the mattress.

"Honoria!" He laughed. What was a man to do? "Your honor…"

She smiled, a wicked, tempting twist. It shot another bolt through him. "Will be there in the morning. Or not. You're leaving our morality to me, remember? Besides, I want you, Lawry. I've seen dogs in the park and horses put to stud. I understand the generalities of what happens between men and women, I think?"

It was clear she didn't. "Not like dogs or horses."

She shrugged. "Close enough. I always looked away. The actions seemed painful and vaguely disgusting, but now I find I very much want you to cover me, Lawry." She paused and raised an eyebrow. "Too blunt for you?"

Yes.

"No."

He swallowed. How was she making him into the prude? Oh, what the hell?

He grabbed her and dragged her down to the mattress, rolling quickly on top of her. "There is a position for pleasure in which a man mounts a woman like a dog, but I prefer to look into your eyes and see your joy rise."

Distantly, he was aware Hercules padded to the door, but he was mired in the emotions passing over her face. He leaned down and meshed his lips with hers once more, felt her flow to meet his body, and pressed his own along her fine lines.

Woof!

He broke away and growled. "Don't move."

He jumped to his feet, crossed to the door, and opened it. Hercules raced through, only to stop and rearrange himself on the flooring just outside the portal. With a contented sigh, he settled into napping again. Lawry shut the door. He shucked his shoes and stalked back towards the bed.

"Where were we?" he murmured, climbing over her again.

"You were about to ruin me."

"Do you still wish to be ruined?"

Her wicked smile spread again. It lit her eyes and his stomach crumbled.

"Yes please."

Who was he to resist?

Chapter 21

When Lawry pressed his lips to hers once more, his kiss was too gentle, his touch too tentative. He explored, while ripples of need washed along her blood demanding more. She groaned as she tried to deepen the contact between them. He resisted by holding his body just out of reach. The business of ruin proceeded at a snail's pace.

Why couldn't he just rip the blasted nightgown from her body and touch her everywhere? She needed to fuse their diverse flesh into one entity. She needed his hands upon her belly. She needed his muscled length dancing upon her softer curves. She needed him to assuage the ache he laid at the very center of her being, where her blood wept with joy and urgent requirement.

Her blood pulsed, her skin buzzed, and parts of her contracted, but no matter how she squirmed or leaned up into him nothing was enough to still the throbbing need. Under her pulling fingers, muscle rippled and resisted, defying her desires. She wound her fingers through his hair and yanked.

In response, his lips broke away to draw down upon her neck. Her pulse beat as erratic as her blood as his mouth raised lightning bursts and star-fire. He trailed his tongue from one point to another. She lay in the midst of a storm, thrumming, before he slipped to the hollow between her breasts. When he did, breath escaped her as he unhooked the three top buttons on her gown. With each one, a part of her let go, fell away from conscious need into an evergreen space of sweetness. Tongue against hard nipples, he unwound her like the pearl buttons, unfurling a stream of budding spring ready to burst through the icy snow. She moaned into the fevered silence, more cry than whimper.

"Steady," he whispered against her skin, a hot mist against the cooling trail.

He moved downward, but the nightgown got in his way. He tore at fasteners, his fingers too clumsy, too slow.

"Lawry!"

He laughed, a ragged edge to the sound. "Patience. Please."

She wriggled from the cloth, tearing a gaping mouth at the final button. The garment fell away from her heated flesh, night air swirling over her skin like fingers as she lay revealed. Never had anyone viewed her naked length, not since she had grown to womanhood.

"Gads, but you are so beautiful." His eyes tarred her body, branding her, as his fingers caressed her so the rush of fire raced like a sharpened arrow to the vee between her legs.

"S-so are you."

He laughed again, his mouth against her bare belly. Slowly, he twirled his tongue down to swirl at her navel, before traveling further. He spread her legs. Some instinct caused her to tighten them.

"This, you will want. Trust me."

His breath fanned against the forest of dark curls so

she opened for him. When his lips wrapped around the secret part of her, everything in her body stilled and then screamed.

The incredible heat rose to impossible heights. She burned alive, the pressure within building until she thought she would explode. And then, she did.

Hurtling pleasure ripped like knives through her entire body, the pieces of her shattered to the edge of the room and beyond. She lay, bodiless, wrapped in pleasure so intense it exceeded her words, and then she came down to lie softly among the pillows once more. He lay still, his head upon her thigh, inhaling her with audible rasps.

In the next instant he was up, his pants undone. The long shaft of him pushed against the hollowed core.

"I'm sorry," he whispered, and leaned in to kiss her mouth once more. Then he pushed, and her world ripped apart again.

He buried her scream in his mouth and held very still. Sweat dotted his brow, a drop falling upon her cheek. Lifting to lean on one hand, he then used her sheet to wipe it away while he stilled and waited.

He was so good, so kind, so solicitous of her every moment. If pain was the only gift she could give him, she would. She moved against him, rotating her hips.

Lightning, sweet and hot, pierced her skies.

He gritted his teeth and groaned, but when she pushed her hips up to meet his, he relented. "My turn."

Grinding into her, in a rhythm unexpected, he touched her again. Fingers. Tongue. The iron need of him drew out the need in her, building her again to the highest, fullest battlements. When she poised upon the edge of falling, he roared. Her explosion followed, spurred by the sound.

Together, they fell into the pillows once more.

Chapter 22

"Are you well?"

Honoria battled against her heavy eyelids to find Lawry studying her. His hair lay in disheveled waves, damp and curling. Her own must look similar. She stretched, feeling the pull on all her muscles.

Their first interlude had passed quick and hot. Afterward, they giggled and tickled and made fools of themselves for the other's pleasure. Their laughter had followed them into another dance, slower and somehow more exciting than the first. Afterward, they had slipped into a sort of contented trance. She smiled. Of course she was well. What woman wouldn't be, after being so entertained?

"Do you wish to play dress-up again, Sir Lawrence, or dress down?" She giggled at the responding twinkle in his eyes.

"Neither right now, minx. I am content to drink you in with my gaze." He leaned over and pressed his lips to the spot between her eyes. "Darling. My love. You are enchantment itself, and I don't know if I wish the hours between now and the next time we couple to fly fast or to drag slow, so I might have an excuse simply to lie here and gaze upon your unparalleled beauty."

"I hadn't realized you possessed so poetic a soul."

"Byron and Shelley have nothing on me."

He touched the side of her face before sinking back upon the pillow, his one arm pretzeled under his head as he continued to assess her. She cuddled closer into him, twisting her leg between his as she laid her head upon his chest. Her fingers played against the light drift of hair trawling his front as he wrapped her within his strong arms.

"Lawry?"

"Mmm."

"I… it was all marvelous."

I love you, she longed to whisper, a silent offering of her soul. Yet she had agreed to marry him, yes, and she had given him her virtue, but some measure of trust must still be withheld from the thief of jewels and hearts lest he run off and take every part of her with him.

"Better than marvelous. Sshh." He stilled her fingers with his own. "I am never energetic after coupling, and you did have me put on quite the show. The corset I modeled for your pleasure—"

"—was not built to your form."

He chuckled as his eyes fluttered shut. "A small sleep. Just a small…"

Honoria tilted her head and watched his lips part. Deep, even breathing told her Morpheus had claimed him. She laid her head back, contented, and closed her eyes as well. She wouldn't sink into slumber. She would just rest her eyes. After all, he had to leave before they were discovered.

****

Woof! Woof! *Scratch, scratch, scratch.*

"Silence, Hercules! I'm trying to sleep. Damnable beast." Lawry rotated. His hand wrapped around a bare silken curve. He awoke in an instant.

Too late.

The door banged open. Colonel Cutworth stood within the frame. His confused expression transformed to fury as his eyes narrowed and his face flushed an angry shade of red and purple.

If a bucket of very icy water had been upturned over his head, Lawry could not have felt more uncomfortable. He spared a glance at Honoria whose lashes blinked a melody.

"Colonel, I can explain."

"Father?"

"Silence!"

His future father-in-law's jowls trembled. Above his menacing frown, the colonel's thick mustache bristled with rage. His slit eyes promised death. Given he had likely done more than polish his boots during his long stint in the army, it took no great stretch of the imagination to picture him skewering the man caught in his daughter's bed. Naked. With said daughter.

Also naked.

Lawry's hand tightened around Honoria's waist. He attempted to sit up, to jump over her and place his body between the irate father in the doorway and his unclothed daughter. The sheets wrapped around his limbs and foiled his efforts. He swore at them.

Hercules barked and danced around the room. He jumped up and placed his paws beside where Honoria lay and poked his nose into her arm.

"Not now, Hercules! Get down!"

The dog sent him an aggrieved look. He jumped down and pranced back to the doorway where he sat, panting, at the colonel's feet.

"Traitor." Lawry mumbled the word, not anxious to let the colonel hear him. The two men locked gazes.

"Get dressed. Library. Five minutes, or by all that is sacred, I will shoot you where you lie and be glad to be rid of you." His words shot forth like rapid bullets from one of Mr. Colt's pistols.

Since he looked serious enough to mean it, Lawry scrambled from the bedding before the door had fully shut behind the man and the traitorous mutt. Searching the room for his trousers, discarded at some point after they had awoken and tickled each other, but before they had fallen back to sleep in companionable bliss, Lawry's gaze travelled past Honoria. And travelled back.

"I'm sorry. I meant to be gone before morning light, but…"

An insistent scratching distracted him. He opened the door for Hercules, who ran back in wearing the largest doggie grin he had ever seen.

"If you haven't brokered a peace, I don't want to hear it." Lawry turned back to Honoria.

"It is not your fault." She yawned widely, clutching the sheet above her beautiful, perfectly sized breasts. "I will come with you. He likely won't kill you in front of me. Probably."

He narrowed his eyes. "Why aren't you more upset?"

"I'm upset. I'm just busy trying to think of the best way to ferret you out of the city until he cools down enough not to be a danger." She peeped at him from beneath her lashes. She opened her mouth, as if she would speak, but closed it without doing so.

He might have commented with some sterling

piece of wit or wisdom if she hadn't chosen to slide from the bed. All he could do was swallow. If not, he would have drooled. Those pink and cream breasts were so beautiful they drew him like magnets, until his gaze slid to her rounded, generous backside as she leaned over to scoop her ruined nightgown off the floor. His hands fisted at his sides as she bent again to tuck the fabric into a drawer. How had he managed to forbear rutting at her like a stag in heat all night long?

The feel of her returned to his palms, the weight of satin measured just to his needs. That's how. The pleasure of simply holding her had outweighed his roguish urgings.

"Oh dear. I'd forgotten the knife." She held up her corset for his inspection. It blocked his view of too large a part of her magnificent form. He lowered his head to the side to see around and beneath the obstruction, but she moved it into his way.

Blinking, he focused on the boning. Last night he had used the small blade he carried everywhere to cut the laces. Well, it would have taken too long otherwise to have divested himself of the garment, and parts of him had been too hard for patience. Between their first mating and the second spilling, to amuse her, he had wrapped the corset around his waist, going so far as to knot each lace. He had used her petticoat as a wig, and a sheet for the skirt as he pranced about the room and pretended to prepare for a ball.

He had been successful, at least. She had laughed until she had gripped her sides. Then he had gripped them for her, along with other parts in a coupling so heated he could barely think of it without blushing.

"I'll buy you a new one."

"Something silk."

"There goes our house budget."

She laughed and he grinned. He ignored the nervous truth behind his jest. How would he ever fulfill his promises to her and still keep her fed, watered, and clothed?

Her father would likely demand the same answers in a few minutes. He might demand them at gunpoint.

Time sped up as he donned his garments and laced Honoria into a loose-fitting dress. More minutes took wing as he spread kisses upon her shoulder until he covered each section of exposed skin with cloth. There wasn't nearly enough once he buttoned the pearl squibs along her back, the high-necked fashion of the time created simply to thwart him.

She grabbed his hand before he could exit. "Lawry, I just want you to know you needn't feel obligated."

"But I do. And if I didn't, you shouldn't have anything to do with me.

He kissed her forehead and took a long breath. He might put on a good show, but this was not how he wished to ask her father for her hand.

Descending the stairs, Lawry carried his shoes. Behind him, Honoria clipped her heels. Just as they reached the main hallway, the colonel exited the library. A long-nose pistol hung heavy at his side. Without a word, he marched back into the room. Throwing the gun upon the desk, he sank into his chair and gestured with his chin to the other two seats fronting the wide expanse of wood.

Honoria grabbed his hand again and squeezed it as best she could around the shoe he held.

"Father, I realize this is not the best way to share

the news, but you must understand. Lawry… er, Sir Lawrence, has proposed, and I have accepted. So, you see, despite the, um, unfortunate way you learned of our intentions, there's no harm done, is there?"

Honoria babbled. Her smile was almost the simper she used to wear. It had rougher edges though. It arose from a wellspring of kindness rather than social necessity. If she ever used her simper again it would only be to cut someone down to size.

He had done that for her. Pride swept over him, starting up from his toes. He had given her permission to be herself, and she, bright star, had run with it. In turn, she had demanded he open himself up to her, to trust her, and to take them into the future. The reward for his own courage was so great he grew teary as he looked at her.

Hercules padded into the room, sniffing at the carpet along his route. When he came even with the desk, he submitted his head for petting by the colonel, who seemed to calm while he caressed the dog. Then, the traitorous mutt curled up at the military man's feet.

"Bad dog." Lawry whispered the words under his breath, and received a soft *woof* in reply.

Ungrateful canine.

The colonel cleared his throat as if shooting a thousand guns at an approaching army. "Honoria, I love you, but this conversation is not your concern. You may stay only if you promise to be silent. One word, and I shall send you to your room. Am I understood?"

"Yes, Father." Her voice was soft, but even.

"Pardon? Did I hear something?" The colonel cupped his ear.

Honoria clamped her lips together.

"Ah, I thought not. Now, Sir Lawrence."

Colonel Cutworth speared him into his seat. Lawry tried not to squirm. He dropped his shoes to the floor and pretended they were on his feet.

"Yes, sir."

"You will marry my daughter both without haste and without prolonging the matter. I will send a missive to the local church, St. Bartholomew-on-the-Field, and requested the banns be waived. We shall see if it is possible. I will allow you each one guest outside of immediate family to witness the ceremony. The reception count will be as Lady Fishbane chooses. We shall leave the matter in her capable hands. I'm of the opinion she will not mind. You, son, will not disappoint her in any manner. Do I make myself clear?"

"Yes, sir." He agreed without any difficulty.

Woof!

"Hercules might also attend."

Snuffle.

"That's not a word." Lawry glared at the dog.

The dog ignored him and turned his head in the opposite direction.

"I envision a simple luncheon. Lady Fishbane and I will coordinate on the menu. As to the financial aspects of this union, had you come to me before sullying my daughter…" The man's skin suddenly flushed puce, the same color as Honoria's ugly dress. "…I would have informed you of the sorry state of Honoria's dowry. You would not have been misled. As it stands, you have made a bad bargain. Seven hundred pounds. That is all."

Beside him, Honoria straightened. She opened her mouth and Lawry shot her a warning glance which she, darling, smart, perfect, female, understood immediately. Her lips clamped shut once more.

"It is a very generous sum, Colonel Cutworth. Had she naught but a small speck of dust to her name, I would still consider the bargain made to my advantage. We shall put the money to good use. Honoria and I have already discussed the purchasing of a small house in the country. I intend to sell some paintings I received to pad our account. With the dowry, we should be able to purchase something not too awful."

"And to live on? What will provide you a yearly income if you spend everything on shelter?" The colonel studied him, eyebrow raised, as if he spoke to a school boy.

Since he felt like one, Lawry didn't take umbrage. Despite telling himself not to, he fidgeted.

"Er, well, I have never been overly blessed with financial savvy. I'm sure the testament is not something a father wishes to hear, but it is the unfortunate truth, and I have vowed to be truthful with Honoria. Miss Cutworth. No, damn it all, I am as good as family now, or near to. Honoria." He looked the colonel in the eye as he repeated her name. "I shall be grateful for your advice, sir. I may not possess much in the way of investing acumen, but I am a biddable sort, and capable of following sage guidance."

The colonel snorted but his hard eyes softened. "So you have no plan."

Lawry swallowed. "Er, well, I planned to set a little by, enough for a year or two, if we're frugal. Honoria has suggested, and I agree, I should be able to start a breeding business. Hercules is past the age to be put to stud, but I suppose he would be willing to offer his services for the sake of England. So to speak. Curly-haired retrievers will become the most popular breed. They're intelligent and loyal and strong, not to mention well-equipped to help out on the hunt. I'm rather hopeful a breeding program will prove lucrative."

He wasn't, but where there was time there was hope.

The colonel groaned and his gaze searched the ceiling, apparently unconvinced. Lawry threw Honoria a glance to see what she thought. She nodded quickly and flashed a small smile. The ragged edges of his nerves soothed under her regard.

"Honoria also believes she might sell her soaps and perfumes."

The colonel slunk back against his chair, wide-eyed. "You intend for your wife—my daughter—to work?"

Shocking, but there it was. It would keep her out of trouble, anyway. Now she had found herself, he suspected she would find heaps of peril too. It would be best to keep her hands and mind occupied.

Unfortunately, the colonel was turning purple once more.

"I don't see her industry as work so much as the fulfillment of a passion. If she might earn a small penny by selling her products, so much the better."

"Hmm."

"We'll be fine, Father."

Honoria gazed at Lawry as if he had set the stars. She must not have minded the speed of the first coupling or the drawn-out nature of the second. Her melting expression hinted she might wish for a third. So did he.

"Neither of us has been traditionally raised, after all, and neither of us gives a fig for Society. We are ripe to slay the modern world."

"Honoria! What are you saying? Slay the world?"

She shrugged. "Figuratively, I suppose. Yes. Why not? Why not embrace commerce rather than disdain it? Why not take our talents and succeed? We shall kill the idea our class is good only for sipping tea and looking lovely."

The colonel rounded upon Lawry. "Is this your doing?"

"I hope so. Isn't she marvelous?"

The colonel rotated back to his daughter. "How have you not been traditionally raised? I brought you up myself to emulate and exhibit all the fine qualities Society expects of a young lady. Even before your dear mother departed this earth, God bless her soul, I overstepped her on certain matters. I dare anyone to say you don't possess the most gracious manners of even the highest born."

Honoria leaned forward and stretched a hand across the desk. The colonel took it within his.

"Father, what other men do you know who take a working interest in their daughter's comportment? Are you aware of even one who regularly accompanies his child to the *modiste*?"

Lawry struggled not to laugh as the colonel's mouth fell open. He gaped like a fish. Having learned to speak her opinions, Honoria was now unstoppable.

She withdrew her palm and sat back. "As for Sir Lawrence, he was raised without a father's influence. I'm sure he simply longs for your tutelage."

She looked at him from the sides of her eyes. He

nodded quickly, if untruthfully. Frankly, he worried sick at what the colonel might do to take him in hand once he became part of the family.

Honoria smiled. "Just as I am somewhat hopeful Lady Fishbane might guide me. You have done everything for me, and I appreciate each one of your efforts, but I do miss a female perspective."

She tilted her head and winked at him. The minx actually winked, which was something no woman of the upper class should ever do.

Was it possible for his adoration to grow? It already reached from toe to crest.

The conversation continued, but Lawry listened with only half his attention. Though he should be sated, all he wanted to do was to take her back upstairs and ram himself deep as her mewl of pleasure spilled over him. Rock hard and uncomfortable, he squirmed in his chair.

Those damned banns couldn't be read fast enough.

Chapter 23

The Rosemere ball was in full swing by the time Honoria and her father arrived. Couples swished around the dance floor like a mad variety of gorgeously hued loose-stemmed flowers swaying in the breeze. Honoria patted her golden harvest skirt. At the base of the dress, two panels of olive green met at a dusky pink satin bow. The top swam with ecru lace and silk, ribbed at intervals with more pink threading. Ornate damask roses hugged the low-cut bodice and mirrored the embroidered cherry blossoms crisscrossed from shoulder to waist.

The dress had belonged to her mother, who had been shorter and thicker. The skirt was not as full as it should be, or as long, but the *modiste* had added matching ecru lace to the side panels and hem. The result proved lovelier than the original. Honoria swished her skirts just for the fun of watching them move before setting her gaze high upon the crowd.

Three days had passed since Lawry had been discovered in her bed. Since the meeting with her father, he had absented himself, though he had sent daily missives assuring her all was well. His last penned note indicated he would meet her at the Rosemere ball. If he was here, he must be hiding. Perhaps under the punch table?

"Do not look so concerned, Honoria. He'll turn up

sooner or later."

Her father's voice, as always, carried at the most inopportune times. As the band finished a piece, heads turned in their direction.

Honoria arrested her automatic simper before the expression completed. She lifted her chin instead and stared down those assessing her. Surprisingly, one by one, they turned away.

Hmph. Who knew it could be so easy?

After her father settled her in the line of wallflowers and took his leave to seek out the gaming tables, she adjusted her skirts over the wobbly chair and tapped her fan against the outside of her thigh. The tiny dance card hanging from her wrist remained blank, but for once she didn't care. She could hum while Lawry danced her feet off in the privacy of her home if she felt the urge to move to music. Once she found him.

"Miss Cutworth."

As her head swiveled, any hope she might have held that Sir Lawrence approached stumbled to its death. The man who bobbed his head stood a shade too tall and was likely to disappear into any mediocre fog. Though he dressed in evening kit of black and white, just as all the other gentlemen did, he nodded to his moniker with the gray bow tracing his long neck. Ice slithered up her spine. She shook it away.

"Lord Meriven. It's a pleasure to see you again."

It wasn't, especially after their last interaction and the way he had treated her.

He took the hand she extended and kissed the air somewhere above it. He assessed her skirts with a studied intensity. "Miss Cutworth, you are looking delightful tonight. What a charming pattern. Quite eastern."

"Cherry blossoms, yes. Thank you for noticing, my lord." Honoria waved her fan to full extension and batted the air. She kept her face expressionless, if only to hide her disquiet.

"I am rather enamored of designs from that part of the world. Though my particular hobbies center around cultures further west, the Land of the Rising Sun has its attractions, I must admit. Their origins disappear into the mists of time. I understand Lord Elgin recently signed a commercial treaty with the shogunate, which means we shall be seeing more of such compositions over the next few years."

He returned his gaze to hers. At some point during his perusal, he had acquired a tightened jaw and lips, but what caused his expression, she couldn't fathom.

"I do adore the pink blossoms, my lord."

Ridiculous words. She searched the part of the room at his back looking for rescue. None seemed readily available.

"I also note your pendant has been recovered. How lucky for you." Though if he thought so, it wasn't apparent in his demeanor.

Honoria touched the gold T-shape, the rough garnets sharp against her kidskin gloves. "Indeed, I feel quite blessed. Sir Lawrence found and returned it to me, though I'm not certain where or how he located it."

Which was the truth. In all the madness following her father's discovery of them together in her bed, she hadn't thought to ask. When she had returned to her rooms after Lawry had gone, she had noted it lying upon her dresser.

"Fishbane recovered it for you." His voice was

even, but something pinched its edges. "How marvelous."

"Yes. Isn't it?" If her tone dripped ice in return, the same frigid solidification creeping up her spine, he gave no appearance of noticing. "I am doubly thankful to him, both for the return of my pendant and for his desire to make me the happiest woman in the world." She paused and swallowed. "We are affianced."

She shivered and tried to cover the involuntary action by beating her fan through the air. If there was a language to fans, and there was, this one had to mean go away. How remiss of her not to have studied the tongue more carefully. Her mother would have known. She would have known how to deal with a maddening marquess whose hands roved too freely and whose attitude required a careful circuitous circuit. The loss of a feminine presence in her life had never seemed the greater.

She watched him carefully, looking for any sign of jealousy that could perhaps explain her sudden atavistic reaction to him. Instead, all she could find was a cold, calculating consideration. He raised his eyebrow, but it mocked rather than questioned.

"Engaged. Well, I suppose congratulations are in order."

"Thank you. Ours is a recent agreement."

She beat her fan harder, so much so her wrist began to ache. Again, she scanned the crowd around his thin, black-clad form, hoping to see someone she knew well enough to warrant jumping from her chair and fleeing The Gray Lord's presence. Her gaze latched upon bright red hair the shade of flames. Marjorie Plimpton. A deep sigh of relief escaped her lips.

"If you'll excuse me, my lord, I see a friend with whom I am most anxious to converse. Do enjoy your evening."

Without a backward glance she hopped up, swished around him, and fled across the room. Even the sight of Mrs. Plimpton, who had never liked her, seemed a boon.

Something about Meriven disturbed her, something more than his disrespect and hubris. If she was completely honest, her initial feelings towards the man hadn't been any different except in degree. There was just something off about him.

Mrs. Plimpton had already moved away by the time Honoria slid up to her friend. When Marjorie began to chatter, the current gossip fleeing from her lips like a pack of foxes before hunters, Honoria took a moment to again scan the room. Where was Lawry? He had promised to be here. And where had he been these past few days? Engaging in thievery? Slipping into other women's beds when caught? Such was the unofficial account of The Midnight Menace, whispered behind raised palms and knowing looks.

For a moment, doubt assailed her. Had she been just another type of acquisition? Was it possible he had taken her innocence like a piece of jewelry, only to skulk off into the night? Her mind flipped through the possibilities, each one a dagger, but each one landing wrong.

No. Despite her fears, the ones that held her back from expressing her love, logic told her he wouldn't be able to get away with such deceit. His mother, for one, would skewer him. Her father would be quick to follow with a deeper blade. Plus, he was too much built of light to engage in such darkness.

Except for The Midnight Menace part of his personality, of course. It was hard to put such endeavors to the side when examining the whole of him.

Snapping open her fan again, unable to remain in place a moment longer, she interrupted her friend's recitation of the artful decoration on Lady Flanders' skirts. "I must go, Marjorie. I must find Lawry."

She took a step toward the dancers when Marjorie's hand locked upon her forearm. Honoria looked down, startled.

"Don't." Her friend's laughing green eyes held a serious note. "It never does to chase a man. While I am grateful to this one for stripping you of that annoying simper, well, I always told you I hated the expression you put on and took off like stockings—"

"Marjorie!" Honoria glanced about to see if anyone had overheard the last word.

"Undergarments are items of apparel. There's no logical reason to dismiss valid terms in the English language simply for what they might lead the mind to imagine." Despite her sentiments, her face flushed red. "Anyway, you must not chase the man, Honoria. He will only run faster."

"I am not chasing him."

Not completely, anyway. Besides, he had chased her first.

"You are. Oh!" Marjorie peered closer, examining Honoria's face in tiny increments. "No! I don't believe it."

"Believe what?"

"Did you… Did he… Are you…" She grew redder

still. Who knew such a flaming color was possible?

Perhaps she herself wore a similar shade. Certainly, her face burned hotter than she could remember.

"You did!" Triumph lit Marjorie's eyes. She extended her fan and waved it furiously, then stopped and leaned in. "Was ruin as exciting as it is described in the penny dreadfuls?"

Honoria tapped her fan upon Marjorie's arm. "I refuse to dignify such surmise with a reply. Sir Lawrence and I are engaged. I would ask you to keep your opinions on any matter related to him to yourself."

Marjorie's eyes grew wide.

Honoria turned and stalked off, not sure where she was going, only that she had to get away. Already, shame at her behavior towards her best friend swirled within her belly, but if Marjorie could so easily spot her spoilation, what did the rest of the world see?

She rushed the floor beneath her satin slippers until she realized she had left the party behind. Without noticing, she had made her way to the servant's domain. The long hallway of the butler's pantry lay before her, tall polished wood, built-in cabinets to her either side. Silver storage boxes lay open upon the counters, ornate forks left spread upon soft cloth. Next to the flatware, jugs lined up like soldiers. The labels upon them read, in order: Chalk, Ammonia, Alcohol. Next to the jugs, a pitcher of fresh water stood at the ready. A deep bucket perched on the extended shelf pulled from within the furniture.

Someone had been cleaning silver, but why the lemons and mint spread upon a hearty plate?

Intrigued, she ran her finger over the divided citrus fruit and pressed the herb's leaves between her fingers.

The delightful, fresh odor spilled upward to her nose and she inhaled deeply. As always, the mint's pleasant smell calmed her nerves.

"What are you doing here?"

Honoria turned toward the rough voice. An ancient man, bent almost double, dressed in old-fashioned garments resembling the servants' plum-colored uniforms, raced toward her as quickly as his infirm legs would carry him. When he reached her, he smacked the mint from between her fingers.

"If you've ruined the oils I'll have to go fetch more from the garden." He turned his attention back to the forks. "There's not enough silver here. Someone's taken it, if you ask me, one of your scurrilous lot, I'll bet. They'll be blaming us, sure enough, and someone's going to swing. Mark me." He grumbled as he shoved her aside by inserting himself into the space she occupied. "I'll tell them, I will. Had to be a guest. Five forks. Gone. Kidney & Johnson, they were. Nice medallion on top. Heavy." He squinted at her. "Are you responsible?"

Honoria shook her head. It was hard to know what to think, let alone reply. She swallowed. "Um…"

He cast her a baleful glance, as if to say she was as stupid as she was ineloquent. Not her fault, of course. It was a rare experience to be berated and accused by someone else's servant. Her glance fell again upon the fruit and herb.

"I, um, I wondered what the lemon and mint were for. The other substances are clearly for cleaning silver—"

"Which I have to do, don't I, seeing as how we're short on service because someone stole five forks. This blasted pattern is different, isn't it, but there's no help for it. No, there's not."

"Yes, of course. I'm sorry. Only, where do the lemon and mint come into play?"

"So, you like the smell of ammonia, do you? Must be. Why else would you be standing in the pantry, ogling the silver, unless of course, you mean to steal more of it?"

She could maintain her innocence, but the way he glared at her made her suspect it would do no good. Excusing herself, Honoria fled the way she had come. On a positive note, she had just learned how to get rid of the terrible smells associated with dreaded household chores.

Something like steel wrapped around her waist. Before she could scream, a soft cloth pressed over her nose and mouth. Inhaling, Honoria discerned something sweet and acrid. Before she could do more than grab at a beefy, hairy wrist, the floor gave way beneath her slippers. The walls tumbled.

They followed her into the dark.

Chapter 24

"It is impossible she is missing. I'm certain she is fine." Lawry's mother wrapped her fingers together. Her knuckles glowed white from her too-tight grip, belaying her words.

Behind her, the fire burned brightly. Lawry suspected the colonel had ordered it lit for comfort's sake rather than to take any imagined chill from the room. The day outside the windows was fine. The sun shone through the glass with mad abandon. Indeed, the temperature was so high he perched on the edge of uncomfortable in his jacket. In the close room, the uncomfortable fast approached downright miserable territory.

He took a deep breath and tried to still his fast-beating heart. "I don't understand. People don't vanish into thin air. There were over two hundred expected at the Rosemere ball. You were there yourself, sir. Someone must have seen her leave?"

The colonel shook his head. "All the servants were questioned. The drivers too. Honoria's reputation will be in tatters now, her name upon everyone's lips. Look. The rags already feature her disappearance on the front page."

He threw a newspaper at Lawry who paced the room closest to the doorway. Lawry plucked it from the air. The headline screamed Honoria's identity in an inflammatory headline. "*Disappearance of Innocence: The Case of Miss H.C., Daughter of England's Finest Defender.*"

Which was bad. Very, very bad. Anyone who had ever crossed her path would recognize her.

He scanned the article once. His blood rushed to his toes, leaving him faint. He gripped the doorframe and then leaned against it for support as he read through the newsprint with greater care.

"Locally famed Miss H. C., she of the puce and turquoise gowns, went missing last night from the ballroom of Lord and Lady R. Lady R remains confined to her rooms, in natural distress over the insult to her meticulously planned event. Last seen holding up a row of wallflowers, Miss C vanished into thin air after having been noted to engage in conversation with none other than the rather dapper Lord M. Has the interest of The Gray Lord been piqued by a gentlewoman whose vibrant shades of skirts might offset his somber demeanor? As soon as she reappears, we shall have to take careful note. We at *The Ladies Periodical of Happenings and Disasters* stand a warning for our dear readers lest they lay any misplaced censure: Lord M is not under suspicion. He was seen to be dancing with Lady S and Lady T well into the night (and see page 2 for a description of their dress), and thereafter he kept the company of Lord S near the gaming tables. The gentlemen, it is said, were engaged until the wee hours of the morning, Lord M having lost seven hands in a row. Scotland Yard has been called in to investigate…"

He didn't bother to read further. The paper flew from his fingers as he tossed it upon the table. He wiped his hand against his pants as he straightened and began to pace again. The article didn't tell him anything he didn't already know.

"She could be dead by now," the colonel whispered, closing his eyes.

"Don't."

It was all Lawry could say as his anxiety choked at his throat. The air he breathed didn't make it to his lungs. The room spun so he clutched onto the back of the couch while he pushed his panic down until it squirmed like a bunch of worms in his belly. Inhaling to the full extent his chest would balloon, he waited. He was used to ignoring trepidation. He would have made a very bad thief if he hadn't been able to control his nerves. This, though…

He pushed the rising panic down again until it stayed where he wanted it. A rolling belly he could deal with.

The thought reminded him of his first dinner with Honoria and their trip to the kitchen to sample the fizzy waters. A wave of longing transmuted into terror. It swamped him yet again, this time too wide and long to be easily tucked away.

"We shall find her, Lawry." His mother exchanged a look with the colonel before returning her gaze to him. "The best officers in the city are searching her out. We must trust they know their job."

He nodded and ran his hand through his hair. Focusing upon the folded paper, he forced his brain to function. "Let's recap what we know. She left her friend, Miss Plimpton, in order to search me out. According to Miss Plimpton, she ran toward the back of the house. The kitchens?"

"Whatever would she do there? No, she must have

been seeking a retiring room, although why she would think..." His mother moved a book upon the table, squaring it. Perhaps she thought the movement would help organize the chaos into which they had fallen.

He tracked her action, fixated. "She has an affinity for creating scents. Perhaps something drew her."

"And why weren't you there?" the colonel thundered, advancing across the room. "You should have protected her better! You're engaged, man! What was so important it kept you from her side?"

The colonel's face had turned an interesting shade of puce once more. He leaned over the back of a chair, breathing hard. For the briefest moment, Lawry hesitated, uncertain, before rushing to his side. He almost collided with his mother who had popped up at the same time.

Honoria's father waved them both off. "I'm fine. I'm fine, damn it to hell!"

Lady Fishbane shrank back and pursed her lips. Her gaze met Lawry's, and she shook her head.

"Apologies," the colonel muttered after he had centered himself once more. With military precision, he straightened his back and patted the lapels of his jacket.

"There is no need for apologies, Henry." His mother threw Lawry another glance before sliding the rest of the way toward the colonel. "You are overwrought, dearest. You are worried. It is natural. Please, Henry, sit down. I have recently read how violent feelings may stop the heart from beating." She stroked his arm. "This is all very upsetting, but I worry about your health."

"My heart is fine. I am perfectly fit." He snapped his response, but allowed Lawry's mother to draw him around the chair. Once seated, he patted Lady Fishbane's hands. His gaze sought Lawry's. "How do you intend to find my daughter and recapture her good name?"

Which was an awful lot to ask, given Lawry's brain had stalled. He paced to the window. To find Honoria, he would have to have some idea of where she had disappeared to, and he didn't. As to her good name, the only thing he could do was marry her as he had long intended. It seemed a long time, at any rate. Forever, really. Perhaps he had known her less than two full weeks, but he had waited for her forever.

Marrying her, however, might not wash this stain. If he got her back, if she wasn't lying dead in a ditch somewhere, perhaps the only course was to flee Society. It was one thing to plan a move to the country, but another to be forced there.

If he could find her.

His heart creased and crumpled. Perhaps he was the one having a crisis of the heart. The idea, when it finally worked its way through his thick skull, touched every piece of rightness in his body. He knew. Suddenly, he simply knew. His back straightened.

"Yes?" His mother sank to the arm of the overstuffed chair and leaned against the colonel. She gazed at him through widened eyes.

"I think, that is, I think I know, where she might be, or, at least, with whom."

"Well, don't leave us waiting, boy! Where the devil is she?" Honoria's father's face turned interesting shades of unhealthy colors once more.

"First, I never sent a note indicating I would be present at the Rosemere ball. I've spent the past few days scouring Kingston-on-Thames and its environs for a suitable location upon which to build. I only arrived home late last night. I've sent Honoria correspondence each day to assure her of my affection, but I said nothing of the Rosemere event."

"Then who did?" His mother petted the colonel's arm as he clutched his chest once more.

"The fiend who took her. It could be no one else. Have *all* of the servants been questioned?"

Again, his mother responded. The colonel looked unable to fix two words together. His shade had dimmed to pasty gray.

"A servant saw her in the kitchen, but he did not see anyone attack her. The man was old and infirm and did not fall under suspicion. He accused her of wishing to steal the silver. The police finally understood she was interested in the making of a silver polish."

Lawry chuckled, despite his disquiet. Of course she was.

The parents stared at him, waiting for his denouncement, waiting for his explanation of who had absconded with his future bride. His mother would understand. He could already see the idea dawning on her face. The colonel though... Lawry flipped through the words he might use to explain his theory. No circuitous route suggested itself.

A bold approach, then. There was no hiding it anymore, at any rate.

Sighing, he dropped himself into a chair caddy-corner to the one upon which the parents sat. Elbows on knees, he attempted to modulate his voice as he explained. "Before I relate my theory, there is something we must discuss first, sir. It's necessary in order to put the rest in context." He took a deep breath. The bald truth, though there would be no going back. "I am a thief, Colonel Cutworth. The Midnight Menace. You may have heard of me? I've become quite infamous in some quarters."

"Lawry!" His mother gripped the colonel's arm so tight the man flinched. He patted her hand.

"He should know, Mother. We're all family now, or will be once I wed Honoria. It is how I have made my living, sir. I suspect the news does not offer any undue shock."

Honoria's father *harumph*ed, but didn't deny the allegation. Indeed, his skin fast returned to normal color.

"Good. I detest drama and recriminations. I promised Honoria I would put aside my immoral occupation, and I will do so. I have done so, even though the Duchess of Shrewsbury and her guests begged to be fleeced. I sat through the most annoying séance ever conducted simply to study them and learn their patterns, and all for naught because Honoria... Honoria is more important."

Lady Fishbane's eyes softened as she gazed at him with a misty expression.

He ignored her. "The point is, sir, I am no longer a thief, but the last piece I stole actually belonged to Honoria."

"I beg your pardon?" The colonel's voice boomed, shaking the pretty ceramic bird sculpture sitting upon a small table next to his arm. He levitated from the chair.

Lawry's mother, clinging to his arm, rose with him. "You must sit, Henry. Allow Lawry to finish. He has a good explanation. He had better voice it well." She glared at him but succeeded in dragging the colonel back down to the cushion.

"I can indeed explain. I stole the T pendant she wears, the one with the garnets, from Meriven. Actually, to be precise, I stole it back from Lord Morray, who had it from Meriven. Meriven was the original thief."

The names stopped the colonel from whatever rampage he had been about to let loose. He snapped his lips closed before opening them again to roar. "Meriven? Lord Meriven, the marquess?"

"Henry! Your heart!"

The colonel's face flashed from red to purple to a nameless color as his mother's eyes grew large as platters. She stroked the colonel's hair as she tried to calm him.

"Why?" the colonel demanded, swatting at Lawry's mother's hand. "Why would a man of his standing and wealth take Honoria's jewels? He isn't even married."

His mother leaned into the colonel again, this time to place her palm against his forehead. "Henry, are you feverish? You aren't making any sense."

"I'm fine, I tell you. Stop that." He removed her hand more gently and folded it between his own. He sighed. "I meant, he might wish to shower his wife with a present, if perhaps she commented upon the piece and he thought to please her. It is what we men do, which is a damned useful trait when presented in a different context." He glanced at Lawry's mother. "Excuse the language."

She kissed his cheek.

The colonel lowered his eyes and shook his head.

"It isn't even valuable. It's hollow." He turned his stare upon Lawry again. "As, I suppose, you know firsthand."

Lawry studied the ceiling for a moment, seeking a calm he couldn't quite find, though he felt strangely better for his confession. When he looked back at the colonel, he used his most reassuring tone. "I am aware, yes. As to why Meriven took the risk of sneaking into Honoria's room in order to steal it is a question I cannot answer. I overheard him in conversation with Morray. I didn't understand their references, but I got the impression they thought Honoria's pendant was important, some sort of key, or a copy of a key."

He explained in more detail about his visit to Meriven's home and how he had taken the pendant back from Morray. His mother fanned her face in response as she grayed. He had managed to avoid relating the details before this moment. Honoria's father looked both thoughtful and deadly. There was something about his fixed stare. It put Lawry in mind of tactical maneuvers wherein many of the enemy ended up dead upon the ground.

"Honoria's honor must be restored."

"Honoria's virtue was left intact when Meriven crept within her chambers. I stood outside the door and would have stopped him if…"

The colonel's narrowed eyes narrowed further. They held him like a bug trapped in amber.

"But the point is, he never went near the bed." Lawry stood. "It means her person is only necessary to whatever his plans are concerning the pendant. He is not interested in her as, well, her."

His mother fluttered. "Have we considered the

marquess might wish to marry Miss Cutworth?" As they both swiveled to look at her, she cocked her chin. "Well, it is one way of taking lawful possession of her property. Many a man finds it an expeditious sort of endeavor. Not everything needs be about skullduggery, you know."

"The only person to wed Honoria will be me, Mother." Lawry squinted back at the colonel, lest the man form the notion that forcing a marriage with Meriven might be the better option. "I shall see the marquess in the ground before anyone takes her from me." He tried to keep his voice steady, but even he heard the ragged edges of his words. "I shall fetch her back here. We may discuss the rest then."

With a slight bob of his head to the older two, he strode toward the door, already planning how to regain access to Meriven's townhouse. The Gray Lord would be expecting him.

"Lawry."

He pivoted. "Yes, Mother?"

"If you find her still unwed, and if she is still willing to wed you rather than the marquess, you will need to travel swiftly to Gretna Green. Though it is no longer the fashion to run off to marry, in my day quite a few couples in unusual circumstances made up for their impetuosity by the several days' trip to the Green. It remains the most romantic cure for ruin."

He met his mother's gaze and his chin trembled. Resolutely, he nodded his head and took his leave, his heart so full of emotion he feared he might leak tears.

Chapter 25

Honoria rolled over onto her back and groaned. Her mouth tasted like sawdust and worms. Her head ached. Prying open her eyes, she studied the gray and rose-striped canopy above. The fabric contained the sheen of expensive silk. Her gaze traveled to the side. Bountiful roses in the same shades of pink flourished against pale yellow walls. The hand-painted designs screamed elegance and opulence. From somewhere below, the faint tinkle of piano keys floated softly into the room.

Where was she? The space was unfamiliar. Lovely, but unfamiliar.

With jerky motions, she managed to prop herself up upon her elbows. The walls swayed like a kaleidoscope so she lay back down again. A funny scent lingered in her nostrils, something sweet and sticky and cloying. She rubbed her nose, took a deep breath through her mouth, and tried to sit up once more.

This time she was successful. She glanced around the large space, noting the cream Aubusson rug with its matching florals and the high sheen of the wooden floorboards and furniture. Perhaps this was Heaven? Had she died during the night?

Sending her thoughts back, she hit a wall of gray. The last thing she remembered was the ball. There had been a funny little man, all hunched over, and he had spoken to her in an impermissible way. Lemons. Oh, yes, and mint. Something about cleaning silver, and then...

She had walked down a long corridor, back to the ball. She passed by the door of some office. There had been a desk. Then...

Honoria sniffed again. The hand. The cloth.

She had been drugged?

Suddenly, she laughed out loud, startling herself with the sound in the otherwise still room. Downstairs, the piano stopped before starting again. She covered her mouth with her hand to hold in the giggles set to escape. The new tune cried mournfully, full of loss, but it didn't settle in her bones, not when she had her own imagination to amuse her.

Marjorie would tell her she had been reading too many penny dreadfuls, and she would be right. Who on earth would drug her? No, she must have fainted, perhaps from the cleaning solutions and their fumes. The Rosemeres must be downstairs right now, waiting for a report on her condition. They seemed a rather nice couple. They had greeted her and her father like old friends though they were only acquaintances. Their gentility had to recommend them as good people.

She slipped her feet over the edge of the bed and searched for her shoes but failed to find them. No matter. Her skirts with the additional lace were long enough to hide her feet. As she stood, the piano stopped once more. She fluffed out her dress and straightened her bodice, startled when a door slammed below. A bit woozy, she picked her way to the window and pushed back the heavy drapery. Her gaze alighted upon a dark-clad male hopping into a black carriage. He wore the typical dress of the day, but otherwise he was too far away to recognize.

He wasn't Lord Rosemere, in any event. Her host had been round, bald, and squat. The figure at the carriage was long and lean.

After letting the curtains fall again, she crossed the room, steadier on her feet with every moment, and exited into a long, wide hallway. Polished inlaid marquetry walls spoke of a wealth she hadn't thought the Rosemeres possessed.

The stairway was tricky as she remained dizzy, but she made her way successfully to the front parlor, only to find it vacant. She passed to the window and gazed out to the front street. It seemed a longer expanse to the sidewalk than she remembered, but really, who remarked such things properly at night, before a ball? The sun shone brightly into her eyes. Too brightly. Her head banged with her own personal drummer.

Resuming her search, she haunted the rooms. Having expected the family to perhaps be gathered for breakfast, or even luncheon or tea, she was disappointed. The dearth of servants, though, was odd. What was one to make of it? Though she and her father had only Giles and Alice, both seemed omnipresent. Surely, the Rosemeres had far more people to clean, cook, and whatnot? And why were the furnishings in some rooms draped with white dust sheets? Was the family planning a long trip somewhere?

Dragging through the ballroom, her limbs strangely heavy, she marked the ceiling. Cherubs gamboled amidst white fluffy clouds and blue skies. They held something. Squinting, she tried to make out just what. Keys? The height was so tall and the objects so small it was difficult to be certain.

Something slithered down her spine, something icy and hot at the same moment. She had spent a good portion of last evening examining the Rosemeres' ballroom. There should be a clutter of chairs unless the servants were so numerous and meticulous they had already managed to rearrange the space. Also, the ceiling, if she remembered correctly, had been plain. Gilded at the cornices, yes, but plain. Hadn't it?

The kitchen. Last evening, she had made her way down the far hall to the butler's pantry. She would find someone there who could help her. Forcing her legs to carry her quicker than they wanted to, she forked off in the direction she remembered. At the far end, a swinging door rested. She pushed it open.

Her heart sank to the bottom of her heels.

It was a kitchen, yes, but not the same one. All these homes more or less resembled each other in layout, and many in design. Materials, however, differed. Last night, the long stretch of cabinets had been made of polished, natural wood. These were painted white. There were doors where last night there had been drawers. She sniffed. A dusty odor met her nostrils, not a hint of ammonia, lemon, or mint coloring it. Had this been the same kitchen, those scents would have lingered to assault a sensitive nose such as hers.

Something like panic gripped her throat. She swallowed it down. Fine. Somehow, she had ended up in a stranger's house, one, moreover, in which she had never before stepped foot. The final lack of cleaning odors had stripped away any of her desired illusions. Still, all she had to do was walk out the door and onto the street. From there she could find her way home. Her father would figure out what had occurred. He would protect her.

Lawry would protect her too, should he ever deign to appear in her life again. What had kept him from the ball?

Thinning her lips, Honoria picked her way through the kitchen until she found a door leading into the yard. Pulling on it, she discovered it was locked. Undaunted, she retreated back to the front parlor, her legs moving more swiftly with each passing moment. When she sighted the portal, she sighed with relief and twisted the knob.

Also locked. The keyhole was empty. As quickly as she could, she searched the hall furniture. Minutes passed as she grew more and more concerned. A sense of urgency sparked through her veins. When she spotted her shoes tucked under the table, she slipped into them, grateful at least to be once more fully dressed.

Retreating again, she stood a moment and gazed about her. There had to be other doorways, but they were likely latched as well. The windows though, surely not all of them were barred?

After the first ten, Honoria admitted defeat. There was no hope for it. Someone had locked her within.

She returned to the front parlor, her blood pulsing. After grappling with her skirts, she removed her hoops and petticoats. The top fabric lay heavy and too long but she ignored it.

Instead, she grabbed a heavy bust of some crowned female sporting long, curling locks from its place upon a side table. The weight dragged her arms down but the piercing alarm rushing through her veins gave her strength. Without pausing, she swung as wide as she was able. The tip of the headpiece smashed into the window. The glass shattered as if the statue been created for just such an occupation. Velocity spun her around twice before the bust flew into the outside bushes.

Tiny shards of glass cut through her gloves and sliced the fabric of her gown. They peppered her chest, and the soft flesh of her cheeks. If she hadn't closed her eyes and instinctively turned her head away, she might have been blinded.

Outside, the tiny slivers of shattered glass sparkled upon the bushes like a Yule tree at night. Pretty though they were, they could also cut her skin. She glanced about and spied a cashmere throw woven in crimson and deep burgundy threads.

She wasn't a colonel's daughter for nothing. She may have been raised all wrong for her social class, but her father had instilled gumption into her very bones. She grabbed the blanket and used the fabric to push out the rest of the pane before spreading it over the bush. Taking one more deep breath for courage, she closed her eyes and dove through the shattered opening. After spiraling to rest at the base of the iron gating, she paused only long enough to tamp down her panic. Decorative balls topped the metal spires. If she used the planter…

It took her three tries and aching muscles, before she cleared the impediment to sprawl upon the walkway on the other side. No sooner did she arrive, but two sets of male hands lifted her from the walk.

Her stomach flipped to her throat. Ruin came in the form of solicitous care.

Hadn't she always somehow suspected it might?

Chapter 26

"I say, are you all right?" An older man stared down from a great height. He sported long sideburns. They ended beneath his chin in a bristle of black and white cobwebs. "I can hardly believe my eyes. Did you just dive through the window?"

"Don't ask her such things, Simon. I'm sure she had good reason for acrobatics. Are you all right, miss? Is any part of you injured?" The solicitous deep tone emerged from a handsome face framed by reddish-gold hair.

"I-I am fine. Quite all right. I-I couldn't find a key." Her voice quavered. She took a deep breath.

The older man released her but the younger one kept his grip. His gaze darted to the house from which she had escaped. He frowned. "I daresay you would like to find your own home. We would be happy to escort you, Miss C…"

"Cutworth, and I would appreciate an escort, if you would be so kind. I'm afraid I'm uncertain of my current location, but I do recall my home address." She tried to smile, but both men's frowns only deepened in response. "I am positive my father will be missing me terribly. There might be a reward?"

Although, she wasn't certain what her father could afford to pay. There was her dowry. Lawry wouldn't mind the lack of a few shillings, would he?

The man named Simon snorted. "Dare say he will be frantic. You're the talk of the rags this morning, Miss Cutworth. You disappeared from the Rosemeres' ball last night. Your father and the whole of Scotland Yard are tearing up the city searching for you. When we saw you fly over the fencing from across the street, I confess, I had hoped you had been found."

Honoria's heart sank down to her toes as her stomach flopped. The man with the golden-red hair released her arm. His eyes looked sympathetic. They should. If everyone knew of her absence, she was ruined. A little public tumbling from a broken window was nothing next to abduction.

"It's all right." The older man smiled. "We work for the queen. We're the essence of discretion."

"Indeed we are, but others might not be so quick as to hold their tongues. We should get you off the streets and back home. My carriage is just there."

The younger man offered his arm for her hand. She wrapped it around his sleeve by habit. She had just mounted the first step, bent to enter the conveyance, when she heard her first name shouted. Turning to look over her shoulder, her heart flipped within her chest as warmth and relief spiraled through her.

Lawry. His hair was disheveled, his collar askew, and his legs spun like a top as he raced toward her. His hat flew from his head but he left it to lie upon the pavement without a backward glance.

"My fiancé." She tried to slip past the two men impeding her descent down to the walk. "Really. It is fine," she added, when they did not move.

It didn't matter. Lawry pushed right through them. He grabbed her about the waist and swung her down, her body sliding tight to his. Clutching her, he drew her through the other two like a battering ram until they stood several paces away. His gaze roved over her skin before he skewered her rescuers with his glare.

"Where have you been? What happened to your gloves? And why are you with these people?" He looked her over quickly once more before returning his excoriating stare to them.

Suddenly, he pulled her back another pace and drew a pistol from his pocket. In the same moment, he pushed her behind him. "Talk, gentlemen, or you will go to your graves mute." He cocked the gun, the heavy metal scrape loud against the quiet chirp of birds and rumble of distant carriage wheels.

Honoria grabbed his arm. "No, Lawry, please. These gentlemen were attempting to rescue me from the walk and return me home. They need to be rewarded, not threatened. I was trapped, so I was forced to dive out the window and climb the fence." She pointed. "See?"

It appeared he did. His face turned as red as she had ever seen him flush. Rage radiated from him in palpable waves. "Meriven."

"Indeed, yes." The younger gentleman bobbed his head. "There is much to discuss, Sir Lawrence, though this is neither the time or place to do so. Meriven may well return soon, and it would be better if we were not here when he does."

Lawry raised the pistol he had begun to lower and narrowed his eyes. "How do you know who I am?"

The red-haired man held up his hand. "No need for violence, Sir Lawrence. Allow me to make the necessary introductions. I am Mr. Alistair Crawley, at your service." He bobbed his head. "This is my associate, Mr. Simon Wilhelm."

The older man tilted his chin in acknowledgement.

"I repeat, how do you know who I am?"

Lawry's voice remained level, but beneath it something growly, maybe dangerous, hunted his speech. It sent a different kind of shiver down Honoria's spine. She had never heard such a timbre from him before. Even when he had held a blade to her throat the first night his tone had been underlaid with laughter. No sign of humor presented now. Instead, his voice wrapped her in a feeling of security, though perhaps it boded ill for others.

She laid her head against his shoulder, uncaring for the moment about the social repercussions of doing so in public. She was already ruined, and anyway, she was tired. Exhausted. Relief had wrung the last drops of energy from her limbs. All she wanted to do was to slip into a bath, then a nightgown, and her bed.

"As it happens, we were going to seek you out later this afternoon," Mr. Wilhelm said. "You shouldn't be surprised as to why."

Mr. Crawley cleared his throat. "Your extracurricular activities, Sir Lawrence. Queen's business, as it were."

"The queen?" Lawry's voice held a sudden note of trepidation as his body tensed further beneath her fingers.

Mr. Crawley nodded. "Yes. I'm afraid so."

Lawry dropped the pistol to his side. He sighed.

"Excellent. We understand each other, Sir Lawrence. Perhaps we might speak after you deliver Miss Cutworth home." It didn't sound like a question.

"We shall follow you there. Understandably, you will have much to do to, um, see Miss Cutworth situated, but I believe you will find the discussion to be of interest."

Lawry shook his head. "The conversation will have to wait. Miss Cutworth and I are off to Gretna Green. Immediately. I'm certain you understand our need for haste, and if you are indeed possessed of the smallest modicum of compassion, I would ask for your discretion in this matter."

Mr. Wilhelm nodded his head.

Mr. Crawley said, "Of course. Except as may be required in any official investigation, our lips are sealed upon the subject of Miss Cutworth's kidnapping and escape."

He smiled at her, his expression kind. She relaxed and smiled back until Lawry's words began to make sense. She pulled away so she could better see his face.

"Gretna Green?"

"We shall discuss it, but I think it the best course." He stroked her cheek with the back of his fingers.

She winced as he scraped over a miniscule splinter of embedded glass. Immediately, his eyes blazed. "You're injured!"

"Just a few tiny shards. I had to break the window and glass flew everywhere."

"Pardon?" His voice ground the word as his jaw clenched.

"Most of the glass landed outside, but some landed in me, I'm afraid. I suppose those are the perils of a solitary escape. I managed all on my own."

She knew she beamed like the benighted, but she was rather proud to have managed her own rescue.

Lawry would be too, once he stopped glaring at her as if the entire situation was her fault.

"Why did you have to break the window?" His voice was sand and fury, more frightening for the restraint he showed.

"All the doors were locked."

His lips tightened further into one infrangible line. "I'm going to kill him."

He started toward the door, tugging Honoria with him, when Mr. Crawley stopped him.

"You must remain with us, Sir Lawrence." The gentleman's tone was mild, but firm. He sounded a lot like her father did before setting the rules. "And we must be off, all of us. If you give me your word you will not do something so foolish as try to escape, you may escort Miss Cutworth. We shall meet up at her residence, and if you'll allow me the liberty, I'll send a note for a doctor we regularly use. I can vouch for his efficiency and discretion. While Miss Cutworth is being tended, we can talk."

"And the Green?" The words emerged like thrown stones from between Lawry's tight lips.

"After our conversation, if it remains your desire to press onto Scotland, we won't stop you. If you cooperate, there's no reason Miss Cutworth's reputation cannot be salvaged."

"And if I don't meet with you?"

Mr. Wilhelm cleared his throat. He looked toward Mr. Crawley.

The red-haired man smiled. It didn't convey reassurance. "Then we shall be forced to conduct the same conversation in a much less hospitable environment. I don't wish to be your adversary, Sir

Lawrence. Don't force me to become it. I despise dirtying my shoes."

Which made no sense, except Lawry seemed to understand more than she did. Well, she was tired. She yawned, and tried to hide it behind a raised fist, but he caught the motion. His expression crumbled before he could right it again.

He nodded his head sharply, an agreement of sorts, before he threw a glowering look toward the broken window.

"Not yet, Sir Lawrence," Mr. Crawley said.

"But soon," Lawry whispered before he drew her close once more.

Chapter 27

The Misters Wilhelm and Crawley were waiting on the walkway outside her home when Lawry's carriage pulled to the curb. Simon Wilhelm held up his hand to help her down. Just as she took it, she chanced to look up, straight at her best friend exiting the front door. Marjorie's eyes grew wide and she clutched the frame before she turned and pushed her mother, Mrs. Plimpton, back into the hallway.

"My hat!" she cried, her voice carrying over the narrow pass between walkway and entrance. "I forgot my hat!"

"Really, Marjorie, it is on your head, you silly goose." Mrs. Plimpton tried to regain her balance by clutching the side of the door frame. "Whatever is wrong with you? What are you doing? Take yourself in hand, at once!"

She tried to push past her daughter and out onto the landing, but Marjorie managed to bob into her path. Finally, the elder Plimpton took her daughter by the shoulders and moved her sideways so she could slip by.

"Sorry! Sorry, Mother!" Marjorie threw herself to the rail as if she tripped in a fit of terrible acting. Her movement managed to keep her mother's attention focused away from the street.

"Marjorie, whatever is the matter with you? It must be this business with the Cutworth chit. It has unsettled you. Well, I always said you should choose better friends." She made a great show of flattening down wrinkles as Marjorie once again stepped between her and the street.

Her friend jerked her chin over her shoulder several times. Honoria was already slipping back into the gloom of the carriage. Marjorie was correct. If they could successfully pretend they had absconded to marry straight from the Rosemere ball, her ruin might end up only a five-minute wonder. However, if they were seen in London when they should be in Scotland, all would be lost.

"No need to explain," Lawry said after she pushed him back in, practically flattening him as she tumbled over his knees. He righted her with gentle hands. "We'll hide here until your visitors have gone. Meanwhile, our two new friends, if we might call them such, seem quite expert at distraction."

Indeed, they had closed the door to the carriage almost before she had backed through. They stood in front of it now debating the benefits and detriments of the length, breadth, and breeding of the horses in loud, excited utterances. No one would even glance at the conveyance for fear of becoming embroiled in the tedious discussion.

Honoria drew in Lawry's expensive scent as she leaned her head against his chest. Peace. Safety. Companionship. Who knew these things could be so important? She had thought to marry for a place in her class prescribed for someone like her. Marriage had seemed the only road to the future, but she hadn't expected it to mean so much. She hadn't expected it to support her emotionally.

The thought of living without Lawry had become impossible. Thief or poor man, it didn't matter. All that mattered was this: she could lay her head against his shoulder and breathe him in like a solace to her very soul. Why weren't women told to want this sort of thing?

His arms tensed as he held her.

"You're thinking of Meriven?"

He nodded. "This must all be about the pendant, Honoria, but I cannot understand the why of it. The lengths he has gone…"

"And you're certain he was the kidnapper?"

"Who else? Wealth and hubris were required to accomplish the task. Plus, you broke out of his home. There is no doubt." He kissed her forehead, leaving his lips in place for longer than was necessary.

She understood. For a moment, when she had discovered all the doors locked against her, she had wondered if she would ever see him again.

"But why did he leave me there unattended? Surely, he must have known a few bolted exits and lack of shoes couldn't keep me?" She tilted her head to stare into Lawry's sparkling gaze.

He slid a loose strand of hair behind her ears. "He would not have expected your intrepid nature, and he might have miscalculated the time you would remain insensate. Meriven has always expected his women to hold less intelligence and competence than his horse. You have surprised him."

"When he finds me missing, he'll be angry." Her fingers reached up to her neck. Where the pendant should hang, she encountered only her own skin.

"I believe he has what he really wanted. I'm sorry

he's taken it again." His gaze followed her fingers before returning to hers. "He didn't touch you?"

She shook her head. Not in any way that mattered, anyway. Indeed, although she knew she should be frightened, possibly catatonic, the entire morning now seemed like an adventure from a penny dreadful. She smiled to show Lawry she was fine.

"I'm so proud of you. You'll never know how much I envy your strength."

Before she could respond, a hearty series of three knocks sounded upon the door before it swung open. With the Plimptons decamped, she descended and accompanied Lawry and the other two men into the house. She stayed only long enough to assure her father she was uninjured except for a few splinters before hastening upstairs to the bath Alice was already drawing. She plopped herself down upon a small bench while she waited for her maid to help with her buttons. She rested, barely able to breathe, her thoughts in a whirl, and her body fatigued beyond anything she could remember.

Still, she had rescued herself. She had faced adversity and won. Though she might sleep for three days, the strength flowing deep inside her would be there when she awoke. It was an amazing feeling.

It seemed forever before she could slip into the tub and out of the whirlwind in her brain, an endless circle to which she could see no end.

****

Lawry paced in front of the colonel's hearth, his second drink clutched in his hand. For once he enjoyed the bite of whiskey. He had never been a teetotaler, but alcohol tended to make him sloppy. In his line of work, sharp thinking was necessary to keep a master thief from the hangman's noose. Now that it seemed his luck had run out, he welcomed the inner sting to keep calm the ants crawling beneath his skin.

What the hell was Meriven up to? Why the interest in the necklace, and did it extend to Honoria, or was she merely an accessory to his obsession with the pendant? He didn't know. He needed to know. If she was in danger, no matter what the queen's gentlemen had to say about the matter, he would kill his old friend first.

Dr. Gibbons stepped into the room, his hat already upon his head. He snapped his bag closed.

"How is she?" the colonel demanded, surging to his feet.

"Fine, fine, no need to rush me." The doctor caught Lawry's gaze. "She wishes to see you, Sir Lawrence. I've given her a healthy dose of laudanum. You should run up while she manages to keep her eyes open, er, with her father's permission, of course. It isn't the done thing, but in certain situations, when the patient is insistent…"

The colonel bobbed his head, though his eyes narrowed with irritation.

"She mentioned you were planning to elope today, Sir Lawrence, but I'm afraid such won't be possible. She'll need at least a night's rest after this upset," the doctor continued.

But Lawry had already set his glass upon the table and was chasing his own feet up the steps. He didn't bother to knock upon Honoria's door. He simply swung it wide.

Not surprisingly, Hercules lay curled upon the bedcover. The dog lifted his head and whined. Lawry scratched his forehead absently as he sat upon the mattress. Honoria's eyes remained closed, her breathing deep and even. Her hair spread around her in a dark circle. One arm crooked upward, wrapped in bandages. Tiny spots of blood spread through to dot the white expanse. She looked so small beneath the covers, so innocent and young, it cracked something in his chest. Her personality was so large, he sometimes forgot how delicate she truly was, how in need of his protection.

"Honoria?"

She didn't respond. He leaned over and smoothed back her hair before pressing a careful kiss upon her forehead. He turned to the dog. "You must guard her, Hercules. She's to be your mother now, and both our responsibilities. We must keep her safer than we've done to present."

The dog woofed softly as if he understood and curled his head upon his legs again.

When Lawry returned to the parlor, the doctor had already gone. Three sets of male gazes skewered him to the spot. He sighed and ran a hand through his already untidy hair. He had refused to speak to the gentleman about the matters they brought until he knew Honoria was well. Now, it seemed, he had no more excuses.

"If you intend to dissuade me from my intention to kill him, you needn't waste your breath. There is only one outcome, and that is for Meriven to pay with his life for these misdeeds."

"Though it may trouble you to hear it, Sir Lawrence, the matter now rests with the authorities." Simon Wilhelm softly voiced the rebuke as if he hesitated to give offense. He cleared his throat. "I'm afraid you're the only one who will suffer if you lift a finger against the marquess. I might remind you he holds an elevated station. Any action taken against him will result in the noose or transport."

"Australia. The climate can be deleterious to gently bred English women. I understand the wildlife is terrifying."

Alistair Crawley smiled. His lips turned in a pleasant expression, but behind the benign façade something watched and waited. It put Lawry instantly upon his guard.

"Don't hang about the doorway like a damp bat, Sir Lawrence. Come in. We've yet to discuss a matter of grave import."

The colonel glared at him, so Lawry squared his shoulders and entered the room. He plopped into a tufted chair and leaned back, before nodding his thanks to Simon Wilhelm who handed him a refilled glass of whiskey. He took a fortifying sip and appreciated the burn.

He turned his attention to the colonel. "Honoria was already sleeping so it was impossible to check her condition. Did the doctor fish out all the glass?"

"The important pieces, anyway. The others, he says, will come out naturally. Something about the body and swelling. Doesn't matter. The good news is she will be fine. Fine enough for the two of you to make haste to the Green tomorrow."

"No need for that pointed look, sir. I am most anxious to make her my bride." He turned his attention to the other two. "I hope we may rely upon your stated discretion. The lady's name has been dragged through the mud sufficiently, through no fault of her own."

"She didn't encourage Meriven?" Crawley's voice

was light, but his eyes snapped. He held up his hand in a placating manner just as Lawry surged forward in his seat. "I mean no offense. We simply need to know what we're dealing with."

"We? The queen's men?"

The colonel sat straighter. "Er, Sir Lawrence, it appears these gentlemen were not conveniently strolling the walk when Honoria threw herself from Meriven's window. They were watching his house in particular."

That stopped him.

Crawley rose from his seat and picked up a brown leather folder from the table. He tossed it onto Lawry's lap before retaking his seat. Carefully, as if whatever was inside might bite, Lawry opened the folder and read the sheaf of papers within.

Laid before him were warrants for his arrest on five separate occasions of theft. Of all he had done, these were the incidents of greatest larceny. For a moment, his mind blanked. He blinked to restore its movement.

"You would hang, should those be executed," Crawley said softly.

Lawry caught upon the sharp point of "would" and "should." He traced the papers. Indeed, they waited for a signature. A cold hand of relief swept over him, though it didn't dissipate the wellspring of horror bubbling up from his gut.

He looked across at the two men sitting loosely upon the couch. "I'm listening. You've captured my attention, as you intended."

"Naturally, we would hate to see a fine, upstanding gentleman such as yourself hang from the gibbet as a result of, let's call it 'youthful exuberance.'" Crawley's voice held a sarcastic note he didn't bother to hide.

Lawry had left thirty well behind him as they undoubtedly knew, and his larceny could not even kindly be attributed to high spirits. "Quite untidy, not to mention your mother's cousin, the Duchess of Shrewsbury, would surely be most put out should your neck stretch. I understand she cares for you. Of course, she doesn't know of your crimes, does she?"

Lawry bit the inside of his cheeks and breathed deeply through his nose. The question wasn't meant to have a response.

"I understand a certain séance at her home recently garnered your attention. Quite a few bejeweled ladies attended, or so my people related. Before that, after a museum lecture on Assyriology and jewelry, you were seen to be sneaking out early. Though we cannot of certain say you stole Lady Ahern's ruby bracelet, it did go missing around that time, and you did sit adjacent to her. Should I continue?"

"No. I understand your point, Mr. Crawley. I've been watched and you know everything." His voice emerged as if dragged over a rocky stretch of pasture. It matched his sentiments.

"I don't doubt your understanding, Sir Lawrence. You can't be stupid. Reckless, perhaps, but not stupid."

Lawry inhaled again and waited.

Crawley drummed his fingers against the armrest of his chair. "Your talents, and they are quite enormous and impressive, should be put to use supporting your government rather than giving the scandal sheets a broader audience. On such point, we three are agreed." His gaze met the colonel's and Wilhelm's in turn, before returning to root out Lawry's own. "Before we speak further, I shall need your vow of silence. We have already taken the colonel's."

He gave it. What else could he do with five warrants awaiting execution and the appearance of more if needed?

Crawley nodded. He raised his eyebrow and Wilhelm bobbed his chin. "We propose you come work for us, Sir Lawrence."

"Us? The two of you?"

Crawley laughed as if his question amused. "Not directly, not in most instances, although I daresay we shall at times overlap our services, especially at first. Mr. Wilhelm and I are merely representatives of a larger, nameless organization whose tentacles stretch across this great country."

"I see." He couldn't say he was surprised. He had always expected the government to contain secret offices designed to execute its more occult will.

"Within the ranks, we refer to our employer as The Office, for want of a better term. We hold no official fiat, but are dedicated to upholding Her Majesty's laws by whatever means necessary. We are directed by the Crown's will, though we admit such to very few people." He winked.

"Something in your eye, Mr. Crawley?"

The crocodile expression returned to sulk under the pleasant smile. "To work for your country and your queen, Sir Lawrence, would bring you honor."

"Should anyone know of my employment, I suppose it would. But they wouldn't know, would they? Espionage by its very nature lurks in shadows."

Lawry turned his glass between his fingers. An organization without official name or fiat meant the two were here to recruit him to be a spy. Spying was dangerous work.

"You're quick," Wilhelm said.

Crawley nodded. "Allow me to be blunt. It is the noose or us. Should you prove your loyalty by using your skills upon the Crown's behalf, and should your work prove satisfactory, we will burn these warrants and arrange for any underlying evidence to be destroyed." He leaned forward. "We have quite a bit of it, I'm afraid, far more than I've mentioned. I assure you, there is no escape except that which we offer."

"A generous proposition to be certain." Lawry's voice crawled through his throat grown too tight. "Though rather open-ended. Is this a life sentence?"

"Five years." Crawley looked at him steadily, studying him. "Such will be the term of your indenture. One year for each incident of theft for which we've overwhelming evidence. Give us that, serve the cause well, and afterward you may stay or go, assured your past has been safely buried."

"And what salary might my future son-in-law expect?"

They all turned to blink at the colonel. He laughed.

"Come, come, gentlemen. You cannot expect Sir Lawrence to live on the streets and yet provide good service. There are standards to be maintained. Am I wrong to assume this position requires a bit of secrecy and discretion, not to mention the ability to mingle with Society when necessary?"

Crawley and Wilhelm bent their heads together. When they straightened, Crawley named a figure Lawry could live with. Indeed, he could live on it a good sight better than he could with what he might make raising dogs.

Only one pressing question remained. "And Meriven? What does he have to do with all this?"

The two men exchanged another glance. Finally, Wilhelm sighed.

"This is a matter of grave secrecy, Sir Lawrence. Colonel Cutworth. We rely upon your discretion in this matter, much as you rely upon ours as concerns Miss Cutworth's adventure."

"We have already given our word." The colonel sat back against his chair, a small smile lighting in his eyes.

Lawry nodded his agreement.

Wilhelm cleared his throat. "Meriven leads an organization of alleged Assyriologists called Veritas. He inherited the position upon his father's death. Since the former marquess's passing, the society's name has been linked to over a hundred disappearances, all of whom were later discovered dead. Indicators point to a darker, more nefarious purpose behind the group's stated educational purposes. We are not at liberty to reveal the specifics. Suffice it to say, The Office is keeping careful tabs upon both Veritas and the marquess."

"And will he hang in the end?"

Crawley smiled his dangerous smile. "Once we gather enough evidence to bring down Veritas, I shall arrange his execution personally. You may help, Sir Lawrence, should it still be your desire."

"Always." His promise was in his whisper.

He took another sip and watched the remaining liquid swirl in the glass. The uncertain date of Meriven's demise nettled. Yet, what could he do? Hang, and leave Honoria to be eaten by Society sharks?

"I have another question. Why Miss Cutworth?

Why her necklace?"

The men exchanged another glance. Wilhelm chose to respond.

"We aren't certain. Our informants say Meriven believes her pendant to be a copy of a key destined to open great treasure. What the treasure might be, we do not know. It is why we approached you now. We intend you should steal the pendant back before the marquess can use it to further his own ends. Whatever he means to do will not benefit England."

Lawry placed his glass carefully upon the coffee table. "You need me to go now, don't you? Before the piece is put to its use."

Crawley bobbed his chin in agreement.

Lawry looked to Honoria's father. "If I leave now, I am playing fast and loose with Honoria's good name. There's every chance I may be spotted in London, at which point the ruse of elopement will no longer work."

The colonel's lips firmed. "Then do not be seen."

Lawry studied the other two. With his options so limited, there was really only one decision he could make. He would have to move fast enough and stealthy enough if he was not to jeopardize Honoria's standing within Society. But to take back the necklace he would have to place himself in the open, allowing Meriven to see the identity of the man who would one day kill him. Then he would slip away like fog to Gretna Green, thereby to re-establish his bride's honor.

He could do it. He had to.

He was out of his seat before he finished the thought and out the door. Patting his jacket pocket, the familiar shape of the pistol fell under his fingers. Maybe he would get lucky. Maybe he could even kill the bastard before the bastard killed him. The Office couldn't blame him if it was self-defense, could they?

The thought warmed him all the way to Meriven's door.

Chapter 28

"Where is he? Where's Lawry?"

Honoria clung to the door lintel as the floor swayed beneath her feet. Wrapped in a nightgown and a robe she couldn't seem to belt correctly, she closed her eyes before prying her heavy lids open once more. Whatever the doctor had given her had made her drowsy, but when she had awakened, alone, she had known something was wrong. She needed to talk to Lawry.

Talk? No, she just needed to be with him, to stop him from seeking vengeance and getting himself killed.

Hercules panted at her side and threw her a look filled with concern. He whined, as if questioning her sanity in being out of bed. He wasn't wrong. She took a step, sagged, recovered.

"You should still be in bed." Her father echoed her own thoughts as he helped her into a chair by the fire.

Through the far window the fine day had turned rainy. A chill hung about the rafters. She sank down gratefully as her eyelids fluttered.

"Lawry?"

Her father's mouth pursed. "Gone. Never mind him now. You need your rest."

"Miss Cutworth, please do not concern yourself."

The voice startled her. She focused upon the red-haired man who stood by the hearth. Two men, really. She hadn't even noticed them. Alistair Crawley leaned against the mantle and watched her with careful green eyes whose color proved so exceptional it was notable even in the darkening room. Mr. Wilhelm sat in a chair against the wall, shelling nuts from a bowl placed alongside.

Mr. Crawley eyed her as if afraid she might jump up and run out the door. "What your father leaves unsaid, Miss Cutworth, is Sir Lawrence has gone to retrieve your pendant. It shouldn't take very long. When he returns, we can send him up to you with tales of his exploits."

Despite her sorry state, her pulse jumped. She studied the gentlemen. Glasses rested within each man's reach. At the center of the coffee table, a crystal decanter of whiskey stood almost empty. Her father was punctilious about such matters as keeping the jars well stocked. They must have consumed a goodly amount in the couple hours she had been above stairs.

And yet, her two rescuers remained in their front parlor. Vigilant. Watchful. Worried.

About Lawry?

She drew herself taller, her eyelids no longer so heavy she couldn't at least put up a good fight against them. "He has gone to beard Meriven? In his home?"

Simon Wilhelm nodded.

"Honoria, such matters are not your concern," her father said, dropping onto the couch once more. "Alice is arranging an early supper which you should take in your bed. We shall retire to the dining room and pass a pleasant evening until Sir Lawrence returns. We shall not do him the insult of worrying."

It was an order. Before she could reply, a steady knock rapped against the front door. Giles rushed down the hall to answer it as the occupants of the room stilled and waited. A moment later, Lawry's mother glided through the doorway. She removed her wet bonnet and coat and handed them to Giles, who waited in her shadow.

"Anything yet?"

Her face was drawn with concern. She twisted her hands, pausing only to send Honoria a brief smile before she glided toward the colonel. He had risen at her entrance so she dragged him back down upon the cushions, her dark blue skirts overlapped his leg upon the small settee.

"No news is good news," Mr. Crawley muttered. He exchanged a pointed glance with Mr. Wilhelm, who also sank back down.

Honoria swung her gaze around the room. In each face, the same uneasiness mirrored. It told its own story.

"Lawry has gone to retrieve my necklace, but how do we know Meriven will even have it with him? How do we know the marquess intends to return to his home at all, rather than run to the Americas or the hinterlands of Japan? Perhaps he meant to leave me in an emptied house to starve and wither?"

Alistair winced about the eyes. If she hadn't been staring at him, she might have missed the reaction. Her pulse, already straining against her skin, sought its freedom with new vengeance.

"An interesting imagining, Miss Cutworth. Quite evocative." Mr. Wilhelm's voice contained a tiny strand of humor she couldn't at the moment feel. "We believe Meriven will have the pendant on his person at all times. He's already lost it once, and now he has risked too much to obtain it to allow it to be retaken once more."

"Yet you sent Lawry." She paused. "Who is 'we?'"

She kept her gaze upon Mr. Crawley. Though he was the younger of the two, there was something in his manner that made her think he was the one in charge. Of what, she waited to hear.

His gaze rippled again, the small little tell he exhibited when distressed, but his voice held steady when he responded. "Who we are is a subject of further discussion. Allow me to put your mind at ease and answer your other questions first. We sent Sir Lawrence because he has the requisite skills and the desire to retrieve your pendant without causing more of a flutter than may be required. We have complete confidence he will best the marquess without the need for bloodshed."

She gasped. Lady Fishbane echoed the sound.

Mr. Crawley held up a hand. "Poor choice of words, though accurate. Sir Lawrence is a professional breaker. There is no need for concern. As to why we believe Meriven will return to his London home, it is because our spies tell us he has only begun to ready his house for an absence. Were I him, I would see a copy made of your pendant posthaste. I would worry."

"Worry I would escape and the police would be called in?"

But Mr. Crawley shook his head. "He would not have expected your escape, Miss Cutworth. You have thrown a stone into his wheel with your daring."

Honoria exchanged a look with Lady Fishbane. As her throat constricted, she saw the same fear echoed in Lawry's mother's face. Lady Fishbane's hands fluttered. The colonel grabbed the butterflying fingers and held them tight within his.

There would be a wedding soon, even if not hers. Would Lawry even come back?

Her father studied her. "Honoria, you and Esmelda, er, Lady Fishbane, need to hear what these two gentlemen proposed to Sir Lawrence. They have agreed you might share the knowledge."

"Which is not in the usual course at all." Mr. Crawley frowned. "However, having studied Sir Lawrence, our investigators assure us he would not keep his counsel from his mother. Or his intended bride. We'll need your oaths. You should know the penalty for the breaking of them is a charge of treason and death."

After they pledged their silence, after Mr. Crawley reminded them several times of how any loose words would imperil Lawry and all of England, Mr. Wilhelm described the deal Lawry had made, along with the difficulties he would face if he failed or refused.

Lady Fishbane leaned against her father as the nature of the work and the terms were explained. Her father put his arm around her shoulders as she sank upon his neck.

Honoria wished Lawry were here so she could do likewise. He thought her strong? She had never felt weaker, as if all she wanted was to crawl under the covers and hide. On the coffee table where Lawry had left it was the leather folder of his warrants. She couldn't bear to look at it, but every time her gaze slid away, it slid right back again.

Refuse? She couldn't imagine Lawry doing anything other than jumping at the chance. To be a spy, a thief, on the moral side of the law, was Lawry right down to his toes. She should be happy for him.

She was happy, or would be once she stopped being terrified.

She tossed the matter back and forth in her brain. There were some holes.

"Why didn't you accompany him, either of you?" She slid her gaze from one man to the other. "Both of you could be there right now, protecting him."

A tiny fidget. A small squirm. She understood. They couldn't afford to be seen, because if for some reason Meriven, a marquess, was not eventually imprisoned or killed for his actions, they, and Her Majesty by association, could not afford to be implicated. For some reason The Gray Lord's kidnap of her seemed too insignificant for the issuance of a warrant against him.

And then she understood something else: bigger fish. They wanted this Veritas organization, not the marquess alone.

A complicated fizzle in her belly, a folding in her chest, told her they were wise in protecting their anonymity. It also meant Lawry was in trouble, maybe more than he knew. Did he understand they would leave him to hang if he was caught? Did he realize they would deny knowing him, let alone hiring him?

She looked around the room again. They would fight her if she told them she was leaving.

Feigning fatigue she no longer felt, not to the same debilitating degree, Honoria excused herself from dinner and retreated to her room. After changing quickly to her at-home dress with its front buttons and ancient, ugly print of purple roses on dull tea-water cotton, she slipped into her garden boots and down the backstairs. She grabbed a cape with a hood large enough to shield her face from London's ever-present rain, and attempted to exit through the kitchen. Before she could close the door, a large black nose pressed into the small space.

"Hercules. I cannot take you. Go back inside. Go on." She urged the dog back in a frantic whisper, but he didn't care.

Instead, he barked.

"Sshh!" She looked around, expecting to see an army charging down upon her. "Hercules!"

No amount of arguing persuaded the dog, whose speech became progressively louder.

"Fine. Come with me. But you're going to get wet, and you had best behave."

Silencing immediately, he wagged his tail and smiled, an unnerving grimace full of long teeth and gums. She let him pass and he rushed toward the street. At the edge of the sidewalk, he stopped next to the nearest carriage to await her.

She gestured him back once she noted it was Mr. Crawley's carriage. His driver sat atop it. In the dimming light, he read a sagging paper sopped from the drizzle. A wide cap protected his face, but would make it more difficult to see her since it sloped at the side. To be certain, she hastened in the other direction, the dog at her heels When she rounded the corner and hurried another block, she spotted a line of carriages for hire.

Time stretched while she attempted to talk one of the drivers into allowing Hercules inside the contraption. Extra shillings were needed to reach an agreement, especially as she could not give him an exact address. Her luck lay in the fact she could direct the man to the general area where Meriven's residence could be found. She would recognize the home by the shattered window.

After paying the coachman, she followed Hercules into the carriage. Over-sprung seats draped in faded and stained crimson cloth met her gaze. The dog must have felt likewise about the conveyance. He shook the wet from his coat, spraying her and the seats.

"That will be another shilling, ma'am," the driver said, holding forth his hand. "I'll have to have the upholstery cleaned."

If not for the fact she couldn't afford to annoy him and lose her ride, she might have questioned whether he had ever cleaned the carriage. She shot Hercules a frown. "You're expensive, doggie." She searched her coin purse and found the requested sum. "We need to be on our way. I'll knock when we arrive."

The driver touched his hat and in the next minute the carriage jerked forward.

Woof.

She leaned in to kiss the dog's soaked head, the acrid smell of wet canine flooding her nostrils. At the moment it was as comforting to her as Lawry's expensive cologne.

Wet, shivering, she pressed as close to Hercules as he pressed to her. Each rounding of the wheels, each clop of the horse's hooves, tried and failed to steady her heart. The ride to Meriven's took forever.

She worried she might be too late.

Chapter 29

Lawry stood with his back to the wall of Meriven's front parlor, dripping blood and water upon the edge of the patterned Oriental rug and polished wooden floor. He might have felt guilt for the ruin if he could hold even one more emotion.

A mad combination of glee, pain, and trepidation held him unmoving as his driver hopped back over the iron fencing. From the sidewalk the man sent him a jaunty wave. Having helped launch Lawry through the broken window, he would now wait in the carriage. If everything went according to plan, which of late was proving less and less probable, they would be back home within the hour.

As blood dripped from the tear in his upper thigh and left arm, Lawry shivered. An icy chill ran up his spine as his leg throbbed. He ignored the pain and discomfort as he focused upon the distant light down the hallway and to the left. If memory served, it originated either from the library or the study beyond.

Meriven was in residence. The absence of servants, though, was concerning.

A board squealed under his wet shoes. He flinched but kept moving. When he reached the library, he hesitated before turning in. Pinching the fabric across his right forearm, he snapped the band strapped under his jacket. A pointed blade slid down into his palm.

Taking a deep breath, he sidled into the room. Books lined each wall to the ceiling, a fortune in leather and paper. Other than the furnishings, the room stood empty.

The light did indeed seep from the study beyond. So did a voice.

"Don't keep me waiting, Lawry. I've plans this evening and much to do before I see to them."

Several curses rose to Lawry's tongue. He bit them all back and pushed the blade back up under his shirt, though he did not fasten it. Patting down his jacket, he donned his best insouciant attitude and sauntered into the study as if he hadn't a care in the world.

Or as if he were assured he might make it out of Meriven's presence alive. He had counted upon the element of surprise, drat it all.

"John. I wouldn't have credited it. How did you know? Have my feet grown too careless and loud?"

He crossed the width of the smaller room and slid into the seat before the desk. Behind it, Meriven sprawled in his chair, for once devoid of his normally perfect posture. The marquess's shirt lay unbuttoned at the neck, his cravat hanging loose, a crystal glass in his hand.

"I expected you. I've done a little research since Miss Cutworth's pendant was taken from Morray. *Tch.* The man can caterwaul with the best of them. Do you realize how much time I was forced to waste consoling him for the loss, all the while wishing to strangle him?"

"Honoria's necklace. You admit you stole it."

Meriven lips tipped upward, an expression filled with contempt but little mirth. He shrugged. "I admit nothing. Ever. You retrieved it from Morray. Anything you say about my alleged involvement will be the word of a baronet laid against that of a marquess. Who do you suppose the authorities will believe?" His villainous smile grew wider. "At any rate, it seems you have made something of yourself since our shared days at Lornings."

Lawry cringed at the reminder of their school, though he had been happy there his first couple of years.

"Too bad you were expelled. I did miss you. Anyway, it seems you've upped your game and transformed into The Midnight Menace. Truth to tell, I never imagined you had an eye for fame and fortune. I suppose I underestimated your enterprising nature." Meriven glanced at his nails, examining them as if they held a key to survival. "Oh, by the by, I'm afraid you'll have to find another fence. Mr. Cartwright—most unfortunate—has passed away."

The blow fell upon the inside of Lawry's chest, caving it. Poor Cartwright. The man had a wife and three tiny children.

"Your doing, I take it? Cartwright's demise?" The edge of his voice trembled and he cleared his throat roughly to push it away. What an idiot he had been to think his old school chum might hesitate to resort to violence. Since when did nobility of title translate to character?

Meriven merely lifted an arched brow before taking a sip from his glass. Still, his gaze remained upon Lawry, unmoving and unblinking as a snake's.

Lawry straightened and slid to the edge of his seat. "So you've found me out. Good on you. What do you plan to do with the information?"

Meriven shrugged and leaned forward to place his glass upon the desk. He fiddled with it a moment, arranging the coaster so it matched the angles of the furniture. When he lifted his gaze, he seemed pensive. "Nothing. I've no wish to discredit you. We were friends once, and although I owe the distance between us primarily to my youthful indiscretions and to your rigid lack of temperance, well, I have never hated you. Pitied, perhaps."

Lawry gritted his teeth. The effort to part them was exhausting. His voice, when he captured it, sounded like it had been dragged over rough gravel. "Save your pity for someone who requires it. I want Honoria's necklace, John, and I want an explanation for why you kidnapped her."

Meriven sat back again and laughed. The sound was entirely without humor.

"You want. Well, your wants don't matter. If it eases your mind, I can assure you with all truthfulness my interest in Miss Cutworth has ended. I will not trouble her again. Indeed, I am rather sorry I wasted the small time I did with her." He pulled out the drawer and withdrew a sizeable velvet pouch larger than his palm. He lobbed it across the desk to Lawry, who caught it easily.

Weighing it, Lawry stilled. The poundage could only mean one thing, unless Meriven had managed to compress a train engine. "What is this?"

"Call it hush money. Call it a bribe. Call it recompense. It is enough gold several times over to purchase a better pendant. I know, let's call it a wedding gift! After all, someone must redeem Miss Cutworth's reputation. The dailies have had quite a go about her disappearance. Did you know several printed an afternoon and evening edition of the papers? Their readers are avidly pondering the nature of her removal from the dreadful *soirée*. Such a dull affair."

"I wouldn't know. I wasn't there."

"Ah, but I led her to think you would be. I wasn't certain it would work, but I suppose you haven't been keeping up with your correspondence. No love notes, Lawry, for Miss Cutworth to learn the shape of your letters?"

"Some." But obviously not enough. He flushed, the heat rising to his forehead. Damn Meriven, and damn himself too for allowing himself to be baited. He gripped the velvet bag so hard his knuckles showed white.

"You think some coins make up for kidnapping a young lady of gentle birth?"

Meriven's eyes narrowed. "I regret the impulse. In truth, I had thought her... seemlier, I suppose. She is beautiful enough, but the sweet smile she used to wear—"

"Simper."

"—misled me into believing her character was of a match. When her expression vanished the day in the shed behind her kitchens, I realized the truth of Miss Cutworth. Beneath her elegant façade, a viper lives." His expression turned sour. "Yet, still I held hope she might be turned back to the lovely creature I had surveilled. You know what they say about hope."

"No."

"It is oft mislaid. The truth became more apparent at the Rosemeres' ball when she fled my presence. I might have simply had her attacked as she made her way to the carriage, the pendant taken, but by then plans had been made. I do hate rearranging carefully constructed strategies."

Lawry turned the marquess's words over his head, looking for a snag he could exploit. Before he could find one, Meriven interrupted his thoughts.

"Look, Lawry, there's nothing to be done. Take the gold and go to your fiancée with my blessing. If you don't, if you try to cause a ruckus for me, I shall ruin her to the point even marriage to you will never wash her blackened name. I will say she followed me home and forced her way into my bed in the hopes of obtaining a proposal. I will say she left her pendant behind in my sheets where it slipped off during a particularly invigorating session of lovemaking."

"You are leaving me with little choice, John."

Lawry drummed the fingers of his left hand upon the arms of his chair. The marquess followed the noise with his gaze. While he was distracted, Lawry slid the blade to the base of his right palm.

"Miss Cutworth loves the pendant. Is there no way to urge its return?"

"An appeal to my sensibilities?" Meriven cocked his head. "Well, why not? I am not the monster you would paint me. I shall return the piece to her in a few days' time. I need some hours to fashion a copy. The reasons for which," he added, as Lawry surged forward to lay his wrists upon the edge of the desk, "will remain my business."

A goad sat upon the edge of his tongue, but Lawry bit it back. He wanted an excuse to shed Meriven's blood, but if he said too much, if he let on he knew the marquess thought the pendant a key of some sort,

Meriven would know others were onto him. Still, the rage was impossible to swallow.

Curse the fiend.

Lawry slid the blade back up his arm and stood. "One day, John, I will see you hanged for your actions."

Meriven laughed and rose as well. He moved beside Lawry and slapped him on the shoulder as if they were the best of friends. "Oh, you do delight! I'd forgotten what a prig you can be. Soames will see you out." He nodded his chin toward the doorway where a butler had materialized as if by magic. "And Soames? Be sure to lock the door behind you."

"As if that could keep me out."

Meriven smiled. "I guess it's just the principle of the thing."

Chapter 30

Honoria didn't bother with subterfuge. She was no good at it, and certainly didn't have Lawry's ability to infiltrate a locked door. Indeed, she had barely managed to escape one. She tugged at the bell pull. Through the heavy portal, the sound of ringing reverberated. Huddling beneath the small overhang so the rain fell down the back of her cape, she waited. Hercules leaned into her legs, threatening to overset her. Finally, what seemed an interminable time later, the door opened.

"May I help you?"

Within the frame, a butler sporting a pince-nez looked down his long nose at her. He turned his attention to the dog and his eyes widened.

She pushed past him, Hercules at her heels, eliciting all sorts of exclamations, but when she threw off her cape the butler settled back. Despite her unfashionable at-home gown, the material and the tilt of her chin were still sufficient to mark her a gentlewoman.

Or so she hoped.

"Please inform Lord Meriven Miss Cutworth has come to call. I shall await him in the front parlor." She glanced down at the wet dog. "*We* shall await him. I noticed you've managed to cover the broken window with wooden boards. We should be comfortable enough."

Without waiting for an answer, she sashayed past him, keeping her chin as elevated as she could make it and yet still see in front of her. When she entered the room upon whose carpet she had earlier slivered shards, she exhaled and sank down upon the couch. In one bound the dog was next to her. He shook the rain from his coat, dampening her gown and the furniture. After turning in four full circles, he slunk into a comma-shape.

She didn't have to wait long before she lifted her gaze to see Meriven studying her from the doorway. He entered smoothly, as if he hadn't kidnapped her and stolen her pendant, or as if she wasn't quite improperly darkening his door. He bent over the hand she extended by rote, wrinkling his nose, probably at the smell of wet canine, before descending into a chair across from her. He eyed the snoring dog before retuning his gaze to her.

He said nothing and waited.

She inhaled through her nose, hoping the action would calm her. It didn't. Her heart beat so fast she could barely breathe. Finally, she managed to force words through her throat.

"If you have Lawry, I ask you to release him. Otherwise, I shall have no choice but to contact the police."

He smiled. He actually seemed amused. "To think, Miss Cutworth, I considered you marriageable material. Despite your impoverished state and lack of title, I thought, 'There, John, is a natural lady born to reduced means. Look at how gently she holds herself in public, and how sweet her smile.' The fact you never tried to capture my attention recommended your character. Not grasping, I said to myself. Now I realize I was mistaken in all respects, which I dislike admitting. In truth, you are a veritable virago, aren't you?"

She returned his smile, using her natural expression, not the simpering one she no longer cared to don. "Thank you for noticing, Lord Meriven. I appreciate the compliment."

"It wasn't, as such."

"Yet for all that, it was. Now, Lawry?"

He waved his hand. "Already departed, I'm afraid. Empty-handed, but for the gold with which I purchased your mutual silence on the subject of, well, let us call it my unfortunate inclinations. Plans, etc. They were already in motion, you see, and I could not alter them. I confess, I had hoped we might enjoy each other's company when I returned from my errand. Alas, you had already fled, leaving much damage in your wake." His gaze flitted behind her to the covered window. He steepled his fingers and gazed at her over the tops of them. "Tell me, do you think it wise to march right back into the lion's den, even accompanied by your attack mutt?"

As if on cue, Hercules snored like a thunderstorm.

Meriven's eyes suddenly glittered. A considering expression crossed his face. "Or dare I ask, did my small escapade catch your attention in a different light?"

"Different light?"

He shrugged. "I understand females are quite naturally attracted to shows of force. Something in your psyches demand it. Nature, I suppose, the weak seeking protection of the strong."

"I can assure you nothing could be further from the truth. Women are enjoined by trust and security, by joy and honesty, not the threat of violence. At least, I am not."

She rose. Hercules jumped to the floor, as if his snores and somnolence had been nothing but show. He kept his keen stare upon the marquess.

"If Lawry has already gone, I have nothing more to say to you, except to entreat you to return my pendant. If you do not wish me to go to the police, that is."

He stood as well. "If you do, I shall ruin you. Do you not comprehend?"

Honoria stepped closer to him, though her skin crawled. She tilted her head to look straight into his gray eyes. "But it may well ruin you too. Perhaps it is you who does not comprehend. I shall not mind withdrawing from Society if it is to see justice laid."

"You would make Sir Lawrence a liar? He gave me his assurances you would remain quiet."

"He shouldn't have done so. I will not follow Sir Lawrence's lead on this matter, nor my father's. You should not rely upon any assistance in taming me. I must insist you return my pendant, Lord Meriven, or suffer the consequences."

He laughed, but sobered quickly enough when she didn't falter. "Well, well." He looked as if he searched through all possible outcomes, but at the end realized she might carry through her threat. His smile evolved into a scowl which he quickly hid behind an uncaring façade.

"You leave at dawn for the Green, you said?"

She swallowed. She hadn't. But of course, they would.

He nodded as if she had replied. "Wait here."

He slipped out the door and she let out the breath

she had been holding. The floor swayed beneath her feet so she held to the chair in which he had been sitting. Hercules snuffled at her boots. When footsteps sounded, she looked up, but not before Hercules slid back his lips. The revealed length of teeth and gums was no doubt meant to threaten the marquess.

"Good dog."

Not a fool, Meriven tossed her the necklace across a span of several feet. She caught it by the chain. Between the glitter of the garnets, a gray substance coated the gold.

"Clay," he said, interpreting her questioning look correctly. "Between Lawry's advent and yours I managed to have made a sufficient mold. Truthfully, I weary of all this intrusion."

"But why? Why all this bother? It is not an expensive piece, or even an interesting design."

"Isn't it?" His gray eyes gleamed with some repressed emotion she could not read. "You would not understand, Miss Cutworth. You haven't the ability to hold deep passion for more than your daily bread. I, however, seek to know the ancient secrets. Your pendant might lead me to them." He leaned forward. "Haven't you wondered at the odd bumps and swirls upon the back of the piece?" Breaking his gaze, he looked into the distance before refocusing his glare upon her once more. "Now, it is time for you to be on your way. I shall allow Lawry to detail our agreement. Should you break it, whatever your threats in return, I shall have no hesitation in ruining both your lives. And the lives of your families. Your friends. I shall be a one-man demolition of any you hold dear to your heart. I beg you not to press me to such an unfortunate end."

He was serious. Anyone could see he would make good his threats. His title alone guaranteed even the wildest accusations would stick. Hercules leaned against her skirt, lightly. He kept most of his weight from her so her stance was not compromised. His stare never wavered from the marquess.

She placed a hand upon his head, the soft fur steadying her. "You said Lawry was your friend. How could you treat him so?"

Meriven swallowed. His face firmed into stone. "He was indeed once my friend, and I did him a great wrong. I beg you not to force me to another." With a bow of his head and a tap of his heels, he exited the room.

Honoria examined her necklace as the dog relaxed. He panted, his tongue extended, and whined.

"Yes, we're going."

The pendant looked much the same as it always had, and yet, it obviously meant a great deal to some very unhinged men. She allowed the butler to sweep them back to the door and through it. When the portal slammed behind them, Hercules grinned and ran to the walk.

No wonder Lawry took him on his nightly excursions. The dog was worth more than his weight in stolen treasure.

Chapter 31

Lawry slumped upon the couch in his front parlor while he waited. His head rested upon the back of the couch; his eyes closed as he studied his lids. Beneath his fingers, Hercules's soft fur rustled. Every time he would stop petting the dog, the beast would snuffle and whine. Sometimes he stopped petting him just to hear the sound.

A grating noise, less pleasant, echoed from the doorway.

"You can't fool me, Smithers. They couldn't have arrived yet. I'd have heard the bell."

His butler's feet shuffled into the room a short distance. "Oh, you're a wondrous detective, Sir Lawrence, even at six o'clock in the morning. Are you aware your cravat crooks to the left?"

Lawry opened his eyes and glanced down. Sure enough, Smithers was correct. His jacket also resembled a pile of wrinkles, and his new shoes, the ones he had ordered a week ago for just this occasion, pinched his big toe.

"I still breathe, however, Smithers. Better a crooked tie than a noose."

"If you say so, sir. Tea will be along in a moment. I thought you might wish to opine on orange cake versus lemon?"

Which was one decision too many. "Both." And

why not? Perhaps Honoria was more capable than he of making a choice.

As Smithers shuffled away, Lawry laid his head back again. When he had returned last night to Honoria's home and given the queen's gentlemen his debrief, they had not been happy. Interested, yes, once he told them the whole of Meriven's words, but discontent he hadn't procured the locket. They had been blunt when they assured him higher-placed heads than theirs would have to determine whether or not he would be allowed to keep his life. Non-performance nullified their employment agreement. Maybe.

Forced by the colonel to leave before he could see to Honoria's continued safety, he had been left to his own thoughts all night long. He had done little but toss and turn, his failures weighing upon him so his successes seemed like fool's gold. The noose still haunted. They had granted him the days to save Honoria's reputation, but then...?

Hercules shuffled his head and laid it across Lawry's lap. He whined.

"Sorry." Lawry resumed his pets.

Through a crack in the drapery, the night lost its battle against the rising sun. It was an ungodly hour to be up.

Snuffle. A wet black nose thrust itself into his palm. Odd, how the cold, slimy thing gave him hope, but it did. It lifted his spirits.

Because yes, it was all his own fault he might hang, but if he hadn't turned to crime, he would have met Honoria only in the normal course, at some ball or rout or dinner. She would have put on her customary graces and airs, and he would have decamped without so much as kissing her hand. As such, one might say his utter recklessness had not only led him to the noose. It had also led him to her.

Anyway, the matter was out of his hands.

"You'll play in long green grass soon, Hercules, and you'll guard Honoria after, won't you? If I'm taken as a thief and strung up?" He ruffled the dog's fur and received a soft *woof* for his efforts.

He closed his eyes once more. They would travel in a separate carriage from their parents and meet at a posting inn along the way. It would be a vacation of sorts while they took advantage of the few days' reprieve granted by the queen's men so he could at least see Honoria safe.

Lord, but he would hate to leave her, even if it meant he would reacquaint himself with Duncan the horse in the great blue sky and green, green grass of the beyond.

The bell rang. The ensuing commotion in the hallway signaled the arrival of his bride and her father. His mother's footsteps raced down the stairs. He opened his eyes just as Hercules barked and rushed the door.

Focused upon the opening, his pulse jumped with the anticipation of seeing Honoria as she sashayed into the room. Those first moments before her gaze settled upon him, when she stood unguarded and bright with her own brand of inner fire, were his favorite ones.

Sure enough, she radiated dazzling colors as she rushed from the hallway. Her face reflected joy until Hercules bounded at her. He jumped upon his hind legs to hug his paws around her throat and succeeded in pushing her down to the floor.

"Sit!"

The colonel's no-nonsense order met with immediate success. Whereas the dog usually decided for himself whether or not to listen to Lawry's commands, it appeared he had no such illusions of free will where the colonel was concerned.

The traitor.

Lawry ambled to his feet, intending to help Honoria back to hers, but her father was already pulling her up. Though it was ill-mannered, he sank back to the soft cushions, the weight of possible worlds holding him down. The parents sank onto the opposite cushions, his mother's face a study of concern.

What could he say in response? That his insides waged a war of equal joy and equal sorrow, surging excitement mixed with absolute terror? He was a mess. Poor Honoria. She deserved so much better than him.

Not intuiting any of his thoughts, she plopped down next to him, her skirts folding over his legs. "Have the queen's men bothered you today?" She pressed a cool glove to his forehead and smoothed back his hair. "Are you well? You look a bit greener than my skirt."

"I must be near dead then." He leaned a bit and kissed her wrist.

Today she wore a bilious dress made in puce and olive, the bands of colors reminiscent of a bilge bucket spilled upon the waves. Despite the unfortunate hues, she was beautiful, a rose grown through rocky ground. So what if she had the fashion sense of a herring? Marriage to him would cure it soon enough when his purse paid the coin, or so a man could dream.

"You, however, look ravishing. A bit—" He

gasped sharply. There, dangling upon a chain around her neck, lay the pendant.

"Before you take breath sufficient to scream, Lawry, you should be aware I may have done something rather vazey. However, my actions garnered some welcome results."

She folded her hands into her lap. As if afraid he would flee before she finished, she rushed the tale of what had occurred at Meriven's. Rage flushed all through him. It battled an illogical terror. After all, she was fine. She sat next to him in perfect health. It was what might have happened that near destroyed him.

From his perch against the colonel's legs, Hercules woofed his agreement, once again reading Lawry's mind. He rolled his shaggy head as if he wearied of their collective ineptitude.

"I agree, Hercules. My daughter's actions chill the heart." The colonel glared at Lawry as if he were responsible for Honoria's ill-witted scheme.

He wanted to object, but couldn't, especially with his mother biting her lips between her teeth.

"That's enough out of you, beast." He contented himself with reprimanding the dog while he gripped Honoria's arm so hard she winced. It was almost impossible to release it. "Don't you ever, ever, do something so foolish again, do you understand me?"

She had the grace to look sheepish. "I am sorry, Lawry. In retrospect, it was rather impulsive of me, but I was terrified he might kill you. As it stands, might we just say all's well that ends well?"

"Ends well for whom?" But already his mind flipped the new information through his brain. He forced his muscles to relax. "None of it makes sense.

Why give you back your pendant, Honoria? You are no threat to him. He could squash you like a bug anytime he likes. And despite his assurances to the both of us, it is impossible he had a copy of the pendant made in the time between your visit and mine."

"Which means what?" the colonel asked.

Lawry rotated his head in a slow shake. "It means Meriven possessed the copy before I sought him out. Yet, he lied to me. Why bother? He could squash me too. Unless…"

The colonel leaned forward. "You think he suspects he is under surveillance?"

"I don't know. Perhaps. I cannot help thinking he knew of my employment agreement with the queen's men and sought me to fail." He drew in a deep breath and flipped through his conversation with his old friend.

Honoria's brow furrowed. "You think he knows you work for The Office? But how could he? You were only just taken up."

"Exactly. Mr. Crawley will find the news most disturbing. It hints at a double agent within his midst, doesn't it?"

The colonel frowned. "You may be reaching."

"Perhaps. Happily, it is not my responsibility to lay out a reason for Meriven's behavior. My assignment was to collect the pendant." He tapped Honoria's knee. "You, minx, for all I wish I were the type to beat you, may have just saved my neck. The pendant you wear means I did not fail. By the time I cornered Meriven, a copy had already been made. Perhaps it had been made before ever I met the queen's gentlemen. One cannot botch a job at which it was impossible to succeed."

He kissed her palm again before laying his head back against the upholstery. He stared at the ceiling, waiting for it to either fall in upon him or remain intact. From what he could tell, Honoria's interference had bolstered the structure. He raised his head. "If you ever, ever, do anything so stupid again, I will lock you in a room for the rest of your days."

Though he made his expression as thunderous as he knew how, she giggled in response. "I'd prefer to be locked up during the nights, Sir Lawrence. With you."

Unbidden, his pants tightened as blood rushed to every inconvenient part of his body. Lawry drew her skirts further across his thighs and hoped they covered the evidence.

After they breakfasted on tea and cake, the colonel slipped his arm around Lady Fishbane's waist. "We should be on our way. I've taken the liberty of securing your writing case, Lawrence. Given Honoria's re-acquisition of her pendant," he glared at his daughter, "I'm certain you will wish to write a lengthy and carefully worded missive to the Misters Crawley and Wilhelm. There are several points along our journey where you might post it. Pointed assurances will aid them in evaluating your future position within the organization."

"From your lips to God's ears." Lady Fishbane rose and shook out her tartan skirt. She had chosen it to celebrate the Scots, apparently.

For a single moment, Lawry relaxed. The weight of the parents' approval lightened something within him.

Honoria leaned her head against him. She ignored her father's throaty growl and his mother's chirrup of disapproval as she snuggled. "I cannot imagine a better position to which you might be suited, Lawry. I wouldn't be surprised if you win awards for your service."

He kissed her forehead. "My secret service. Awards would ruin the point." He paused. "You will not mind when I am sent forward upon dangerous maneuvers?"

She pulled away. "Mind? What did you feel when you heard of my little outing last night?" She waited as his stomach flipped and turned. "Exactly. Multiply your feelings by a thousand. Yet, the job suits you, Lawry. It suits you down to your bones. I would be a fool to deny it."

Not long afterward, they found themselves bouncing along the path to Gretna Green. Hercules rode with them and took most of one seat, giving them the excuse to kiss and cuddle the entire way to their first stop. At a small country hitching post they used facilities, gathered a small basket for lunch, and allowed the dog to run free in an adjoining field. They resumed their positions and slumbered into one another until they reached the first inn at which they would sup and pass the night with their parents.

After posting his long missive to the queen's men, Lawry joined them for a hearty dinner of cold meats and stale bread. Their parents looked as if they may have spent their hours in their coach also kissing and cuddling, for his mother's careful hairdo had devolved into a bird's nest of quickly gathered tresses.

He burst into laughter. He couldn't help it. Despite his worry, he was happy. The government might execute him upon his return, but right now, at this moment, with his newly extended soon-to-be family surrounding him, his blood buzzed with anticipation and light.

When the colonel met his gaze, Lawry nodded. "I suppose, sir, if you had been chasing us with a shotgun, this journey might have proved less restful or pleasant."

"Lord save us from the thoughts that pass through your head, Lawry." His mother frowned and cast a quick glance toward the colonel. "As if we would wish Henry to shoot you dead."

He reached across the table and patted his mother's hand. He might be a trial, but she loved him. She, in turn, leaned in to whisper in the colonel's ear. The military man flushed to his forehead. Lawry chuckled again and wrapped Honoria's hand within his. He brought her fingers to his lips and appreciated her glow.

They would rest overnight, continue the journey, and arrive the third day at the Green. He gazed at Honoria. She was so perfect his teeth ached.

She leaned into him and tucked his hair back. Her fingers tickled his lobe and her breath sent shivers racing down his spine. "Do you think Hercules would mind very much if we locked him in our parents' carriage tomorrow?"

As if he understood, Hercules, who lay at her feet, growled low in his throat and sent up a resounding *woof*. The empty plate between his paws vibrated against the stone floor.

"He should be paid for how well he performs his chaperoning duties. Wait until we're married. I'll lock him from the chamber every night." He exchanged a stare with the dog who didn't seem at all threatened. "For part of the night, anyway. I shall rely upon his discretion to absent himself during key moments."

The dog stood, stretched, turned in three circles, and lay down again, his back to his people.

Lawry was not the only one who laughed.

That night, between cool, crisp sheets, the colonel snoring in the other small bed installed within the chamber, he lay staring at the ceiling. His arms missed Honoria. Odd, how she had grown so quickly into another appendage, one he could not do without. He gave a silent thanks to whatever higher power had put her in his path and fell asleep, wondering at his good fortune.

Chapter 32

Six days later, Honoria rose from her bed within Lawry's home for the first time. Their bed and their home. What was his was hers, and vice versa. They had arrived in London late the prior evening, both of them exhausted and contented. Though they maintained separate bedrooms as was the custom, Lawry had already declared his intention to return to his room only to bathe and dress. As she found utter bliss wrapped in his arms, she applauded his decision.

Trying not to wake him, she slipped into a nightgown and robe. Foregoing slippers, she crept through the door and down the stairs. Early light already chased the shadows under her bare feet. The crisp tang of a summer morning brushed against her face. She entered the dining room and found her father sitting there, flipping through the morning paper as he sipped his tea.

He wore pajamas and a robe.

"Darling!" He put the paper aside and rose to kiss her cheek. "Er, I didn't expect to see you this early." He turned his head away, but not before Honoria noted the flush tiptoe up his features. "Er, should I ring for a fresh pot? I forget the girl's name. Cook's helper. They do keep a full staff, do they not?"

"They do. It is lovely, and an easy thing to become accustomed to. Let us hope Lawry retains his employment so we might keep them all."

After taking a cup and saucer from the sideboard, she poured herself tea. The brew didn't even steam. Some things needed to be sorted, although she hesitated to step upon Lady Fishbane's toes.

She sank into the chair across from her father and looked at him evenly. His mustache quivered. He shot a glance toward the hall. He fidgeted in his seat. He grumped and mumbled something incomprehensible.

Honoria laughed. "Never mind, Father. I'm happy to see you. I was going to stop by later to see how you fared, but I see my concern you might be lonely was misplaced." She paused. "Ours—yours—is a drafty old place. No wonder you chose to sleep here."

His expression softened and his eyes grew misty. "I admit I am grateful not to wake to an empty house, well, excepting Giles, of course, since only he remains now you've brought Alice here. I don't suppose a butler counts as company. At a certain age, one longs for someone to chat with across the table. Can you imagine if I invited Giles to share breakfast?"

His eyes twinkled, as well they might. The very thought of their proper butler sharing a meal and conversation with his employer was laughable.

"Is that what you seek here? Conversation? I fear Lady Fishbane will be disappointed. I believe she holds other intentions." She tried to don her most innocent expression, but snickered as his face fell.

"Lady Fishbane, er, the Dowager Lady Fishbane, I suppose, given you're Lady Fishbane now. In any event, we are all adults. You're a married woman, so you understand, er, certain… things." He mopped at his brow with his linen napkin. Then he pulled at the collar of his pajamas. "It is frightfully warm this morning, is it not?"

"I suppose it must be."

She took a sip of the tepid brew. Tannin bit her teeth. She placed the cup upon the table. Certain household chores already suggested themselves, but she should make a list.

"And Lawry? He, um, he's been treating you well?"

"He always has."

It wasn't what he meant and she knew it, but there was no way to describe to her father the utter bliss of lying and waking in Lawry's arms these past days since the simple ten-minute ceremony had legally joined her to him.

Her father nodded. "I told you dogs don't make cats. Fine moral backbone, that one."

"Father."

He shrugged. "Excepting a certain proclivity, which we shan't discuss where others might overhear."

Smithers passed through the door. He set a fresh pot of tea atop the sideboard, snapped his heels, bobbed his head, and retreated. They waited a few more moments.

Her father continued, "I had suspicions about Lawrence's occupation, of course. Having studied his finances as best as I could, I noted certain discrepancies. I imagine The Office noticed the same ones. We all believe we act in private, but I daresay the government is ever upon us like hawks before field mice."

She toyed with her cup, rotating it one way and then the other. "I fear they will pull Lawry apart. Have you heard anything?"

"No, but I feel certain they'll contact him soon, one way or the other. As I said, we are but field mice before their talons. We must hope they choose not to swoop, and maintain a contingency plan should they do so."

"Do you have one?"

He shook his head. "No, but I am certain Lawrence does."

"Let us hope all they do is watch. Lawry will give himself to the noose if it means easing my path." She rose from her seat and circled the table to place a kiss upon his leathered cheek. "I shall be in the greenhouse."

"The heather?"

He knew her so well. The lavender and pink flowers grew in swathes across the grassy fields and mountains of Scotland, bright in the morning dawn and blued in the afternoon gloaming. Their scent was redolent of earth and herbs rather than sweet like a floral. She couldn't wait to discover if her surmise was correct: the fragrance would make an interesting middle note if combined with grass as a top note. But, what to use for the bottom?

Without quite realizing how she had gotten there, she found herself gazing about the small arboretum abutting the stone wall. Within the decrepitating room, upon raised tables, hopeless stalks withered into dry earth. Still, once the windows had been cleaned of grime and the beds cleared, the room would work well as a distillery. On the table closest to the door, a small trunk of heather blooms waited to be transmuted into potions.

Honoria rolled up her sleeves and shifted pots,

straightened boxes, and pulled at dead things. Distantly, she realized Hercules had come to watch her. He lay upon a lap rug she placed in a spot of sunlight and began to snore.

The peace captured her completely as she set the planters right. Remembrances of her wedding trickled through her brain. The ivory skirt dotted with tiny seed pearls. The gossamer sleeved jacket that matched. A bouquet of the same heather she hoped to transplant and grow here, a tiny sprig inserted into Lawry's pocket. Words had been said. She had been too nervous to understand them, but she assumed they meant she was well and truly wed. With their parents looking on, they had shared a chaste kiss, and at night, in the privacy of their own room at last, they had shared so much more.

When a hand brushed the hair from the back of her neck, she smiled, assuming it was Lawry, but when she rotated her head, it was Meriven who leaned over her. He backed up as she abruptly surged away.

"My lord!"

Hercules scrambled to his feet. He growled low in his throat and approached on careful paws.

The marquess ignored him. "My apologies, Lady Fishbane. You looked so intent, so lovely in the dappled morning light, I quite forgot myself. Perhaps I let you go too precipitously."

His gray eyes shone, but it didn't look like desire resting there. She had seen passion's heat in Lawry's gaze enough times to recognize it. Meriven's expression looked more triumphant, and a lot like possession.

He took a step closer and she backed up until her spine hit the table, stopping her. A sense of déjà vu

Judy Lynn Ichkhanian

swept over her as he placed his hand upon the box of dirt and leaned in.

"You are not dressed for gardening."

Hercules barked. Once. A short, staccato sound of warning.

She looked down at her *dishabille*. Dirt smudges dotted her bright red robe. The belt had come loose so a line of soil-streaked white nightgown peeped through the opening. She set about pulling at the cord and tightening it.

"I started quite early. I meant to only be out here for a moment, but could you back up, please? You are crowding me in a manner most uncomfortable. You seem to possess the tendency."

"Ah. There's the tart tongue that lost me." He stepped back and pivoted away, his gaze roving over the space until he angled back. "I wished to let you know I have decided to leave England for a time. The desert sands call to me. Mysteries of the past, you see. I have decided to heed their urgings."

"How lovely for you."

"You wonder why I tell you this."

"I wouldn't have credited you as being so observant, my lord."

He scowled. "Lawry should beat you. There was potential there before he ruined it." He drew in a deep breath and shook his head. "No matter. It is for the sake of my friendship with him I tell you of my impending absence. I am certain he worries I shall attempt to steal you away."

"I doubt it."

He glared again. "Nevertheless, I also wished to ascertain you have kept your agreed upon peace."

"Have constables knocked down your front door?"

Honoria smiled. She enjoyed baiting the marquess. It might not be well done, but it was fun.

Fury flashed up his face in a red haze and disappeared the next moment.

As her smile dropped, icy fingers crept up her spine. His self-control should be laudable. Instead, it had an atavistic effect. Even Hercules must have been disquieted, because he nuzzled up beside her and growled low in his throat.

For a moment she thought Meriven would growl back, but instead he turned his gaze to her chest. Instinctively, she grasped for the pendant she always wore. Last night, she had gone to sleep with it still attached upon its gold chain. Her fingers came back empty. She gasped.

"Lose something?" He smiled. There was no kindness in it. He gazed toward Hercules's feet. "Ah. It appears your dog has stolen it this time."

Honoria glanced toward the ground. Indeed, the chain rested bright against the hard-packed floor at Hercules' feathery paw. Several inches away, the pendant lay pulled from the chain. She looked back to Meriven, wary now. She held his gaze.

"The clasp must have loosened."

He smiled.

She swallowed. "Something has been bothering me. Why tell Lawry you hadn't made a copy of the pendant when you already had?"

He smiled, a long, cold slash reminiscent of a serpent's expression. "Did I tell him I hadn't? I don't recall." He caressed the edge of the table. "You know, sometimes the best way to throw one's enemies off the scent is by undertaking puzzling and seemingly nonsensical actions. Most people, especially those in government who tirelessly gather strands of information, tend to look for a holistic explanation. They construct a narrative. They act upon it. But what would happen if some of those strands were false?"

He waited. She shrugged.

"I suppose the narrative would prove false as well."

"Exactly. It becomes flawed. Useless. The reliance upon logic creates failings an intelligent man might use to his advantage." His gray eyes glittered like diamonds.

"And you enjoy exploiting failure."

His grin turned genuine. It sparkled in his rainy-day eyes, warming them to smog. "I do, as it happens." He tipped his hat. "Well, I must be off. There's ever so much to be done before a voyage, even with the most trusted servants doing the necessaries. I bid you good day, Lady Fishbane, and much happiness in your marriage."

Without another word, he slithered from the room. She watched his back recede, wanting to make certain he was truly gone before she bent to pick up the necklace.

There was no point giving him any advantage. She didn't trust him in the least. When she held up the pendant to examine it, her fingers trembled.

****

Lawry's hand fisted around the fork he had picked up just as Honoria began describing what had transpired in the greenhouse. When she finished, he forced some conciliatory words past his closed throat. Everything in him tightened as he resisted drawing her into his arms.

He wanted to. Seated at the head of the table with her caddy-corner, he could reach out with ease. He could smother her in his embrace and never let her go again out into the dangerous world. His backyard.

He refrained. He couldn't lie to her, but he couldn't coddle her either. She was strong enough to resent being treated like a child. Hell, she was stronger than he was.

He cleared his throat of the gruffness lining it. "There is nothing to be done. As everyone reminds me, his is a station well above ours, and there are the various agreements to hold me back from killing him outright."

The agreements didn't prevent rage from sweeping through every part of him. It pulsed into his fingertips. It battled against the worry swamping him all over again because of the things that hadn't happened but might have. He took a deep breath through his nose, trying to capture his equilibrium once more.

"I know. I am safe. He only meant to taunt and…"

"I promise you, my love, the moment The Office gives their permission, I shall rid this earth of him."

He stepped over her words in an effort to wipe away the distress creasing her brow. She had waited until they sat to luncheon before delivering news of what had transpired earlier and he was glad of it. Any sooner and he might have missed breakfast as well.

He placed his fork along the side of his plate and forced his fingers to unclench enough to leave it there. Banked by Pompeian red walls, the color too reminiscent of blood, Honoria looked fragile in her ivory day-dress. The color blended well with her skin and set off the ebony of her hair, though the style was at least ten years out of date and just a tad too tight around the bodice.

"I wished to tell you earlier…"

"But didn't, because you didn't know how to remind me we are barely wed and I've already broken my promise to keep you safe. I am aware. The knowledge slices me. Here." He drew his hand across his chest and took another long breath.

"I am beginning to believe nothing will stop Meriven if he wishes to act. The fault is not yours, Lawry. He is crippled with some odd form of insanity. However, if he meant what he said, and I have no reason to doubt him, he will no longer be a concern. His absence will be reason enough to celebrate." She leaned sideways towards him.

He met her halfway and kissed her brow, despite the fact displays of affection outside the bedroom were frowned upon. But that's why she loved him, he hoped. He had vowed to keep her at the center of his heart and he would do so. Always. And she, bright sun, rescued him over and over again with her intrepidness.

They sat at luncheon, just the two of them, as the colonel and his mother had gone off to her favorite restaurant in Pall Mall. *Verrey's* was one of the few dining establishments in London in which a woman could be seen enjoying a meal without the pall of wagging tongues turning the food to dust. With every passing day, however, dining out gained fashion.

With a reluctance to break contact, Lawry sat back and took up his fork again, but only to push the cold beef to the side of his plate. With the fingers of the other hand, he tapped a rhythm upon the starched cloth. Despite his assurances, Meriven's gall in accosting

Honoria demanded a reaction. If nothing else, he would have to contact Crawley and Wilhelm once more about Meriven's latest intrusion.

They would not be pleased. Though they had just agreed not an hour since he could not be blamed for Meriven's successful copying of Honoria's pendant because they had recruited him too late, the stench of the affair still covered him. His occupation was not yet secure.

And now what?

Honoria touched the pendant. It dangled halfway between her bodice and her chin. She frowned.

"Would you mind undoing the clasp?" She turned to enable him to do so.

When he complied, she stared at it. "It felt different from the moment I put it back on. But I'm certain. I don't know how, I just know I am." She met his gaze. "This is not my necklace, Lawry. It is slightly heavier. And see, the stones are just a bit darker, especially this bottom one, here. And this one had a small inclusion." She pointed at both places. He looked, but could see nothing amiss.

"The differences could be your imagination playing tricks upon you."

She nodded, but seemed unconvinced. "Perhaps. Yet he touched my neck, an odd sort of gesture from any man not my husband, and then later drew my attention to my necklace upon the floor. The pendant was loose from the chain, which I don't believe could happen if it simply slipped to the ground. Also, my pendant had a tiny scratch, up here, along the fob. This one doesn't." She fingered the chain. "This appears to be original."

"Hmm." No one could blame her for imagining hobgoblins and intrigue where none existed, especially as so many others did. Yet, her level head was one of the many attractive qualities.

"You don't believe me."

"No. I mean, yes." He shrugged. "Of course I believe you. I'm only wondering why he would give the original back to you in the first place if he meant to take it again. It is the same size, you say?"

"Yes." She shifted in her chair. "You all believe Meriven thinks my pendant a key to treasure. If so, he would want the original. I didn't mark it in the context earlier, but he said he enjoyed placing false strands among those his enemy collected because the government was hampered by logic. And when I went to his home, he knew I was to leave for Gretna Green at dawn. I could keep the pendant safe, out of the country, while he made a copy so perfect, only I would recognize the differences."

He nodded. It made sense, if one was Machiavellian in his thinking and action, and not afraid of a little risk.

"The piece would stay with you in Scotland, away from the gentlemen of The Office. Meriven could collect the original upon your return before they did. Meanwhile, he could lay 'strands' to confuse his enemies. Illogic mixed with logic. It might draw them away from correct conclusions."

"He wanted the original all along. He was just willing to wait to get it."

"John always enjoyed games." He sighed. "We shall have to write the gentlemen yet another missive, I suppose."

He took the pendant from her and threw it upon the table. If Meriven had decamped there was no great need to solve the mystery of him now. Not for him, at least, though The Office would feel otherwise. If Meriven wanted to open all the locked doors throughout the desert countries, so long as Honoria was safe with him in England, Lawry would cede him the trinket.

He lifted her hand, a long line of delicate skin and bone, and brought it to his lips. He glanced at Hercules, curled upon the sofa in the sitting room and just visible from where he sat. Perhaps he might share Honoria's attention with the dog, who was doing his best to guard her safety. But just a little of it.

"Come," he said, rising and drawing her up. "All this talk of keys and chains has given me an idea."

"What kind of idea?" Her eyes narrowed.

He drew her into him, the motion sharp so air whooshed from between her lips. He bent down and kissed her, savoring her sweetness until his body urged him onward. He spun her around and dragged her up the stairs. She giggled all the way, lightening something dark in his heart. When they reached the bedroom that was, nominally, hers, he pushed her gently down onto the bed. She lay staring up at him, smiling and trusting.

"It has come to my attention certain ladies enjoy being tied up while their husbands administer to their pleasure."

He paused and waited, but when her smile froze in place, he reconsidered. Slowly, he unwound the cravat from around his neck. It was pale blue silk, the shade of a robin's egg.

"I had a different thought, however. If certain ladies enjoy being restrained, perhaps others of a more intrepid nature might prefer tying up their very willing husbands instead."

There it was. The thoughtful gleam he had hoped to see from his first suggestion now lit her like some magic kind of glow.

He kicked off his low shoes and stripped the clothing from his body, piece by piece while she watched, her eyes hot, her lips open. She raised herself upon her elbows to get a closer look.

Perfect. Every move she made was perfect.

He left attached the cotton pants he wore beneath his trousers. She should have something to remove, if only so he could rejoice in the touch of her fingers against his skin as she popped the buttons. He approached the bed and tossed the strip of blue silk to her belly. She snatched it up, then caught him about the waist and drew him the rest of the way to her. Surprising him, she wrapped her leg around his and twisted so he fell across the spread. Hovering above him, she smiled once more, her turn of lips both wicked and provocative.

"I've never been very talented with horses. Perhaps I should practice."

He swallowed against the sudden lump in his throat. Pressed to her softest parts, he hardened to a pole. "Please do. I vow, husbands should be made to serve some useful function."

Deftly, she maneuvered him to a position where she could tie his hands through a decorative niche in the headboard. Unfortunately, she left a lot of room for him to slip out of the rings about his wrists, so he grasped the silk between his fingers to make certain he didn't escape.

She edged away from him and stood. Just as he had done, she slowly unbuttoned the top part of her dress and shimmied it from her arms. The endless line of small pearl fasteners running the length of her waist to hips took longer. Each second drew him further into an agony of wanting, so he gripped the silk tighter to assuage the ache at the other end of his body. It didn't help.

Her skirts pooled to the floor. She released her petticoats, one at a time. Her chemise followed. She stepped from the mix. Clad only in her open drawers, tied-stockings, and corset, she pivoted.

"You'll have to untie my strings." She shot him her sternest look over her shoulder. "No other touching. Understand? I shall be very displeased if you ignore my... desires."

He wiggled his fingers. "And how shall I accomplish your laces, tied as I am."

She turned her head away and sighed. When she faced him again, she stroked a hand over her cinched middle, the expression on her face contemplative and just a little bit sly.

Gads, he loved her when she was minxy.

Slowly, her fingers rose to the hollow between her breasts, stroking the edge of the corset where it mountained.

He groaned. Sweat dampened his forehead as he strained against the small linen covering.

"I'm going to disgrace myself, Honoria, and loose my seed without a single touch from you."

"Then I shall be very, very angry." Her voice purred, sending waves over his skin. She couldn't know her words were those of a practiced courtesan, and yet, from her lips, the playact suddenly had meaning.

He jerked against the linen again and bit his lips.

She sidled up to him and placed one knee upon the bed, then the other. On all fours, she crept up to almost the level of his straining member. High and rigid, he jumped with anticipation. Instead of lowering herself upon him, she straddled his thighs, sat her linen-covered bottom upon them, and ignored the part of him begging for attention.

"My strings, Lawry. You'll need to untie them."

"Yes. Come closer. Please."

The word was gruff as a whispered prayer. She responded with another sly smile. Instead of leaning over and touching him where he needed touching, she rotated so her back faced his chin. Skimming in reverse, folding his pole toward his belly as he groaned with delicious agony, she stopped when the vee of her hovered just above his chin.

Staring toward the most beautiful part of her which he could almost see, half-dumb with astonishment at her daring, he licked his lips. Before he could bend his head far enough to taste her flowering center, her words halted him.

"Remember. No touching."

Which was impossible. She was a fiend. Love her? How could he, when she would torture him like this?

She stayed there, just out of reach as he died a little more each second.

"The laces, Lawry? Can you reach them?"

"Not unless you bend toward my fingers." Which should just about put her where he wanted her.

Instead of complying, she slid to the side and sat next to where he lay. Laughing gaily, she leaned over and pressed a kiss to the center of his chest, then moved down the length of him, her lips delicately tracing a path.

If she touched him there, now, he would explode. Gads, he hoped she would.

She ignored his clear desires and continued her kisses down the length of one leg, to the top of his right foot, and up the other.

"Sit over me, Honoria," he demanded, out of patience. He would be damned if he would spill his seed without the benefit of touching her. "I cannot take this torment any longer."

"Ah, well, if I torment you, I should put an end to that, shouldn't I?"

He nodded and closed his eyes, waiting. When nothing happened after a few moments, he popped them open. She was gone.

"Honoria!"

"Husband?"

Her voice came from the direction of the windows. He turned his head to see her sitting upon a chair, smiling like a loon. Well, she wouldn't be so pleased with herself in a moment. Two could play, though he didn't like his chances for the game lasting longer than a few seconds.

He slipped his hands from out of the ties, her exclamation of surprise music to his ears as he stalked to where she sat. Falling to his knees, he dragged her hips to the edge of the seat.

"Lean back."

She complied, and he buried his head in the gaping space between the linen. Modern conveniences. What did husbands do when drawers had been constructed of a solid piece of fabric without the benefit of sweet openings?

All too quickly she cried out.

He was on his feet in the next instant, turning her so her knees pointed toward the back of the chair. He pulled his linen down and entered her on a slide of heated honey, the relief and the agony mixed until he could bear no more. One thrust, and he was done, spilling into her like a tide rolling into shore.

When they crumpled to the floor, he pulled a blanket from the back of the chair and covered them.

Lord love a minx. He certainly did.

Chapter 33

Supper was a light affair with just the four of them present. Five, if one counted Hercules, who really should have a chair of his own. As had become their custom, they ate at the center of the long table so as to be able to converse in easier fashion. This time the gentlemen took one side, the ladies the other. The dog was required to skirt under and around in order to effectuate his begging to maximum effect.

Honoria glanced at Lawry, whose foot stretched under the linen-draped wood to meet her own. He grinned as the tip of his shoe rose up her ankle to her calf.

She moved her leg just far enough he couldn't touch. "Do you think we would be considered too eccentric if we allowed Hercules a seat at the table?"

Her father grunted. "The English have always been mad for dogs." He patted his lips with his napkin. "This soup is marvelous. I've forgotten its name, but the spices are excellent."

Lawry grinned and moved his toes next to hers again. To reach, he was required to sit a bit sideways in his seat and closer to its edge. "Mulligatawny, an import from India. I think it a splendid idea to grant Hercules a chair, my love. Perhaps next to you so he does not continuously pester me."

Her father grunted and slipped the dog a slice of

315

buttered bread. Hercules downed it with benefit of chewing.

"Manners, Hercules," Lady Fishbane admonished.

The dog looked over the table at her and moved his jaw three times.

Honoria burst out laughing. Lawry took the opportunity to raise his shoe up past the inside of her calf to the beginning curve of her thigh. She gasped, gurgled, choked, and reached for the wineglass. Under guise of lifting the crystal, she used her free hand to push his foot down. He laughed as well and relented.

Lady Fishbane glared at her son as if she well knew what he did. To his credit, he did not color. He merely lifted his own wine to sip.

"I forbid it. The dog will not have a seat at the table as if we are some deranged family possessed of degenerate manners."

The dowager's voice was as stern as translucent fluff. Laughter could be heard through it.

"Why, what if someone should happen by and witness such goings-on? Bad enough we've only three courses." She tapped the table near Honoria's hand. "I'm afraid, my dear, Lawry has already become a terrible influence on you with his slipshod ways, though I noted the tea earlier was finally warmed. I thank you for it. So many chores have been needed I could not keep up with them all."

Honoria exchanged a look with her husband. He certainly was a bad influence, but also an excellent one. Her cheeks heated. Had she really tied him up? His tongue touched the top of his lip. Quickly, she looked down at her soup.

He laughed again. "Who would come to call,

Mother? No one interrupts supper. It would be rude."

Lawry's foot slid along her own, even though he had to slide in his chair to accomplish the reach. She kicked it aside but he returned it to push against her instep.

The ringing of the doorbell interrupted his foray. The four of them exchanged startled glances.

"I say, Lawry, perhaps you should join Madame Rose in her occupation. You seem to have grown psychic abilities in the inverse." Honoria stepped lightly upon his instep with the heel of her slipper and giggled as he winced and withdrew.

His mother nodded. "He is always wrong with his predictions."

"Sometimes, delightedly so." He smiled at Honoria.

Smithers entered the room in a wash of propriety. His frown ended somewhere about his starched and tailored knees. "The Misters Crawley and Wilhelm to see you, Sir Lawrence."

Lawry stilled for only a moment before patting his lips upon his napkin. He threw the material down upon the table. "I'll see them in my office, Smithers."

"Is it secret we cannot hear?" She was his wife, after all.

He rounded the table and placed a kiss upon her forehead. "I shall relate all later. Let us give the appearance of normality. A man is expected to keep his own counsel as well as that of others. Mostly."

When he had gone, the three of them looked at each other. Hercules woofed as if disgusted not to be included and took off after his master. At least one of them made no pretense of wanting to overhear what the queen's men had to say.

"You know, Lawry's office has terrible acoustics. Why, the sounds carry quite clearly through the room's chimney into the bedroom above." Lady Fishbane looked at both of them in turn.

Her father raised his eyebrows. "We shouldn't. A man should have his privacy."

"We definitely shouldn't, but we will, won't we?" Lawry's mother turned to her. "Well?"

Honoria jumped from her seat so quickly her napkin dropped to the floor. Ignoring it, she sped out through the sitting room into the hall and up the stairs. Her father and mother-in-law processed on her heels.

"This one," the older woman said, brushing past Honoria as she stood deliberating between two doors.

Once they were ranged around the hearth on their knees, she discovered her mother-in-law had spoken true. The voices from below were not only audible, but clear.

"The matter is of greatest urgency. We understand from a source within Veritas they intend to leave with the item for Baghdad at dawn. Whatever they believe the key to open, we must not allow them to use it. Murders most foul have been done in the name of their quest. We might finally fathom the nature of their leanings."

"That's Crawley." Honoria mouthed the words to her father, who nodded.

Her mother-in-law put a finger to her lips. As if she needed the reminder sound would carry both ways!

"If murder has been done and you know about it, then why haven't the authorities moved upon the members?" Lawry sounded piqued. Perhaps it was merely the echo of the chimney. "I still believe the gambit short-sighted, especially now your big fish is swimming for the sands."

"What you must understand, Sir Lawrence, is the upper run of Veritas is comprised of high nobility of every rank and level. *Every* rank and level."

"Wilhelm." She narrowed her eyes at Lawry's mother before she could finish raising her finger to her lip. She exaggerated her silent words. "I know."

Lawry's mother wobbled her head.

Wilhelm continued, "There is no question of prosecuting some, or perhaps even any. Not yet, and maybe never. Instead, we must foil their plans until such a time as Her Majesty relents, or those higher placed than even Meriven stumble into a grave, taking whatever mad quest they pursue with them."

"Higher placed than even Meriven?"

Lawry's soft repetition echoed the shock clapping Honoria. Few men held such position. To think their leaders, those Society looked up to and respected, could be harbingers of evil was a daunting realization.

"Which is why hanging is impossible. Of course, graves might be filled by less public means, should Her Majesty relent."

Several moments of silence followed Crawley's dry observation.

Wilhelm cleared his throat. "In the meantime, this is your next assignment, Sir Lawrence. Kindly burn the paper after you've memorized its contents and address."

"Shouldn't we develop a code instead of consigning directives to the fire? What happens when my memory turns for the worse?"

Lawry. Even if she hadn't known the timbre of his

voice, the sarcastic, laughing tint coloring it would have alerted her to his identity.

"Once we are assured of your undivided loyalty, we shall see you are given it."

Crawley. Amusement edged his tone as well.

Honoria sank back upon her heels. Perhaps they might become friends in time, Crawley and Lawry. Honoria huffed through her nose as the rhyme hit her brain. She pressed back the laugh as Lady Fishbane rotated and narrowed her eyes once more.

Still. Lawry needed friends possessed of a similar sense of humor, and they needed couples to invite for dinner parties. Was Crawley married? She would have to ask. Perhaps she might invite Marjorie Plimpton over for tea and arrange for him to be present. If he was eligible, of course. Two redheads, though their shades varied. Still.

As she pondered a dinner, a series of noises drifted from below. Rattles. Swishes. A door opened, the hinge requiring oil. Honoria made a mental note to see it done. Mumbled conversation, but it was too difficult to make out individual words.

"They're leaving."

Her father ambled to his feet. He stretched out a hand to help Lawry's mother off the floor, only then offering assistance to Honoria. For the briefest moment, a pang of something like pain arched through her. He had never put her second before, not for anything or anyone. Not in her entire life.

She pushed the feeling away, but perhaps it showed upon her face, for he sent her a sympathetic glance and patted her cheek before turning away. The three of them rumbled down the stairs, coming face to face with the

Misters Crawley and Wilhelm as they gathered their hats at the door.

"Checking for mice, Mother?" Lawry asked as he leaned against the doorframe. He addressed the gentlemen. "One must do what one can to avoid an infestation. Rodents will take up residence if one isn't careful to set clear boundaries."

Her father *harrump*hed, but refrained from reply.

"Mr. Crawley, are you married?"

As a one, they all turned to stare at her. Only Hercules ignored the impertinent question, but only because he still dozed beside the office desk.

"Er, I was only thinking we might have you to dinner, and I wondered at the number." She caught the movement as Mr. Wilhelm pivoted away. Before he managed, his face flushed. "And of course, you too, Mr. Wilhelm. I'm sorry. I just, um, assumed you would be wed."

As all three men jumped into the embarrassing pause, their voices creating a cacophony of incomprehensible sounds, Lady Fishbane sidled up beside her and took her arm. Patting her hand, she sent Honoria a sympathetic glance before turning to the rest.

"As Lady Fishbane suggests, a dinner would be a lovely way to get to know one another better. A capital idea."

As she took up the conversation and received their direction, the men falling into politeness by habit and convention, Honoria settled back and met Lawry's stare. His lips tipped up and he winked at her.

Was it possible to love her new family this much?

When the gentlemen had taken their leave, Lawry glared at each of them in turn. "*Tsk, tsk*. The fireplace.

You do realize you all bear traces of soot about the knees, don't you? It is lucky the lads aren't familiar with the acoustics of this house or the wonders of my office's chimney."

"What will they have you do, Lawry?" Honoria asked, lacing her arm around his waist. She leaned into him. "I hope it's nothing dangerous."

He kissed the top of her head. "Only to break in and steal back your original necklace. Not from Meriven himself, thankfully. An informant has reported the pendant lies within a safety box located at the club offices. I shall wait a bit and then tiptoe in and retrieve it."

"Tonight?"

Honoria's stomach sank. She looked at her husband, but could find no trace of hesitation in his expression. Instead, he looked excited by the prospect of sneaking, entering, and stealing, a full use of his unusual skills.

There was nothing she could do. She hadn't married a gentleman farmer, whose only chances of injury and death outside of old age lay at the feet of some cattle and goats. She brushed back the hair from his forehead and lifted on tiptoe to kiss his lips.

In the next instant, he scooped her up in his arms and rushed back up the stairs. He ignored the gasps from their parents. She waved at them over his shoulder.

"What are you doing?"

"Taking you to bed. I've an hour or so before I leave, and I need to change clothing. You'll help me, won't you?"

"To dress you?"

"To undress me." His eyes glowed and his smile sparkled. "I believe you were going to show me what happens when a husband is tied to the rails."

Gads, but she loved this man.

Chapter 34

Lawry didn't spot his front door again until after four in the morning. Exhaustion weighted his limbs, and his eyes held all the grit of the sandiest of deserts. No need for The Office to traipse through those exotic locales, the ones circled on maps spread across Veritas's walls. They could dig much closer, though they would have to tie him down first.

He almost laughed at the images his brain conjured. His wife had done just that, tied him down and shown him what she had intended the first time before she had lost her nerve. He had almost been forced to crawl out the door to the Veritas assembly room, his legs had shaken so much from his release.

She was amazing.

Distant faint light was already slipping around the dark when he let himself through the front door. He crimped his way towards the staircase when a loud *clink* from the back of the house arrested him.

Instead of proceeding upstairs, he made his way towards the sound. Even from a distance he could see a brighter light sneaking under the kitchen door. As he approached, he heard voices.

Pushing through the portal, he discovered his wife, mother, and father-in-law gathered around the small table. In front of them, tall glasses of fizzy water and syrup stood in various states of consumption. Hercules opened a tired eye, an empty saucer lying at his chin.

Woof.

"Lawry!"

Honoria jumped up, nearly upsetting her chair. Only her father's quick reflexes kept it standing. She rushed to him and threw her arms around his waist.

"I was so worried! I mean..."

"You mean you had complete confidence in my abilities, but had a small hankering for a fizzy water and decided to cover-up your gluttony with silly professions of concern."

She looked into his eyes and smiled softly. "Exactly." She backed up a small pace and examined his face. "You look exhausted."

"I am," he admitted, rubbing his thumb along the ridge of her rose-petal cheekbone. "I had the most difficult time finding the safe, and was almost discovered by the guards twice. I was lucky the lock was easy to pry open. For a secret organization, their security is lax. I don't suppose they imagined anyone might have the temerity to slip in."

"They misunderstood the daring of The Midnight Menace." Honoria bopped him on his nose with her fingertip. "Foolish murdering scoundrels."

He bent and kissed her lips, only removing himself from them when a gruff throat-clearing reminded him the parents were present. Well, they always were, weren't they? He rather appreciated their company most days.

After grabbing a chair, he slunk into it as Honoria worked the machine. She placed a lavender-hued drink before him.

"I've concocted an herbal remedy for relaxation.

We've all agreed it is quite delicious. Lavender and berry. Take a sip. Tell me what you think."

He did. "It's lovely." He rubbed his eyes.

"Was the mission successful, son?" The colonel's loud voice boomed in the small space.

"It was." He retrieved the original pendant from his pocket and held it up. "I must give the bauble to Crawley. I'm sorry, Honoria. I know it has sentimental value, but they'll need to take it apart, to see if there's more to it than meets the eye. Meriven's latest attempt and his words, well, they'll need to dig deeper."

He thought she would become upset, but she simply nodded. "Of course. I have this new one, anyway, though I confess I may put it in my box and forget it for a while."

"Capital idea, my dear." His mother reached out and took Honoria's hand. "It is part of the old you. Let's focus upon a new day, shall we?"

The colonel cleared his throat once more. As he reached for Lawry's mother's hand, she let go of Honoria's. "Speaking of a new day, we have a bit of news we'd like to share."

Honoria slipped into the chair next to his. She placed her palm across his leg.

"I have asked Lady Fishbane, er, the Dowager Lady Fishbane, to be my wife. She has graciously accepted."

Honoria removed her hand from his thigh to clap for them. Lawry exclaimed with the most delight he was capable of showing, which was a goodly amount, although not as much as he might show tomorrow after a long rest.

After the congratulations had tapered off, his

mother faced Honoria. "Since I am to be your mother, dear, I wondered if I might broach a sensitive topic?" Still glowing, she appeared suddenly uncertain.

"Of course."

His mother nodded. "Well then, I have noticed the fabric of your gowns is generally quite, er…"

"Loud? Blinding? Uglier than sin?" Lawry supplied all the helpful adjectives he could manage at the late hour.

Honoria punched him in the arm. He winced. She hadn't held back her force.

"Yes, well, I was searching for more descriptive and less insulting terms, but there you have it. Dear, I don't know if you're aware of my hobby. I generally try to keep it secret as it is not at all proper for a female of my standing." She paused and bit her lip, casting a glance at her future husband.

"She doesn't act upon the stage, if you're worried." Lawry shook his head.

His mother made it seem as if she might. She frowned in his direction.

"I don't act, of course not, but I do enjoy a bit of sewing, now and again. Something a bit more plebeian than embroidery."

Lawry studied the two Cutworths. Neither seemed scandalized by the unlikely hobby.

"And I thought, since I have a goodly supply of fabrics at the ready, I might make you something in a… subtler color? Perhaps a nice navy?"

"Wonderful idea, Mother. She can match you and the drapery."

His mother ignored him. "Or I've some lovely yardage in a soft green, though I don't suppose it's truly your color, is it? I do have a crimson…"

"To match the dining walls. Excellent. We'll throw wonderful dinner parties, dress Honoria up, and stick her to the wall, see if anyone can find her."

"Do be quiet, Lawry! Ooh. Or the rose! Yes, with a bit of lace, and perhaps some trim about the hem in a daring black to match your hair. I have some silk roses…"

"You're in for it now." Lawry bussed his wife's cheek as it flushed the color of the proposed dress. "You'll either match the walls, the appointments, or the living rose hedge along the back wall. Your choice."

His mother gave him the fisheye. He laughed.

"I would be very grateful for such aid, Lady Fishbane." Honoria's eyes had grown glassy. "If it's not too much trouble."

"Of course it's no trouble, my dear. It will bring me joy. I've always wanted a daughter. And you must call me Mother, if you would. I am, after all, to be installed in such capacity. Not that I would dream of trying to take your own dear mother's place. Not at all. It's just…"

Honoria leaned across the table and took her free hand, the one her father did not already hold. "I would be delighted, Mother."

The colonel gruffed. "And you must call me Henry or Father as you prefer, son. I can't take your father's place, Lawrence, but I am always available should you require paternal advice or support."

Despite his fatigue, a sudden contentment spread along Lawry's bones. It warmed him like a fire from within. As they discussed the future and the wedding, he exchanged a look with his father-in-law. The grumbling man winked at him, his eyes moist.

Lawry squeezed Honoria closer and kissed her cheek once more as she laughed with delight at something his mother said. Hercules, settled in the corner, woofed softly.

He played with his wife's hair, the long black length a fall of silk through his fingers. He kissed her cheek yet again. The soft skin played like satin against his lips.

"I love you, Honoria. So much. I just realized I haven't told you properly. I'm a terrible husband."

She glanced over her shoulder and held his gaze, an enormous smile still stretching her lips. "Lucky thing I know how to punish. Anyway, I love you more, Lawry. Terribly much more."

"It is to be a competition, then?"

She laughed, a delighted trill, before she leaned over and pressed her lips to his. Soft and warm, honey and home. She was everything he had never thought to look for and always wanted to find.

When she stroked his cheek and retreated, he settled back in his chair once more. The future was going to be grand. He couldn't imagine how he had gotten so lucky, but he intended to hold onto the love and the laughter surrounding him now for the rest of his life.

The Midnight Menace threw his arm around his wife's shoulder. He chortled and joked with the rest of them as his father-in-law, soon to be stepfather, cracked a quip.

It just went to show anyone could win the prize if they were brave enough to enter the race and smart enough to spot a diamond. He gazed at all the faces surrounding him and wallowed in the joy. Marrying a mealy-mouthed miss had been the best decision of his life.

Even if he had been the last possible choice for bridegroom upon her list.

A word about the author…

Judy is a sort-of retired litigation attorney, a current homemaker with a propensity to ignore any and all domestic chores, and the mother of an outrageously comedic teenage boy and a fur-baby named Chocolate-the-Dog, so named because he thinks he's a cat.

Judy has been writing since she first learned to read, and has stories constantly going through her head. With a passionate interest in archaeology, most especially alternative archeology, she still hopes to one day uncover the true history of the world. She is also the author of *Arabella's Assistant* (Raised All Wrong, Book 1) and *Primrose and Promises* (Jellybeans and Spring Things series).

As a graduate of Mount Holyoke College with a degree in Art History, when she ventures away from books, it is to find the nearest art museum or purveyor of High Tea. She has lived in four states and in France, and currently makes her home in North Carolina, which she loves, except for the bugs, snakes, and humidity.

****

https://www.judylynnichkhanian.com

****

If you enjoyed this story, leaving a review at your favorite book retailer or reader website would be much appreciated. Thank you!

Thank you for purchasing
this publication of The Wild Rose Press, Inc.

For questions or more information
contact us at
info@thewildrosepress.com.

The Wild Rose Press, Inc.
www.thewildrosepress.com